THE

NO-END

HOUSE

THE

MATCHMAKER

GROUSE

THE

NO-END

HOUSE

JEREMY BATES

KENSINGTON
PUBLISHING CORP.

kensingtonbooks.com

KENSINGTON BOOKS are published by

Kensington Publishing Corp.
900 Third Avenue
New York, NY 10022

ISBN: 978-1-4967-5552-0 (ebook)

ISBN: 978-1-4967-5551-3

First Kensington Trade Paperback Printing: July 2025

10 9 8 7 6 5 4 3 2 1

Printed in the United States of America

The authorized representative in the EU for product safety and compliance
is eucomply OU, Parnu mnt 139b-14, Apt 123
Tallinn, Berlin 11317, hello@eucompliancepartner.com

For my parents, Linda and Gerry,
and my wife, Alison, with love.

Chapter 1

"There is no end without a beginning."
—The Book of Nine

Memories are a double-edged sword.

I have beautiful ones of my late wife, Jen, and I have terrible ones, as well. I can recall her face and smile and laughter whenever I want, but I can recall the accident and her slow death whenever I want, also. Often I don't have control over which memories, the good or the bad, will fill my head on any given morning, afternoon, or night; they simply appear, uninvited, and in the case of the bad ones, they stick around for far too long.

I began thinking about Jen this evening because I knew how much she would have loved Barcelona. She liked cities with character and charm, and Barcelona had that in spades on every landscaped boulevard and down every twisting back alley.

Jen would have insisted on browsing through every bohemian knickknack shop we passed. She would have found us a hidden-away café where we could enjoy a bottle of wine and nibble on seafood paella and other local dishes. She would have made me snap photos of her with all the costumed buskers along Las Ramblas. Hell, she would probably have convinced me to take one of those city bus tours, where she'd insist we sit at the front of the open deck so we'd have the best view of everything.

Gradually and inevitably, these thoughts turned to the accident that ended her life three years ago. She had been flying her final one-hour supervised flight in a Cessna 172. When she and the instructor landed, she had attempted to walk around the plane to thank him—and walked right into the still-spinning propeller. It sliced off half of her face, took off much of one shoulder, and severed her left arm below the elbow. Somehow paramedics got her to Arizona State Hospital alive, although her injuries were so severe the ICU doctors put her into a barbiturate-induced coma—only it wasn't temporary. The brain trauma she suffered meant she would live the rest of her life in a vegetative state and require a ventilator to keep breathing.

The neurologist withdrew life support three days after Jen was admitted to the hospital.

Walking into a spinning propeller was a terrible way to die—but more, it was such a *stupid* way to die. I know I shouldn't be angry at Jen, but I couldn't help it. I was also angry at myself for buying her the Learn to Fly Solo flight course. She'd had two dreams she talked about since we met on Valentine's Day in 2014: earning her pilot's license and flying to all fifty states, and signing a record deal.

Although she was a talented singer and songwriter, she never found an equally talented band (in my opinion), and never landed a record deal. So I bought her the fifteen-hour flight course for Christmas.

More than anything, I was angry at the instructor for taking her out on that final lesson after dark. If he'd scheduled it in the daytime, like all the previous lessons, she would have seen the propeller, wouldn't have walked into it, wouldn't have *died*.

I suppose I was angry at just about everybody and everything when I thought about Jen, the good times we had together, the future we should have had together. Her death seemed so pointless and unfair.

I tipped the bottle of beer I was nursing to my lips and watched the activity on the street. The coffee crowds and window shoppers were gone, replaced by people who all seemed to have somewhere they needed to be. Shorts and singlets had been exchanged for pants and Polo shirts and breezy dresses. Flip-flops and sneakers for leather and heels. Even the dozen or so twenty-somethings that were gathering on the sidewalk out in front of the hostel (no doubt for some soon-to-be-messy pub crawl) were all dressed spiffily. It amazed me that they prioritized precious space in their backpacks for multiple pairs of shoes and fancy clubbing clothing.

In contrast, the items that rotated in and out of my backpack (which was considerably smaller than the gravity-defying Mountain Co-op ones you saw these kids lugging across Europe) were limited to a toothbrush and toothpaste, a stick of deodorant, three T-shirts, three pairs of shorts, three pairs of boxers, three pairs of socks, a journal, a Kindle, a first aid kit, and my phone and charging cable.

For chillier evenings like tonight, there was also what I was currently wearing: jeans and a long-sleeved white shirt. I also had a light tent and sleeping bag I attached to the bottom of the backpack, but those were necessities, because I wasn't jumping on and off buses and trains: I was walking everywhere, and more often than not, I'd go days without a proper bed or roof over my head.

Two months after Jen's funeral, I decided to walk around the world. It took me that long to realize I couldn't keep going into the real estate office every day and pretending everything was all right. It took me another month to plan the trip, the route that would take me across every continent with as little bureaucratic red tape as possible, the allocation of finances to support me for several years, all that stuff . . . and also to get my head in the right place. I wasn't stepping out for a Sunday stroll, after all.

I started the journey on a Sunday morning from my house in Green Valley, Arizona, and spent the next year walking south to Panama. From there I flew over the Darien Gap (a dangerous stretch of jungle where I was advised with much confidence that I would be robbed, if not murdered, if I attempted to cross it on foot), and I spent another year walking from Bogotá, Columbia to Montevideo, Uruguay. I caught a plane to the Argentinian-administered Marambio Base in Antarctica at the beginning of the summer and walked to Esperanza Base, a year-round civilian settlement, where I organized the necessary paperwork to travel to Europe. I landed in Scotland in September and wound my way south to Spain. I'd been in Barcelona for a week now. Next I planned to cross over to North Africa, travel through Morocco, Algeria, and Tunisia, and then crisscross back north through Eastern Europe. Eventually I'd reach Western and Central Asia. From there I would fly to Australia, and then—finally—back to the US.

Yes, some days my feet hurt, and some nights my knees hurt more. Yes, when I get caught in a torrential rainstorm, I wonder what the hell I'm doing. And yes, I get homesick when I think about my family and friends so far away. But at the same time, I've never been as fit and healthy as I am now, and I've never felt so free. Visiting Peru or France and lounging by the pool in a Hyatt is not the same as walking across a foreign country, from town to town and city to city, seeing how the locals live, understanding the world outside of *my* world, committing to something that only a handful of people have ever accomplished and ever will.

I'll put up with sore feet, a bacterial infection or two, sunburns, rain, and whatever else nature throws my way for that. I have to now. I've gone so far that quitting is no longer an option.

For the last two days, I'd been at a place called Hola Hostel, and like most European hostels, it was tidy and offered a shitty but complimentary continental breakfast. Also, it had a bar in the lobby that opened at seven p.m. and sold cheap beer. I was currently on my second bottle of Hoegaarden, and that would likely be the last.

The twenty-somethings on the sidewalk were growing in number and getting louder and more boisterous. The guys were high-fiving, shoulder-bumping, and chugging beers while trying to outwit each other (some of their comments were so outrageous that they were actually funny). The girls gossiped about friends and enemies and just about anybody who wasn't there to overhear them.

I was forty-four, probably nearly double the age of most of them, and while forty-four wasn't too old, I felt old right then. Hostels did that to me. Because barring the occasional bare-footed, stoned-eyed hippy, I was usually the oldest person in every hostel. Sometimes I'd see a married couple in their fifties checking in or out, or someone in their thirties or forties scratching the backpacking itch later in their lives. But the majority, by far, was the early twenties crowd, recent college grads who didn't want to give up the party they'd been living for the last three or four years.

Which was why I was intrigued by the woman with the orange hair seated at a nearby table.

She had been there ever since I sat down half an hour ago. A laptop was on the table in front of her, along with what looked like a mai tai. I'd guess she was a little younger than me, maybe forty.

Aside from the attention-getting hair, the rest of her didn't look like someone you would find in a hostel. The champagne-colored blouse and black dress pants were too sophisticated. Her jewelry looked expensive. And the laptop was a late-model MacBook Pro.

She lifted her eyes from the screen and caught me studying her. I looked away and sipped my beer. The twenty-somethings were finally moving on to start their night. I wondered how many of them were going to make it back to the hostel before dawn and whether I was going to be taking a shower tomorrow morning in a puke-splattered stall.

I took another sip of beer and could still feel the orange-haired woman's eyes on me. I was sure I was wrong; she was probably looking past me. Yet my curiosity got the better of me, and I glanced at her.

She was indeed staring directly at me.

I didn't know what to do but look away again. I felt myself blushing . . . and when was the last time *that* had happened?

I took another sip from my beer and found it empty. I hesitated a moment, then got up without looking at the woman. I went to the lobby, past the bar, and pushed the button for the elevator. At the last moment, I turned around.

She was still looking at me . . . but now she was grinning.

The blush in my cheeks dialed up to a ten, and I finally identified the emotion I was experiencing: intimidation.

The elevator doors pinged open, and I thought, *Fuck it.* I went to the bar, bought another Hoegaarden from the German guy manning it, and returned to the patio.

I stopped at the orange-haired woman's table and said, "Mind if I have a seat?"

"Please do," she said.

Chapter 2

"Dreams dance on stage only when there is
nobody awake to watch."
—The Book of Nine

Now that she'd won the battle of wills—or whatever the
hell had just happened—and had me sitting down with
her, she quit it with the crazy Jedi stare and turned her attention to her laptop. She clicked the mousepad a couple of
times before closing the screen. She wrapped her lips around
the straw sticking out of her mai tai and sucked until her
cheeks dimpled. Then she said to me, "Are you always this
forward?"

I laughed and said, "*I'm* being forward?"

"Walking over to a strange woman's table and asking to
join her. Seems pretty forward to me."

"I—" I shook my head and sipped my beer. She knew exactly why I had come over. "I'm Joe."

"You look like a Joe."

"What does a Joe look like?"

"You."

My jaw tightened. I didn't know what was going on. I'd

thought the Jedi stare was a come-on, and while I had no interest in a relationship, or even a one-night stand, I wasn't averse to spending an evening with an attractive woman, even if all we did was chat.

Walking around the world on your own was a lonely business. But now . . . well, I wasn't sure if I was the butt of some obtuse joke. I decided on bluntness. "Have we met before?"

"Ooh. I thought you'd have a better line than that."

"I mean, do you know me?" An idea was forming in the back of my mind: somehow, she'd heard that I was walking around the world. When some people learned that, it made them act a little weird. Back in Chile, I was invited to a local wedding by the groom, and the guests began lavishing me with so much attention that my presence overshadowed the newlyweds, and I left before the cake was cut.

"I know you now," the woman said.

"What's your name?" I asked her.

"Helen."

"You don't look like a Helen."

"You know many Helens?"

"No."

"Then how do you know I don't look like a Helen?"

"I was referring to Helens from popular culture."

"I'm intrigued. Which Helen from popular culture do I not resemble most?"

I wasn't slow-witted, but right then my mind was racing to keep up with her pointed questions. "Helen of Troy."

The woman's brown eyes sparkled. "Touché, Joe. I *don't* resemble the most beautiful woman who ever lived. I don't know whether you're purposely disparaging me or simply sticking your foot in your mouth."

Hell, I didn't know either, but it was likely the latter.

"And what's more," she said, still smiling, "I don't think Helen of Troy was black."

"How about we start over?" I said.

"Sure," she said. "Let's." She extended a lithe hand. A silver bracelet engraved with the double Gs of Gucci encircled her wrist. "I'm Helen."

I accepted her hand. "I'm Joe."

"You look like a Joe."

"You look like a Helen."

Her eyes sparkled again. "Any in particular?"

"Helen of Troy."

She tilted her head back and laughed, an unexpectedly sweet and girlish sound, and it was then I decided to stick around until I finished my beer.

I ended up sticking around for a fair bit longer than that. Another four beers, to be exact, and when I checked my wristwatch, I was surprised to discover it was almost midnight.

"Time flies," I said, thinking I hadn't stayed up this late in months.

"When you're having fun . . ." Helen said. She had matched my four beers with four mai tais, but if she was feeling a buzz, I couldn't tell.

"To be honest . . ." I said.

"I like honesty," she said.

"When I first sat down, I didn't know what to make of you."

"Oh?"

"You were intimidating."

"Don't mince words."

"You were a bit full-on."

"Just say it."

"Say what?"

"You thought I was a bitch."

"I didn't think that."

She gave me a droll look, as though she knew what I was really thinking and was waiting expectantly for me to say it.

"All right," I said. "Maybe it crossed my mind."

She slapped the table. "You *did* think I was a bitch!"

"I didn't know what to think. I thought a lot of things."

"I'm only teasing you, Joe. I know what I can be like. I live with myself every day, don't I?" She shrugged. "I don't mean to be bitchy. I don't *want* to be. It just happens when I'm nervous."

I was surprised. "You were nervous . . . ?"

She shrugged again, a cute lift of her shoulders accompanied by a self-deprecating smile. "A little bit."

"You seemed pretty confident to me with that whole Jedi-stare thing."

"Jedi-stare thing! Are you going to tell me I look like Yoda next?"

"Yoda crossed with Helen of Troy."

"That's a little better—I'm seeing . . . God, I don't know. I turn dumb when I'm drunk."

"You don't seem drunk."

"I'm good at covering things up."

She had revealed little bits about herself like this over the last two hours, and it was endearing . . . so much so that it was becoming scary.

I looked at my beer bottle; it was empty. I checked my watch again. It was now five past midnight.

"Somewhere you have to be?" she asked.

"I should call it a night."

The surprise that flashed in her eyes disappeared in a blink.

"I'll—uh, walk you to the elevator," I said. "What floor are you on?"

We both stood up.

THE NO-END HOUSE   11

"I'm not staying here," she told me. "I'm at a hotel down the road."

Now it was my turn to show surprise. "They don't have mai tais at the bar there?"

"I was walking past this place. The patio was enticing, and it wasn't filled with all those kids then."

I frowned, feeling suddenly self-conscious about staying at the hostel. If Helen were staying at the hostel, too, that would be different. But she wasn't, and I'd never mentioned the walking around the world stuff, and that made me just some middle-aged chump who couldn't afford a proper hotel room.

It was especially ironic considering that in my previous life, I owned a closetful of tailored suits, drove a BMW, and had enough money banked to dabble in the stock market and not worry about whether I was any good at dabbling or not.

I cleared my throat. "All right . . . um . . ."

"You could walk me to the elevator in my hotel if you'd like?"

I hesitated. "I . . . can't."

"Can't?"

"It's complicated."

"Complicated. Right." She lowered her eyes. They might have gone to my ring finger . . . which wore no ring. I wasn't advertising that I was single. The journey I'd embarked on was, in part, an effort to move forward with my life, and seeing that ring on my finger every day had made moving forward really tough.

When Helen's eyes met mine again, there was nothing in them. It was like we were strangers. "Good night, Joe. Enjoy your time in Barcelona."

"Good night, Helen," I replied, and watched her walk away.

*   *   *

I wasn't surprised I dreamed of Jen that night.

Helen and I were on Hola Hostel's patio, as we had been earlier in the evening, and Helen noticed someone standing across the street, watching us. She urged me to find out who it was, so reluctantly I went.

The person wore a monk-like robe that covered their body and face. As I approached, I asked them who they were and what they wanted. They didn't answer. I stopped directly in front of them. For some reason, I couldn't see into the cowl. There was only darkness where the face should have been. I yanked the cowl free and discovered Jen staring back at me.

At that moment, my heart felt like a small bird that had flown down my throat and died in my chest, because Jen was missing the parts of her face that had been sliced off by the propeller. That included most of her mouth and some of her jawbone, which was why she hadn't answered me. She recognized me, though. I saw that in her eyes, along with stark terror, as if she were back on that tarmac in Arizona, knowing she was about to walk into the propeller but unable to do anything about it.

I was horrified to see her like this, but I was also so grateful she was alive that I wanted to throw my arms around her.

Now, as I lay awake on the lumpy hostel mattress and recalled the dream, it occurred to me that the real reason I never embraced Jen was that I knew, beneath the monk robe, she would be missing much of her left shoulder and arm, the wounds would be raw and unbandaged and unforgiving, and any kind of hug would end with her screaming in pain.

A couple of the twenty-somethings with whom I shared the small room were talking in the dark. It was their voices that had woken me, I believe.

"He was munted, bro," said one of them in a New Zealand accent. "It was all bullshit."

"But five *grand*," said his buddy, attempting to whisper. "Just for some internet challenge."

"He didn't say it was an internet challenge."

"Why else would someone dole out that much loot? They prolly got a million YouTube subscribers. They'll make heaps more than five grand by filming and posting us all scared and shit."

"Scared? It's a fucking haunted house, bro."

"Exactly, cuz. It'll be a piece of piss. So let's do it."

"We're going to Madrid tomorrow."

"Bugger that. We put it off for a day."

"Nah, bro. It's sus. I ain't wasting my time."

"He said the place was across from the Picasso Museum. That's by that tapas bar where we met those Swiss girls."

"So?"

"It's not far from where we gotta catch the bus to Madrid. So we check out the house, and if it's sus, we get on the bus."

A grunt.

"Yo, yo?"

Nothing.

"Cuz?"

No reply.

"Cuz?"

And then silence, finally.

I tried getting back to sleep.

I was woken a second time that night by a different kind of talking. It was a guy trying to get into a girl's pants—literally. They were on the bunk above me. They weren't there when I went to bed, so they must have come in at some point during the night.

They were speaking quietly—much more so than the two Kiwis—and I probably wouldn't have heard them if they hadn't been right on top of me.

"Come on," the guy said.

"No . . ." the girl said.

"Come on."

"Then, a bit distressed: "Stop."

"Come on."

"I'll take off my top, but that's all."

"Come *on*."

"Stop *that*."

"I'm not doing nothing."

"Not *there*."

"Come on—"

"Hey, pal," I said loudly and sharply, and there was noise above me like one or both of them had shot up straight. "She said no. Understand?"

I heard little more after that except for someone, at some point, descending the ladder by my feet, and then the door to the room opening and closing . . . although by then, I was half asleep and dreaming once more.

Chapter 3

"A soul burns bright, but two burn brighter."
—The Book of Nine

No puke greeted me in the shower stall in the morning, thankfully. I soaped up, shampooed—these things were luxuries when you couldn't do them every day—and toweled off, drying my shaggy brown hair as much as possible. Back in the room, I pulled on dark jeans, a long-sleeved shirt, and a light jacket. I withdrew an orange pill bottle from the rear pocket on my backpack and frowned when I saw that it was empty. I'd been meaning to stop by a pharmacy and refill my prescription, but I hadn't gotten around to it. The prescription had been written by a doctor in the States, and I'd had no problems so far using it in any of the countries I'd passed through.

I produced the little tattered piece of paper with the doc's scratchy handwriting on it from my backpack, stuffed it in my pocket along with the pill bottle, and went downstairs to fuel up on the continental breakfast. I toasted and buttered a couple of slices of white bread but ignored the electric kettle, the jar of instant coffee, and the little box of dried milk. My sleep had been lousy, and I felt like a double-shot espresso to get me going.

When I stepped through the glass doors to the patio, my eyebrows jumped. Helen—I didn't know her last name, I realized—was sitting at the same table as the previous night, with a newspaper open in front of her. She glanced up at me, smiled, said, "Oh, hi, Joe!" and then nonchalantly returned her attention to her laptop.

A dozen questions crossed my mind. The one I asked was, "You haven't been here all night, have you?"

"What? Don't be silly. I just got here."

And it was a silly question. She was dressed much more casually than she had been the night before, in tight faded jeans and a cozy cream sweater.

I said, "What are you doing?"

"Reading the news."

"I mean, *here?*"

She raised a paper cup, presumably filled with coffee. It was plain white and identical to the ones inside the hostel, stacked next to the electric kettle. "I noticed last night that breakfast opens here at six. I was up early, nothing near my hotel was open, so I stopped by for a coffee."

"No coffee in your room?"

"I drank it all before going to bed to sober up."

I frowned suspiciously. It made sense . . . I guess. And what was the alternate explanation? Helen came here specifically to bump into me?

I said, "I'm going to look for a Starbucks or Costa. Care to join me?"

"God, yes," she said, slapping the laptop shut. "Hostel coffee should be tried for crimes against humanity."

We walked east to Passeig de Sant Joan and followed it south through the Gràcia district until we found a Starbucks near

Casa Milà, a curvy stone building designed by Gaudi. Helen ordered a cappuccino and a blueberry muffin. I ordered a latte.

When she tried to pay for mine, I said, "I think I should be the one paying."

"Don't be so old-fashioned."

I found us a corner table—the place wasn't too busy, as it was only a quarter past seven—and took out the red journal that I'd started writing in a few months after leaving Arizona. It gave me something to do when I wasn't walking and was therapeutic at the same time.

When Helen joined me with the drinks, I took the latte and said, "Thanks, Hilda." That was the name the barista had called out.

Helen rolled her eyes. "How do you get Hilda from Helen?"

"It says that right here." I pointed to the name scribbled on my cup.

"I didn't write that. She did. You have a diary?"

"It's not a diary. It's a journal."

"Same difference if you ask me."

"Little girls write in diaries."

"And big, manly men write in journals? What were you writing about?"

"It's private," I said.

"Me?" she asked.

"Was I writing about you? No."

"I bet you were."

"Okay, I was." I opened the journal to a random page and feigned reading: "I went to Starbucks today with a rather pretty woman."

"*Very* pretty."

"She's at the counter now paying for our coffees. You can't really miss her with hair that color of orange."

"Joe!"

"I've never seen anything like it. It's almost as though she's got a radioactive pumpkin on her shoulders—"

"Okay, whatever," she said. "You've made your point."

"What's my point?"

"That your diary is private. What you write in it isn't my business." She looked around the café. "Do you really want to sit in here? Let's go for a walk. It's such a nice morning out."

"I'd prefer to sit for a while. I've been doing a fair bit of walking lately."

So we sat and chatted and sipped our coffees. The conversation was easy, fun, breezy. If Helen had felt stood up the night before, she'd gotten over it. At one point she took a little orange bottle just like mine from her handbag. She twisted off the cap, shook out two pills—a round blue one and a larger pink capsule—onto her palm. She slid the capsule back into the bottle and said, "Want it?"

I was amused. "You some kind of drug dealer?"

"Yup." She popped the blue pill into her mouth.

"Xanax?" I asked.

She nodded. "I have bad anxiety. Do you want one or not?"

I shook my head. "What are the pink ones?"

"Aren't you nosy? Do you want me to itemize my medicine cabinet next?"

"Sorry," I said, embarrassed for prying.

"I'm kidding, Joe. I don't care if you think I'm a fucked-up crazy girl."

I didn't reply, as I figured she was poking me to get a response; she seemed to enjoy creating awkward moments.

"The pink ones are for my mood disorder," she said.

"Oh."

"Do you want to know what kind of mood disorder I have?"

"Nope."

"If you told me that you had a mood disorder, I'd like to know more about it."

"Well, I'm not you, and I don't want to know more about yours. But I do what you do."

"Do what I do?" She laughed. "You mean, have mood disorders?"

"Mix pills in the same bottle."

She appeared surprised. "You're on meds, too?"

"Not really."

"Not really?"

"I have a prescription. But I'm weaning myself off it. After . . ." I almost said *after my wife died* but caught myself. "After some stuff that happened in my life, my doctor prescribed me benzos."

"And?"

"And?"

"What else did your doctor prescribe? You said you mix your pills in the same bottle, hence there's more than one kind of pill."

"Who's looking into whose medicine cabinet now?"

"You don't have to tell me . . ."

After a moment I said, "Zoloft."

Helen's eyebrows went up. "You have depression?"

I shrugged. "It comes and goes."

"But you don't take anything for it anymore—I mean, regularly, at least?"

"I don't like how it makes me feel. It changes me . . ."

Helen was nodding. "I know what you mean. And I wish I could do that, just dump all my meds down the sink and never take another one. But I don't think I ever could, because they change me, too, only they change me for the better . . ." She tucked the bottle back into her handbag and looked at me with a crooked smile. "Jeez, Joe, that was weird."

"What was?"

She shifted in her seat, crossed her legs beneath the table. "Opening up like that. I don't usually do that with strangers."

"I'm still a stranger, am I?"

"We only met last night."

"I guess you're right," I said, and I didn't think she was quite the private person she was making herself out to be. She had no problem taking out the pill bottle right in front of me, after all.

"But a *good* stranger," she said.

"Thanks, Helen." I wanted to change the topic. "Anyway . . . what were we talking about before . . . ?"

"I have no idea. Oh, how dry this muffin is." She pushed the blueberry muffin toward me. "Try it."

"No, thanks." Then I remembered. "The Kiwis last night."

"The two guys who woke you up?"

I finished telling Helen about their conversation, and then I told her about the guy trying to get into the girl's pants, and she told me I should have punched him in the face, but she seemed more interested in the Kiwis.

"Let's go," she said.

"Where?" I asked.

"The haunted house. The Picasso Museum is only a few blocks from here."

"I don't need money that badly."

"We'll just knock on the door, check it out."

"No thanks."

"Why not?"

"I don't want to."

"That's it? That's your reasoning?"

"Do you know what 'munted' means? That's how the Kiwis described the guy who told them about the house. *Munted*. In other words, completely off his face on drugs or booze or both. The house doesn't exist, Helen. And if it does, it's probably some drug den. I wouldn't be surprised if that fucked-up guy went around to hostels trying to lure backpackers to the house so he and his addict pals can rob them to pay for the next hit."

"You sound scared," she said.

"You sound naïve," I said.

"It will be fun, Joe. What else are you going to do today?"

"Rest."

"Rest! You're not an old man." She studied me. "You never told me last night why you're in Barcelona."

"You never told me why you're in Barcelona, either."

"You never asked. UNICEF transferred me here last month. I'm an education specialist."

I raised my eyebrows. I had never met anyone who worked for UNICEF before, and for some reason, it impressed me. "Do you get transferred around a lot?"

"I spent the last two years in Libya. Before that, Turkey. Aside from those assignments, though, I've always been based in Chicago, where I grew up. Now you."

"I used to be in real estate."

"Past tense?"

"I quit."

"To travel around the world?"

"Something like that."

"Stop being so mysterious, Joe! I feel like I'm talking to Harry Houdini."

I sipped my latte. Was I being mysterious? I didn't think so. In general, I didn't like talking about myself, and that extended to my sojourn around the world. When I was out on the road, that was different. People would see the backpack, the tent, and the sleeping bag, and they'd ask me where I was heading, I'd tell them, they'd offer a few words of encouragement, and that would be that. But when I was in a big city and kicking back in a hostel for a few days, I preferred to fade into the background, to be anonymous. This didn't mean I wouldn't tell someone I met in a hostel what I was doing if they asked. I would and had done so many times. The thing with Helen, I suppose, was that if she'd asked me right off the bat what I was doing in Barcelona, it would have been no big deal. But the fact that I'd spent hours chatting to her and was now hanging out with her for the second time in as many days, and the fact I'd never mentioned I was walking around the world . . . well, busting something like that out would be a little weird, wouldn't it? Like I'd been trying to keep it a secret or something.

Even so, continuing to keep it a secret would be even weirder, so I told her.

"Is that so, Joe?" Helen said, clearly not believing me. "First off, that's physically impossible, unless you're Jesus and can walk on water."

"I fly across the oceans."

"In an aircraft, I hope you mean."

"Look, you asked, and I told you. I left my house in Arizona more than two years ago and walked south to Mexico, and now here I am, in Spain, with half the trip behind me and half to go."

She was still studying me—*scrutinizing* might be a better way to put it—and her eyes narrowed. "What was the exact date you left your home?"

I shrugged. "It was a Sunday in September. I don't recall the exact date. Mid-month sometime."

"Wouldn't you remember such an important date?"

"I think I'll remember the date I return home. That's a little more important, don't you think?"

"Tell me all the countries you've been to, in the order you visited them."

"Really?"

"If I told you I was swimming across the English Channel, would you believe me?"

"If I was in a boat, and I saw you floating in the middle of the English Channel, yeah, I would."

"You're stalling."

"From Mexico—Guatemala, El Salvador, Nicaragua—Managua—Costa Rica, Panama. That was just Central America. Want me to keep going?"

"Stalling . . ."

"Colombia, Ecuador, Peru, Bolivia, Chile, Argentina, Antarctica—not a country, obviously, but I'm planning to hit six continents—Scotland, England, Belgium, Luxembourg, France, and now Spain."

"And the rest?" she pressed, although with less swagger.

"From here I take a ferry to Morocco, then it's on to Algeria, Tunisia, Italy, Austria, Slovenia, Croatia, Bosnia and Herzegovina, Montenegro, Kosovo, Albania, North Macedonia, Greece, your former home, Turkey. Keep going?"

She was shaking her head. "My God, Joe . . . You *are* walking around the world! So you know what my next question is going to be, right?"

I thought I did, and this was probably the real reason I'd kept her in the dark until now. Strangers don't typically ask follow-up questions. Strangers don't ask *why*. Helen and I, on the other hand, hit it off quickly last night. She was smart and curious. She was full of *why*s. Her "next question" had always been inevitable.

I said, "My wife was in an accident. She passed away.

After that . . ." I swallowed tightly. *Three years and I can still barely get a fucking sentence out.* "I'm, um . . . I needed a new perspective on life, I suppose. I decided I needed to do something different with my life."

"Oh, Joe . . ." Helen's hand cupped mine on the table. Maybe she felt it flinch, because she released it the next moment. Then she said, *"Oh. . . . !"* with exclamation, and I think that was her understanding why last night ended the way it did.

I said, "Let's go for that walk, after all."

Chapter 4

"Her glory is wasted on the blind who walk
straight past."
—The Book of Nine

We walked and talked and found a waste bin for our empty coffee cups. I wasn't leading the way; I wasn't even thinking about where we were going. Helen might have been leading, however, because twenty minutes or so later, we ended up on a medieval street in front of the Picasso Museum.

The museum was housed in several linked buildings that had once been the palatial homes of wealthy merchants. Through an archway in the somber stone façade, I could see an old courtyard wrapped by an exterior staircase that led up to the main floors. A blue sign with an arrow read: ENTRADES ENTRADAS TICKETS.

"Well, surprise, surprise," I said, giving Helen a wry look. "Funny how we just happened to end up here."

"I was following you," she said.

"Right."

"Honest."

On the opposite side of the road was another archway that led to more linked palaces, these housing the Museum of World Cultures.

"I don't see the drug den anywhere," I said.

"It's a long street. Let's have a look for it."

I shrugged. We were here. Why not?

The stone buildings lining the narrow alley-like street— CARRER DE MONTCADA, I read on a small stone plaque— showcased a mix of relatively well-preserved Romanesque and Renaissance architecture. The ground-level businesses ranged from a dingy souvenir shop and discount pharmacy to trendy boutiques, funky eateries, and natty little bars. Eventually the cramped street emptied onto a larger boulevard.

"No haunted house," I said.

"We must have walked past it," Helen said.

"We didn't walk past it."

"Are you sure the Kiwis said it was this street?"

"They didn't mention the street name. They only said it was across from the Picasso Museum."

"So maybe they were mistaken. These old streets are like a maze. Let's keep looking."

"Nah."

She blinked at me. "Nah?"

"This is supposed to be a restful day for me. And I'm in the middle of a good book."

"So?"

"So I think I might head back to the hostel."

Helen appeared indignant. "You would leave me here on my own? You would *abandon* me?"

"You live in Barcelona now, Helen. I don't think I'd be abandoning you."

"We walked here together, Joe. If you decide to walk away on your own, then yes, you would very much be abandoning me."

"I'm more than happy to walk you back to the hostel. In fact, I'll even walk you to your hotel."

She clenched her jaw, and I suspected that if I ever got to know her better, I might learn she had something of a fiery temper.

"Why don't we have one last look up this street?" I said to placate her, pointing the way we had come. "We have to head north again anyway."

"That's gotta be it!" Helen said excitedly.

We were standing in front of one of those archways that led to the characteristic set of courtyards and palaces.

"What's special about it?" I asked her, puzzled.

She pointed at a bronze plaque on the keystone. "*The No-End House*," she read. "Tell me that's not spooky."

"It's not spooky."

"Please, Joe. This is one hundred percent the haunted house. Can't you feel it?"

"How did we miss it before?"

"That plaque's not exactly a marquee with flashing lights. Let's go knock."

"And say what?"

"That we heard they were offering five thousand dollars to anyone who made it through their haunted house."

I shook my head. "I'm not doing this, Helen."

"Don't be a scaredy-cat."

"I'd prefer not to become an internet meme."

"Why? Because you're *famous*? You believe this will hurt your reputation?"

I frowned. "What are you talking about?"

"I bet you're documenting your walk online, and you have thousands of followers."

"Uh, no."

"Facebook . . . ? Instagram . . . ?"

"No."

"YouTube?"

"I don't use any of that stuff."

"So what's the big deal if we become a meme?"

"I don't have any urge to share my private life with strangers—"

"Private life? Please, Joe! It would just be you and me walking through a few dark rooms with people in rubber masks jumping out from behind Styrofoam tombstones. You're overthinking and hyperbolizing."

"You go knock if you want, and if they invite you inside, I'll wait here—"

Helen snatched my hand and dragged me through the archway.

The central courtyard was greener and lusher than any of the others we had glimpsed. Ferns and flowering shrubs and well-established palm trees grew everywhere. Out-of-control vines scaled the columns and arches of the staircase as well as the stone walls, some snaking up to the corniced roofline. A twisted and gnarled olive tree that almost certainly predated the palace dominated the center of the open space. Just visible through the overgrown vegetation was a series of shadowed arcades, which I presumed had, at one point, served as stables. Tall rectangular windows with semicircular pediments and shallow wrought-iron balconies looked down on us from the upper floors. I saw no shady characters peering out ominously from behind parted curtains.

"It's like the Garden of Eden," Helen said, and the reverence in her voice was clear. She sounded as though she were standing in the hallowed nave of a venerated church.

"Or a German fairy tale," I countered. "And you know how most of those end . . ."

She released my hand and went to the staircase. I followed. At the top, we crossed a pointed-arched gallery decorated with flamboyant Gothic sculptures. We arrived at a large oak door embellished with the monogram *NEH* set into an oval medallion. Below this was a weathered knocker. The ringer was clenched between a gargoyle's jagged teeth.

Helen glanced apprehensively at me.

"Go on," I told her. "This is your show."

"You're the man."

"Don't be old-fashioned."

Rolling her eyes at the gibe that recalled her earlier sarcasm, she rapped the ringer three times against the brass plate. The sound wasn't as heavy or loud as I'd expected it might be.

"Put some muscle into it," I said.

She didn't reply, and I got the feeling she had finally and rightly become uncomfortable with this audacious plan.

"Want to leave?" I asked.

She struck the ringer against the plate three more times, and now the *knock-knock-knock* sounded properly imposing.

A moment later, the door opened.

The woman inside the entrance was tall and oldish but not frail.

She stood straight and regal, as if her mother had made her walk around as a child with books balanced atop her head. Her body looked as though it had been poured into her skintight crimson gown. I found it hard to judge her age, however, because her jet-black hair was long and lustrous (and surely a wig), and she wore enough over-the-top makeup that she might have been auditioning for a turn as the macabre matriarch of a new Addams Family reboot. Her green eyes studied us indifferently.

"*¿Les puedo ayudar?*" she said, raising one pencil-thin eyebrow.

"*Buenos días,*" Helen replied. "*¿Habla usted Inglés?*"

The woman continued to study us silently for several uncomfortable seconds before replying simply, "I do."

"Oh! Well, that's a relief. My Spanish isn't very good. I've just moved here . . ."

Helen paused, and if she was waiting for a response, she didn't get one.

"My friend and I," she went on, "we heard—umm, you know what, we might actually have the wrong house?—but we heard there was a kind of contest being held here? Or around here? Like a haunted house contest?"

Those green eyes didn't blink. "Who told you this?"

"Um, these . . . two guys?"

She looked at me for help. And while it was amusing to hear Helen floundering—she was practically speaking in questions—I decided a prompt exit would be best for everybody and said, "Look, I'm sorry we bothered you. There was a misunderstanding, and we'll be on our way—"

"Who told you there was a competition here?"

The woman didn't raise her voice, but something in it had changed—hardened—and while my instinct was to leave, and quickly (why I might have felt threatened by an old woman, I didn't know), I didn't, not yet. I would leave on my terms, not be chased away.

Jen used to tell me I was too stubborn for my own good, and she was often more right than wrong.

"I overheard a couple of backpackers talking about a house across the street from the Picasso Museum," I told the woman. "They mentioned it was holding some sort of contest. We found ourselves down here this morning, saw this house, and thought it might have been the place. Again, we're sorry for bothering you." To Helen, I added, "We should go."

"No, do come inside," the woman said, and she smiled for the first time, her red lips parting to reveal very white but crooked teeth. "You found your way here, and that is not something many people do. You are my guests."

"So there's a competition here, after all?" Helen asked.

"There is, indeed," the woman said, still smiling, and the smile was pleasant enough to quiet the small voice in my head that said going inside The No-End House was the last thing we should do.

"And there's a prize?" Helen pressed.

"There is that, too."

"Ha! Told you, Joe."

She snatched my hand in hers again, and we entered the house.

Chapter 5

"A house lives and breathes only when a warm
heart beats from within."
—The Book of Nine

You wouldn't be blamed for confusing the entrance hall of
The No-End House with one belonging to a château on
the grounds of the Palace of Versailles. Although the painted
coffered ceiling was clearly from the Middle Ages, the rest of
the room was a sumptuous mélange of different European
periods. I was particularly impressed by the silvered mirrored
panels that could be lowered by a crank to obscure the windows. I'd never seen such a thing and thought it was a creative substitute for blinds, especially since the mirrors would
reflect the flames from all the candles in the room, and there
were candles everywhere.

Our host showed Helen and me to a settee upholstered in
silk. She sat in an armchair next to a floor-standing candelabra and crossed her legs. "I am Isabella Dávila y Osorio,
Eleventh Marchioness of Astorga," she stated.

"I'm, uh, Joe," I said, feeling a little like I was sitting down for a job interview for a position I knew nothing about. I hooked a thumb. "This is Helen."

"You are both American, *sí*?"

"I'm from Chicago," Helen said. "Joe's from Arizona."

The woman weaved her fingers elegantly together on her lap and said nothing more. The flames from the gilded candelabra's tall white candles flicked shadows across her face, adding uncanny animations to her still features.

I couldn't help feeling she was scrutinizing us, judging us, and I didn't like it.

"So . . . how does this work?" I asked bluntly to end the uncomfortable pause.

"What have you heard?" she asked.

"That anybody who stays here overnight receives a cash prize," Helen said.

"Yes . . . and no," replied the woman. "There are nine rooms within The No-End House dedicated to what you, señorita, previously referred to as a competition, and what I refer to as a challenge." She spoke in fluent English, although her Spanish accent was stiff and lilting.

"Is there a difference, Señora . . . Osorio?"

"You may call me Doña Isabella, that is fine."

"Doña Isabella, okay. So what's the difference between a competition and a challenge?"

"A competition implies that you would be competing against others. That is not the case within The No-End House. Here, you will face a series of events that are intended to persuade you—*sí*, to challenge you—to perform actions that you otherwise would not perform."

"Such as . . . ?"

"That will be for you to find out for yourself."

"How about some broad instruction then?" I said, amused by her cloak-and-dagger routine. "Can you at least give us that?"

She pinned me with her heavily mascaraed eyes, and I sensed more scrutinizing and judging, as if she'd detected the condescension in my thoughts that hadn't been in my words. "As I mentioned, there are nine rooms within the walls of this house, Señor Joe from Arizona. Each one contains a specific challenge that must be overcome before progressing to the next room—or, in the case of the final room, the exit. There is no time limit. The challenge will take however long it takes."

"And the prize?" Helen asked.

"That depends on the contestant."

"It's different for everybody?"

"It is."

"What would ours be . . . if we were successful?"

"What would you like?"

"A new iPad," I deadpanned.

Helen shot me a disapproving look. Doña Isabella waited patiently.

"Ten thousand dollars," Helen announced.

If the number shocked the old woman, she didn't show it. She said simply, "That is more than most ask for."

"I've just moved to Barcelona for work. I'm still living out of a hotel. I could use some help paying the first and last month's rent on an apartment. And Joe . . . well, he has a lot of traveling ahead of him. So we could both use the money."

"It is lucky for you then that money is something I have to spare." A curt bob of her head. "Ten thousand dollars, agreed."

I blinked. "Just like that?"

"I believe you both will make worthy participants."

"What I meant was," Helen said, "ten thousand—each."

A ghost of a frown tugged at the edges of Doña Isabella's red lips. "I am a generous woman," she said evenly. "But I am not a foolish one, señorita, and I do not wish to be treated as such."

Helen twisted her mouth, then found something interesting to study on her lap.

"What are the odds that we make it to the exit?" I asked.

"That would be up to you."

"Based on how past participants fared . . . do we have a fifty-fifty shot? More? Less . . . ?"

"The challenge is not impossible, Señor Joe. But it is by no means a trivial undertaking, either." She stood abruptly. "I see you remain undecided, so take a few minutes to discuss what you will in private. When I return, I will expect a decision."

She left the room.

"Ten thousand dollars!" Helen said. "That's double what she was offering those backpackers."

"Ten grand—for what?" I said. "Simply getting through her haunted house?"

"Look around, Joe. You think ten thousand dollars means anything to her? She's loaded. She's blah-buh-blah-blah Marchioness of whatever."

"What the hell's a marchioness, anyway?"

"The wife of a marquis . . . or the widow. Yeah, Izzy looks like a widow. In any event, she's an aristocrat with a pretty impressive pedigree."

"Right, so why's she doing *this*?"

"Because she has millions of dollars and she *can*. She's gotta be, what, eighty?"

"I'd say more like . . . sixty."

"Sixty! She had more lines on her face than a road atlas of Europe. Seventy—at least. And people that age with money do weird shit. They go on never-ending cruises. Shuffleboard and comedy skits and amateur musicals until the end of days, that's their thing. And this is *her* thing. Better than sitting in a rocking chair and staring out the window all day, right? Have you ever done an escape room?"

I had. Four years ago, almost a year to the day of Jen's death, we had been in Los Angeles for no other reason than to get out of Arizona for a weekend. We'd done all the touristy stuff we could fit into a couple of days: the Hollywood sign, the Getty Center, Madame Tussauds, Muscle Beach. On Saturday night, we'd eaten at a Korean BBQ restaurant in Koreatown and were walking back to our hotel when we passed a sketchy building advertising an escape room. We were both a bit tipsy and decided to buy tickets. The gist of the story was that we were abducted by a cannibalistic serial killer and locked in the basement of his deceased mother's home, and if we didn't escape in time, we'd be his latest meal. The set was straight out of a horror movie: dark, gritty, oftentimes gross (and there was even a live actor involved—a freaky yet charismatic fellow—who offered some assistance when we got stuck). Which happened a fair bit, because the bulk of the gameplay centered on finding objects and puzzles hidden everywhere.

I'd never considered that The No-End House could be one big escape room, and I told Helen as much.

"You heard Izzy," Helen said. "*Challenge, challenge, challenge.* She wouldn't shut up with that word. So she's pretty excited about whatever she's put together. Actually, I wouldn't be surprised if she hired some legit escape-room company to operate out of her house so she can have a front-row view of the action. Maybe she's even the game master."

"We never asked her if she's going to film us."

"So ask her when she comes back, Joe. Does it even matter? She's clearly not some YouTube or TikTok influencer who's going to post you all over the internet. She's a lonely old spinster who doesn't mind shelling out her inheritance for entertainment. Don't you want the money?"

"It's not about the money, Helen. Ten grand would be great—or five grand, after we split it, I guess. What I'm more concerned about is—"

The door to the room opened, and the noblewoman Doña Isabella entered, her petite and svelte figure made larger-than-life by the Cher wig and Morticia makeup and slinky red gown.

Before I could get a word in, Helen said, "We accept."

Doña Isabella led us to an adjoining room. It might have been her study, and it was just as over-the-top and glamorous as the entrance hall. The showstopper was the faded remains of a full-wall fresco that depicted a battle between angels and demons with gods and goddesses watching down from the clouds. In fact, I noticed a religious motif throughout the room, from the artwork and statuary and vases to the cherubs and crucifixes carved into the antique furniture. There was also an arched door with giant cast-iron hinges from which spread black, creeping tentacles that ultimately encircled an elaborate *1* carved into the solid wood panel.

Doña Isabella went to a rolltop desk and withdrew a piece of paper backed in triplicate from one of the drawers. She beckoned us over with a smart curl of her finger and said, "Please read this contract and sign the bottom when you are finished."

Helen picked up the contract, and I read it over her shoulder:

THE NO-END HOUSE
Service Agreement

This agreement is made and entered into by and between Isabella Dávila y Osorio, 11th Marchioness of Astorga, hereinafter for convenience called MANAGE-MENT and (name) _____ hereinafter for convenience called SECOND PARTY.

SECOND PARTY agrees to participate in The No-End House Challenge and accept the outcome on (date) *October 2025*

For the above service MANAGEMENT agrees to pay SECOND PARTY *$10,000* made payable to _____ immediately following the conclusion of services provided.

SECOND PARTY agrees on forfeiture of the cash prize if he/she chooses to withdraw from the challenge before exiting Room 9 or if he/she fails to reach Room 9.*

Subject to the provisions set forth above, the agreement is legally binding and shall become effective immediately upon execution by both parties.

Accepted and Agreed to by:

Isabella Dávila y Osorio   *Oct '25*
Isabella Dávila y Osorio, 11th Marchioness of Astorga   Date

For Second Party:

_____
Signature   Date

*In the event of the forfeiture of the cash prize, the undersigned also forfeit the eternal rights to item 1, hereinafter referred to as SOUL to MANAGEMENT. At the time of the undersigned's death, SOUL will become property of The No-End House to trade or sell as MANAGEMENT sees fit with no regard to time or universe.

Frowning, I said, "What's the difference between with-drawing from the challenge before reaching the end of it or failing to reach the end? Isn't that the same thing?"

"I am not a lawyer, Señor Joe," said Doña Isabella, "but that seems like lawyer gibberish to me, no?"

"Whatever," Helen said. "If we don't complete the compe-tition—sorry, *challenge*—then we don't get the prize. That's fair."

"What does that say?" I asked, pointing to the footnote that was written in a much smaller font than the rest of the legalese. "I can't read it without my glasses."

Helen squinted and said: "In the event of forfeiture of the cash prize, the undersigned also forfeit the eternal rights to item 1, hereinafter referred to as Soul, to Management. At the time of the undersigned's death, Soul will become the property of The No-End House to trade or sell as Manage-ment sees fit with no regard to time or universe."

I laughed. "Did you just make that up?"

Helen shook her head. "That's what it says."

We both looked at Doña Isabella.

She smiled pleasantly. "A little dark humor, *sí*?"

"Dark humor or not," I said, "I'm not signing my name to anything that requires me to forfeit my soul, thanks."

"Oh, come on, Joe," Helen said. "She's just trying to psych us out." She pointed to a cobalt blue inkpot and glass dip pen on the desk. "Can I use that?"

"Please."

Helen scribbled our names where required (she had to ask me for my surname, and I had to spell it out), and then she signed and dated the bottom line. She handed me the pen.

I hesitated to take it. A primitive, ridiculous dread pre-vented me. I knew the footnote clause was a joke. It was part of the game, no different than the "disclaimer" that Jen and I had signed in LA absolving the escape room company of any liability if we were eaten by the cannibal. As Helen said, it was meant to psych us out—or get us psyched up—before entering the challenge.

Yet even though I understood all this, the dread remained; it was powered by gut instinct, not reason.

I glanced at the door with the elaborately carved 1, then back at the contract. A droplet of ink fell from the pen's metal nib and struck a top corner.

"Come *on*, Joe," Helen said. "What are you waiting for?"

Reluctantly, I took the old-fashioned pen and signed my name to the document.

Doña Isabella left with the whacko contract in hand, telling us she had to get things ready and that it wouldn't take too long. We paced in the study, too anxious to sit. At least I was anxious; Helen might have simply been interested in all the museum-quality furnishings and knickknacks. She was, I was learning quickly, impulsive and a little fearless, and I wasn't sure what to make of that. After all, fear is meant to keep a person's most foolish and self-destructive impulses in check.

About thirty minutes after the old woman left us, electronics whirred inside the door with the carved 1, followed by the sharp *clack!* of a dead bolt releasing. The heavy door swung inward a few inches, revealing a strip of very black darkness.

"Finally," Helen said.

"After you," I said.

Chapter 6

"A room is infinite space if not corralled by
walls."
—The Book of Nine

The door closed and locked on its own.

"No turning back," I said, rattling the brass handle futilely.

"Why would we turn back?" Helen said. "We're just starting."

"This isn't a room," I said, looking down an arched stone tunnel that funneled away from us. Candles in cast-iron wall sconces illuminated pockets of orange light in the darkness, although they were placed at far enough intervals to ensure that plenty of shadows thrived in the spaces between.

"Do you want to hold my hand?"

"No."

"Then stop sounding so scared, and let's find the first room."

The passage wasn't wide enough to allow us to walk abreast, so I followed Helen. The only sound was our footsteps on the stone pavers. The tomblike quiet surprised me. No discordant, creepy music playing over a crackly PA system? No sinister laughter and terrified screams and other shock sound effects?

"Maybe we weren't supposed to enter yet?" I said.

"The door opened, didn't it?" Helen replied over her shoulder. "And these candles are all lit."

We came to a set of steep stairs. There were no handrails, so we proceeded down them cautiously, bracing our hands against the cool stone walls. At the bottom, a thick white fog covered the ground and swirled around our knees.

"Dry ice," I said. "That's more like it."

"More like what?" Helen asked.

"A haunted house."

"I'm still waiting for a jump scare—"

She froze abruptly. I bumped into her back.

"What?" I said, confused.

"*Something brushed my leg.*"

"*What?*" I glanced at the dry ice, reliving a scare I'd had as a kid in a lagoon filled with eels. "What was it?"

Helen laughed in that girlish way of hers, I berated myself for falling for the gag, and we continued walking. Soon we came to a T-junction. To the right, in the center of a dead-end alcove, a human skeleton was positioned on its hands and knees. Two skeletal legs, feet skyward, were braced against its shoulders. The rest of the second skeleton was obscured by the white fog, but my imagination had no problem visualizing it on its back, in a variation of the missionary position.

"Oh, Izzy!" Helen said, pressing a hand to her chest in amusement.

I went to the morbid, erotic display (those two adjectives had no business hanging out in the same sentence together) and swiped my arm through the dry ice, briefly revealing a pair of skeletal hands gripping either side of a moth-shaped pelvis—

Red lights flashed in the kneeling skeleton's globular eye sockets. Its hips thrust back and forth in a jerky, unnatural rhythm. A woman's orgasmic squeal burst from hidden speakers. The squeal tapered to a moan and then played again on a loop.

I had leaped backward in surprise when the skeleton first moved, and Helen was laughing again. Whether it was at my reaction or the tasteless display, I wasn't sure.

"Didn't expect that . . ." I said, and whatever else I'd been about to say died on my lips.

"It's great!" Helen said. "And the bones look realistic, too. . . . What?"

I was staring past her at a huge man—he must have been at least six and a half feet tall—who stood directly behind her. He wore a burlap sack over his head and denim overalls with only one strap hooked over his broad, bare shoulders.

Helen turned and gasped and jumped about twice as high as I had moments earlier.

I said, "Hey, buddy."

The man didn't reply, and I wondered if it was an animatronic puppet like the skeletons. However, I dismissed the idea almost immediately; the eyeball peering through the single slit in the burlap sack was far too lifelike.

"Where did you come from?" Helen demanded, sounding angry at being startled.

I noticed the man held a hatchet in each hand—they were vintage and real, certainly not plastic props—and despite knowing he was an actor, someone harmless hired to frighten us, I felt a sense of foreboding in the isolated and claustrophobic passageway.

"I think we'll be on our way," I said, and placed a hand against the small of Helen's back to guide her past the thug.

He remained mute, but the eyeball peering out of the slit followed us.

When we were a dozen feet away, I looked back.

The guy faced in our direction, his large frame filling the tunnel.

"What a freak," Helen whispered so her voice wouldn't carry. "I didn't even hear him sneak up on us."

"Pretty quiet for a big guy," I agreed.

"Where did he come from?"

"Behind us through the door with the *1*?"

"No, where did he *come* from? Izzy didn't know we were coming today. How'd she get him here so quickly?"

I shrugged. "We were in her study for a good half an hour. He probably lives somewhere close by."

"That mask or potato sack or whatever it was . . ."

"A Jason rip-off is what it was."

"*Friday the Thirteenth*, Jason? He wore a hockey mask."

"In the second film, he wore a sack with an eyehole. The writers switched it to a hockey mask because some other movie around the time had an actor who wore a sack. They wanted to be original."

"What did Jason wear in the first film?"

"If you don't know the answer to that, I think you should watch it again."

"I never watched it in the first place. I hate horror movies . . . Joe!"

She pointed at a hatchet protruding from the wall a little way down the tunnel from us. The blade, we discovered, was wedged in a crack between two stones where the mortar had broken away.

Pinched between it and the wall was a Polaroid photograph.

Helen plucked it free and said, "That's *us*!"

It was indeed a shot of Helen and me from earlier when we were standing in the courtyard.

"Who took it?" she asked, flipping it over. Nothing was written on the back. "Izzy?"

The perspective suggested the person had been above us, looking down, and I said, "They would have been up on the second or third floor."

"I didn't see anybody in any of the windows."

"A motion detector in the courtyard might trigger a camera automatically."

Helen frowned. "But why?"

I shrugged. "To mess with us? Anyway, it's yours now. A memento of our time together."

She tucked it into a pocket. "I'll cherish it forever, Joe. Thank you."

I looked behind us again. I didn't see the big guy. Either he'd returned to the palace, or he was still back there in the tunnel, still facing us, concealed in the shadows.

The image unnerved me, and I said, "Let's keep going. The room can't be too much farther ahead."

We reached it a minute later, after a descent down another steep staircase. An arched doorway led to a small room with a vault ceiling supported by thick stone pillars. A two-tier medieval chandelier hung from where the four arcing faces met in the middle of the ceiling. The many burning candles revealed some sort of stagecoach parked against the far wall . . . although it more closely resembled a tiny mountain hut on wagon wheels, as it featured a shingled roof and iron chimney. The rear double-leaf door was open, and a preposterously obese man sat on a plank between the two panels, which contained all sorts of little shelves and drawers and pigeonholes overflowing with trinkets. Salted fish and links of sausages and a smoked leg of ham (with what appeared to be a large bite torn free) dangled from hooks and chains above him.

The man wore a bejeweled necklace and flamboyant rings. Beneath a fur-trimmed sleeveless emerald coat, a stained white tunic was stretched to the seams to contain his grotesque belly, which hung over his waist almost to his knees. Skintight beige breeches outlined his groin in unabashed detail and showed every crease and fold of fat in his legs. His ankles and bare feet appeared blotched and swollen.

Despite the awkward seat, the man seemed perfectly comfortable, with a leather-bound book propped open in one pudgy hand and a cigar in the other.

In front of the stagecoach stood a large table covered in an oilcloth patterned with whimsical creatures. On it were half a dozen oblong bronze boxes that resembled miniature caskets.

Helen and I stopped in front of the table.

The man, who until then had ignored us, looked up from his book. A Cheshire grin spread between his fleshy jowls. "My young friends!" he said, with a Spanish accent similar to Doña Isabella's. "What took you so long to find me?"

"Who are you supposed to be?" Helen asked, easily slipping into the spirit of the game.

"Supposed to be? I am who I have always been, señorita. But if you mean what it is that I do, I am but a humble merchant."

"I imagine you don't get too many customers down here under the palace."

"Now and then, somebody comes my way," he said, and puffed on the cigar.

I glanced at the bronze boxes. "What do you sell?"

"Anything you wish, señor. But *that*"—he waved an arm expansively at the table—"is not merchandise. That is my dinner."

"Your dinner?"

He bobbed his head, his chin dipping into the other two.

"I am somewhat of a gourmet, my friends. I use only the finest ingredients in my meals. Some time ago I was harvesting autumn truffles from a grove of oak trees. Unknown to me, the land—and the truffles—belonged to an evil sorceress. She cast a spell on me, and ever since, I cannot trust my sight and smell to identify food. A very curious and cruel spell to cast on one who considers himself a gourmet, would you not agree? So now I must rely on the kindness of wanderers such as yourselves for help with my gastronomic endeavors."

"So there's food in those boxes?" Helen said.

"Only the finest ingredients," insisted the fat man.

I'd watched enough reality TV to guess where this "challenge" might be going, and I said, "I'm not eating cockroaches or cow testicles."

"Yuck!" Helen said, looking appalled. "Is this one of *those* games?"

"I have no idea what game you mean, señorita. But you need not taste anything. All I ask is for you to identify the ingredients I have collected." With an aggrieved groan, he hefted his massive bulk and descended three steps, which creaked precariously, at the back of the stagecoach. He tossed away the cigar, retrieved a stack of ivory envelopes from a pigeonhole in the door, and waddled to the table. He placed one envelope in front of each of the six bronze boxes.

They were stamped with gold fleurs-de-lis and labeled with different—and presumably human—organs.

"Due to the sorceress's spell," said the fat man, "what I have written on the envelopes is what my cursed senses tell me is in each box. What I need one of you to do is to tell me, by touch alone, the true ingredient."

"And if we play the game?" I asked.

"I will show you what you seek."

"The way to the next room?"

"Exactly, señor! But there is a caveat." He smoothed his

hands together like a villain reveling in his sinister machinations. "For each ingredient you guess incorrectly, you will forfeit one of your organs of my choosing."

"Great," I said. "First our souls, now our organs."

Helen wrinkled her nose. "I bet it's going to be some gross stuff in the boxes. You can do this one, Joe."

"Excellent!" The fat man stuck out a heavy hand. "A gentleman's agreement, consummated by a gentlemanly handshake."

What the hell, I thought. And shook.

The obese lord—I couldn't help but think of him simply as "Lard-Ass," as he bore a resemblance (although he was much older and much, much fatter) to the pie-eating character from the Stephen King movie about those four boys— opened the lid of the first bronze box. It lifted on hinges toward me to stand in a vertical position, preventing me from seeing what was inside the box. I reached my hand over the top of the lid and averted my eyes so I couldn't be accused of peeking. *Eyeballs* was written in a careful script on the box's corresponding envelope, and what I felt were slippery and wet and very well could have been eyeballs. They also could have been olives. That was going to be my guess, but at the last second, I changed my mind and said, "Pickled onions."

"Pickled onions," said the obese man. He used a quill and inkpot he'd retrieved from the stagecoach to jot down my answer in his leather book.

After I wiped my hand on the oilcloth to rid it of whatever foul juice had been poured over the "eyeballs," I went on and guessed the contents of the next five boxes.

"Bravo, señor!" Lard-Ass said gleefully when I'd finished. "The sorceress's spell holds little sway over one as skilled as yourself at identifying food!"

"Joe's a man of many talents," Helen said dryly.

"I think I did a pretty good job," I told her.

"Let's find out then, shall we?" said Lard-Ass. "Señorita, would you please open the last envelope first?"

Helen picked up the envelope labeled *Heart* and slid out a plain white card on which was written *Chicken breast.*

"Bravo again, señor!" exclaimed the fat man. "How I could ever mistake a tender, juicy chicken breast for a human heart . . . that is the tragedy of my curse, no?"

I couldn't resist and said, "Did you really need my help when the answers to your dilemma have been written inside the envelopes all this time?"

Helen swatted my arm and said, "Be a good sport, will you?"

The fat man merely smiled at me . . . and there was something in his eyes that hadn't been there a moment before, or perhaps it was a *lack* of something, a lessening of the phony enthusiasm.

Helen opened the next four envelopes, and my guesses were all correct: ground beef (brains), dried apricots (ears), sliced banana (tongue), and sweet corn (teeth).

"Are teeth even organs?" I asked.

"They're composed of enamel and other tissues," Helen said, "and if the definition of an organ is a collection of tissues that perform a specific function, then yes, Mr. Smarty-Pants, they are."

"Señorita, please," said Lard-Ass. "The final envelope."

It was the one labeled *Eyeballs.* Helen slipped free the white card and said, "Peeled grapes. Ha, Joe! You got it wrong!"

"Five out of six isn't bad," I said.

"It certainly is not," said Lard-Ass. "Nevertheless, per the terms of our agreement, you are in debt to me one organ of my choosing."

"How about a tooth?"

"No way," Helen said. "He's going to want your brain or heart—still beating, presumably."

"That is a decision I will make shortly. But now is the time for me to uphold my end of the bargain."

He waddled back to the stagecoach and closed the double-leaf door.

On the back of it, painted in thick black brushstrokes, was the number 2.

Chapter 7

"To get lost and give up, or to give up and get
lost, both are a union made in hell."
—The Book of Nine

"Check it out, Joe!" Helen said. She was crouched inside the stagecoach. "There's a hole in the wall that
leads to another tunnel!"

I climbed the wood steps, ducked below the dangling spec-
imens of cured meat, and crouch-walked into the carriage.
The shelves lining the interior were crowded with all sorts of
vials and jars containing spices and dried herbs and other
ingredients. Other glass containers held a variety of living
insects—which, who knew, might have also been culinary
ingredients. There wasn't much room for furniture, but Lard-
Ass had managed to fit a writing desk and stool in one corner
(no regular chair with arms could ever accommodate a back-
side as impressive as his), as well as a small cast-iron stove. A
sweet-sour smell permeated the dark and cluttered space, and
I did my best to hold my breath until I reached the hole in the
wall.

The hole was a crumbling jaw of broken stone, clearly not

part of any original design but rather made with brute force. Helen had already slipped through it. I followed feet-first, dropped a short distance to the floor (piled with rubble that had once been part of the wall), and found myself in another vaulted tunnel. It was similar in height and width to the previous ones, but the tightly fitted stones were larger and much more crudely cut. Although there were no longer candles to light the way, a burning torch was secured in the ornamental bracket of a lone wall sconce.

Helen plucked it free. The stave was the leg bone of a deer or other similarly sized animal, and the combustible end burned bright and high. I wondered who had lit the wick, because there was no way Lard-Ass could have fit through the hole in the wall to reach it.

Helen whooshed the torch this way and that. "It's heavier than it looks!"

"It suits you," I said.

"What does that mean, Joe?"

"You're a bit savage—it suits you."

"Savage? You said I look like Helen of Troy. She's hardly savage."

"That was then. Now that I've started to get to know you better . . ."

She thrust the torch at me. If I hadn't flinched away, she might have singed off my eyebrows.

"Hey! Watch it!"

"You don't know me at all," she said, and started down the tunnel.

I hustled to catch up. She didn't say anything more, and I wondered if I had genuinely ticked her off.

"One room down," I said, to say something. "Eight to go."

Helen said nothing.

I glanced sidelong at her. Her face was impassive.

"What?" she said.

"You seem pissed off."

"It wasn't funny."

I played that know-you-better remark every which way in my head, and I couldn't figure out why it might have been so offensive to her. I was clearly kidding around.

We walked in silence, and my thoughts ended up on a girl I'd once known named Lisa Barlow. This was a couple of years before I'd met Jen, and I'd been single and dating a fair bit. I was living in a condo in Flagstaff, Lisa lived on the floor below me, and we became elevator acquaintances. One Friday she invited me to her place for a drink. I already had plans for later that night but told her I'd come by before I went out. This ended up becoming a regular thing: every Friday or Saturday night, we'd have a few drinks together at her place or mine before we went our separate ways. We got along great, we were similar in age, we had stuff in common. We probably would have made a good couple. I think we remained platonic, however, because we'd missed our window; we'd remained friends for too long to become anything more than friends. Because how do you kiss a friend? And what happened to the friendship if the romance was miscalculated or if it died? In retrospect, maybe I had been overthinking, and things would have turned out great between us.

The point was, we never got together . . . but our friendship still went pear-shaped in the end.

One weekend I had no plans, and instead of stopping by Lisa's place for one or two drinks, I ended up getting smashed there. She got smashed, too, because she was mixing a new Filipino cocktail she'd discovered, something called a weng weng, which was essentially a Long Island iced tea on steroids. At one point—details of the evening remain foggy—she suggested we go out somewhere, maybe to dinner, and I jokingly told her we couldn't because we weren't *friend* friends, just *neighbor* friends.

Well, that was it. She shut down. I felt like I was suddenly in a stranger's home, and after making up some excuse, I stumbled back to my condo and passed out.

Lisa never got over the innocuous remark. She never invited me over to her place again; she never returned any of my calls or messages. Bumping into each other in the elevator became such an ordeal that I ended up moving out of the building.

In the end, it had all worked out for the best, because I'd bought the house in Green Valley and met Jen at a local Zara boutique. (She'd asked me to try on a sweater because I was the same size as her "boyfriend," although as I found out after we struck up a conversation and went for coffee, she never had a boyfriend to begin with . . . but those were memories for a different time. . . .)

Right now, I wanted to figure out why Helen was so pissed off at me, and while I didn't think she felt romantically snubbed like Lisa had, it was pretty clear a mental switch had been flicked.

What might have triggered that, I had no fucking idea, but it would be best to tread carefully on the topic . . . or maybe not tread on it at all.

I decided on the latter approach, and we continued walking without speaking to each other. I was looking forward to the next costumed actor or animatronic prop or whatever to inject some levity into the sullen silence.

What greeted us first, it turned out, was one of those funhouse mirrors that distorts your image. It was large, almost six feet from top to bottom, and affixed to the stone wall on our right. Helen's reflection looked as though a giant had grabbed hold of either end of her and pulled with all its might. Mine featured legs that went to my neck.

I was about to crack a joke about Helen's elongated midsection—*So you finally grew a spine, hey*—but given how she'd reacted to the know-you-better comment, I figured it would be more prudent to pick on myself.

I said, "I look like one of those aliens from *War of the Worlds*."

"Never saw it."

"Not even the Tom Cruise one?"

"Nope."

Curt, quiet, cranky.

I tried my best Travolta *Saturday Night Fever* dance move, hips swinging, fingers pointing skyward. My leggy doppelgänger looked so ridiculous that if Helen hadn't laughed, I would have considered our relationship irrevocably broken and called it quits on The No-End House challenge right then.

Thankfully, she did laugh. Then she passed me the torch— it was indeed heavier than it looked—and did a pretty good "Gangnam Style" interpretation, which made me laugh, too.

When we started walking again, Helen seemed back to her old self and said, "I can't decide if this is the worst or best haunted house I've been to. I mean, the palace was cool, these tunnels are cool, and the fat dude was top-notch. But the skeletons? Come on. And that Jason copycat didn't even say a word. And now a single carnival mirror?"

"I think you spoke too soon." I pointed ahead of us to where the torch's jittery flame revealed several more mirrors affixed to the walls of the tunnel.

As we passed them, more and more appeared, one step ahead of us, one step behind the continually retreating darkness. They were all shapes and sizes, encased in a variety of frames, and arranged haphazardly. Each one reflected warped images of Helen and me, so depending on our perspective, we might have anything from a Cyclops' eye, triple eyes, puckered fish lips, blown-up cheeks, bulging foreheads, mangled limbs, caricature expressions, anything.

Helen said, "It looks like the mirrors just keep going."

I said, "This is getting a bit creepy now."

"They're just mirrors, Joe."

"There must be hundreds down here, Helen. Yeah, Izzy is eccentric, but this is eccentric even for an eccentric. Where do you get so many mirrors? It's not like they're all off the same production line. Each one is different—and old." I trailed my free hand along a gold-leaf frame on my left. "No dust."

"Dust doesn't usually form underground. On the surface, it comes from pollution or pollen or soil particles. There's none of that down here, and no wind to blow it around even if there was."

"Inside it comes from dead skin cells."

"And hair and clothing fibers and other stuff. But these tunnels aren't exactly Grand Central Station. Nowhere near enough people would pass through them to leave behind a noticeable amount of dust."

"Why are we talking about dust . . . ?"

"You brought it up."

"Where's this fucking next room?"

"What's the rush?"

I shrugged. There wasn't a rush, of course. I had nowhere else I had to be. But you didn't have to be in a rush to want to get something done, and I was starting to get tired of walking aimlessly around Izzy's basement . . .

Suddenly my hand was in Helen's hand, and she was squeezing it tightly. She pointed to a mirror on our left.

Someone was inside it and trying to get out.

First, the someone was a midget. I thought his diminutive size was due to the mirror's distortion effect (a non sequitur, because he was *inside* the mirror), but then I noticed the surface of this particular mirror was neither concave nor convex, and his limbs and other body parts were all in proper harmony.

Second, he was dressed as a Nazi. His uniform was mostly black, from the military-style peaked cap down to the calf-high jackboots.

The only spots of color were a red swastika armband and a tan shirt beneath the greatcoat. A silver and gold pendant depicting the twin SS lightning bolts swung wildly from a chain around his neck as his fists pounded the inside of the mirror. His face was a maelstrom of rage, his lips mouthing words we couldn't hear.

"Jesus! That nearly gave me a heart attack," Helen said, releasing my hand and going to the mirror. She examined the plain black frame. "A TV in a frame—pretty neat, Izzy." She stepped back and studied the furious Nazi. "And a pretty spectacular picture."

"I've never seen any TVs with that shape," I said. "It's a lot more rectangular than square."

"What are you saying, Joe? It's not a TV? A midget Nazi is actually trapped inside a magic mirror? Hold on—let me test it. Mirror, mirror on the wall, who in this land is fairest of them all?" She clasped her hands dreamily against her chest. "Oh, why thank you! Did you hear that, Joe? The midget just told me *I'm* the fairest lady in the land!"

"Dwarf."

"Don't call me a dwarf, you ogre."

"I meant—"

"I know what you meant. And give me a break. Even midgets call themselves midgets."

I stepped close to the mirror and drew my finger from side to side, the way a cop might during a field sobriety test.

The midget's eyes didn't follow my finger.

When we began walking again, Helen said, "My feet hurt."

I looked at her feet. She wore beige wedge sandals. "You should have worn something more comfortable."

"I thought we were just going for a stroll."

"Ah, right, I forgot."

"It's true, Joe. I didn't lead us here. We just ended up here."

"Do you want to back out?"

"Of the challenge? No way."

"We haven't even found the second room yet. Your feet are going to get more tired."

"Feet don't get tired. They get sore. And for ten grand, I can put up with sore feet."

"Five grand."

"Not if I kill you and take your winnings for myself."

I frowned at her.

"I'm teasing, Joe. Get into the macabre spirit of things. Oh, great."

We stopped at an intersection in the tunnel. Mirrors covered the walls of the three new passageways.

I said, "Left, right, or straight ahead—?"

Glass shattered from somewhere in the dark behind us.

Helen and I exchanged concerned glances. Before either of us could say anything, a shrill German voice shouted, "*Verdammt!* I am finally free of zat prison! Ant now I am coming for you, my darlink! Do you hear me, *die Schlampe*? I. Am. Coming. For. YOU!"

"Holy shit!" Helen said, looking bloodless in the torchlight.

"Sounds like I'm safe," I said.

"Was that a recording like the skeletons, or do you think—"

"He actually broke out of the mirror—"

"An actor's coming after us?"

"I am going to count to five!" shrieked the voice. "And zen you are mine, *die Schlampe*! One . . . ! Two . . . !"

Helen snatched the torch from me and took two quick steps into the convergence of tunnels. Her eyes darted between the three options. "That way!" She pointed to the left passage.

"Three . . . !"

"Joe, let's *go*!"

"I'm not running anywhere—"

"Four . . . !"

"*Joe!*" she said, and took off running, leaving me alone in coffin blackness.

"*Five!* Ready or not . . . *here I come!*"

"Fuck," I mumbled, and ran, too.

I caught up to Helen at the next intersection of tunnels. She had stopped to decide which passageway to take and must have heard me coming, because she whirled around and said in a breathless, frightened voice, "Joe?"

"Yeah, it's me," I said, stopping as I entered the cone of torchlight in which she stood. "And for future consideration, it's pretty dark down here without that torch."

"I'm sorry, I panicked . . ." She stood stiff and erect.

"Hear anything?" I asked her.

"Shhh!" After several seconds of nothing, she started down the rightmost passage and added, "Hurry, before he finds us."

I hustled to catch up and said, "Maybe we're not supposed to lose him. He might have a clue to the location of the second room."

"You can go back and ask him for a clue if you want. He's not after you."

"What's he going to do, Helen? He's an—"

"Actor! I know that! But look." She thrust out a hand. It

was trembling. "I can't help it. Maybe it was his stupid costume or his voice. I don't know." She shivered. "But I felt . . . violated. Like it was personal. Like he really wanted to . . ."

I frowned, surprised at how shaken she was. "If you want to quit this thing—"

"I don't. I've already told you as much. Let's just . . . keep walking. I'll feel better in a minute." She took the little orange bottle from her handbag and shook the remaining pills onto her palm: two blue, two pink. "Only two Xanax left," she said. "Want to split them?"

I shook my head. Although benzos did little more than make me feel kind of floaty, I wanted to keep my wits about me until we left The No-End House—especially now that there was a psycho midget on our tail.

Helen popped the two blue pills into her mouth and swallowed. Then she held out the pink ones for me to take.

"Right," I said.

"Go on," she said. "You could use a mood adjustment."

"What's wrong with my mood?"

"All your talk about giving up and going home is a bit of a downer."

Helen returned the pink pills to the bottle and the bottle to her handbag, and we kept walking.

I said, "Why don't you ever take the pink ones?"

She shrugged. "Like I told you. They change me."

"For the better."

"Yeah, well . . . not always. And I like who I am right now. I like the time we're spending together. So I don't want to change."

I left it at that.

The torch burned brazenly in the darkness. The reflected flames bounced from mirror to mirror, so we were constantly surrounded by figments of fire. I thought a bit more about the midget Nazi—I didn't blame Helen for feeling the way she did; he really had sounded batshit crazy—before turning my attention to our predicament.

We were no longer in the cellar of The No-End House. We had walked—and run—too far for that to be possible. If we were on the surface, we would likely be a block away from the palace by now.

Suddenly the stroll through the Gràcia district earlier this morning—the warm sun and the blue sky and the bustle of people—seemed a world away, and I wondered why I'd let Helen talk me into this stupid game. At the pace it was unfurling, we still had an hours-long slog ahead of us.

"Not to be the apparent downer that I am," I said eventually, "but you know we're no longer in The No-End House."

"Really?" Helen replied sarcastically.

"I think the cellar ended at the hole in the wall. This tunnel must be part of the city's old drainage system."

"I don't see any water, do you?"

"Sealed-off drainage system," I amended. "I doubt Izzy would have stored her prized collection of mirrors in tunnels that flood with water every time it rains."

"Or maybe we're in a crypt like the ones beneath Paris."

I had visited the City of Light's infamous underworld when I'd passed through Paris two months ago. The circuit open to the public contained thousands upon thousands of bones retained in backfill areas by walls made from rows of tibiae and skulls. Seeing so many jumbled mortal remains was a pretty heavy and introspective experience, but it was also an educational one. An audio guide had explained the history and story of the ossuary, and I said to Helen now, "The catacombs were initially quarry tunnels before they were a mass grave."

"The French don't appreciate cemeteries like the rest of us?"

"Their cemeteries were overcrowded. People were being

buried one on top of the other in shallow graves. Sometimes a storm would wash corpses free."

"Cool."

"Cool?"

"In a nasty kind of way . . ."

"So the graveyards were condemned, and millions of bodies were dug up—always during the middle of the night, so people didn't freak out—and dumped down old quarry wells."

"Who arranged them into those decorative displays?"

"City officials thought it would make for good tourism."

"People are morbid. Who wants to look at piles of bones?"

"Says the girl participating in a haunted house contest."

"*Challenge*, Joe. You'll piss Izzy off if she's listening to us. And I'm only participating for the money—that's it."

I had a thought and said, "After the Nazis took over Paris, they used the catacombs to move around the city. I wonder if that's where Izzy got the idea for the Nazi actor?"

"Can we not talk about him?" Helen glanced over her shoulder into the sepulchral darkness behind us. "He still gives me the creeps."

When we came to yet another intersection, I said, "Any particular tunnel take your fancy . . . ?"

Helen harrumphed. "We're getting lost."

"I think we *are* lost. It's a maze down here."

She perked up. "Hey—what if *this* is the challenge?"

"A maze?"

She nodded. "Maybe there's no Room Two. Maybe we're already in it."

"Should I start touching the wall?"

"Whatever gets you hot, Joe."

"That's how you find the exit to a maze, isn't it? You keep one hand in contact with the same wall and walk until you get out."

"That's silly kid talk. The only guaranteed way to exit a maze is the old-fashioned way." She passed me the torch, opened her little black handbag, and withdrew the brown paper Starbucks bag that contained her half-eaten blueberry muffin.

"Breadcrumbs?"

"Muffin crumbs, in this case. We leave a trail of them behind us. If we end up backtracking, we take the passage without crumbs."

"And if we backtrack to where all the passages have crumbs?"

"We choose a random direction and leave a new trail next to the old one. The cardinal rule is never select a path that already contains two trails."

"Cardinal rule, huh? Is this a theory or science?"

"It's based on a mathematical algorithm, so I suppose it's a science. Do I impress you?" She broke off a crumb from the muffin, dropped it by our feet, and started down the passageway on our right. After a few yards, she stopped and turned around. "Are you coming or what? I can't see in the dark."

I didn't have much confidence in her so-called algorithm, but some sort of plan was better than no plan, so I said, "I'm coming, Gretel, chill out."

Ten minutes and numerous passageways later, we were more lost than ever.

"This is driving me nuts!" Helen said, her fists planted defiantly on her hips. We had stopped at a new fork in the tunnel. Both passageways disappeared into blackness. They still featured mirrors, but far fewer than the earlier tunnels. "How far could these tunnels possibly go?"

I shrugged. "The ones under Paris stretch for two or three hundred miles."

"We're not under Paris. We're under Barcelona. And I've

never heard of tunnels beneath Barcelona—certainly not hundreds of miles of tunnels."

"All I'm saying is that if these tunnels are even a fraction of the size of the Paris Catacombs, we could be walking for days. Anyway, what I'm more worried about is this torch." I gave it a little heft. "It's not going to last forever. And when it goes out, it's going to be pitch-black."

Helen shook her head. "This can't be right. Why would Izzy make a maze with no end?"

"Considering what she'd named her house . . ."

"She wouldn't put us in a maze that went for miles and miles with a torch that could burn out and leave us in perfect darkness."

"That's exactly what she's done."

"No, we've screwed up—"

"We can still follow the muffin crumbs back—"

"I mean the *challenge*. We screwed up the challenge."

"I'm pretty sure we should have talked to the midget."

I slumped to the ground with my back to the stone wall. Helen sat against the wall across from me. She closed her eyes and tilted her head back.

"I'm exhausted," she said. "Wake me up if you figure out how to get us out of here."

I brainstormed that for a little, made no progress, and took my journal from my jacket pocket. I wrote in it for a good ten minutes, detailing what we'd experienced so far in The No-End House, when Helen finally opened her eyes.

"Writing about me again?" she asked.

"How do you spell *corral*? One *r* or two?"

"Like where goats graze?"

"Yeah."

"Two. Why are you writing about goats?"

"Writing is therapeutic. You should try it sometime . . ."

Suddenly and terrifyingly, something familiar scuttled

deep inside my skull. I rubbed the center of my forehead with the heel of my palm, hoping against hope. The little circles did no good. The dull ache was already sharpening to a needle-like point, and I prayed: *Not now, goddammit. Jesus Christ, not now.*

Prayers, of course, were nothing more than optimistic thoughts. They didn't save Jen from her coma. They didn't improve my state of mind when it had been at its lowest in the years after she passed away. And they certainly never prevented one of my migraines from tearing through my skull when it so pleased. Regardless, I continued to pray, because my migraines weren't the run-of-the-mill variety; they were the equivalent of a brood of maggots hatching inside my brain—only each maggot was on fire and trying madly to escape.

My vision wavered and darkened, and I lost Helen in a hazy fog. She reappeared, still talking, but much more loudly now, her voice like broken glass dragging on a chalkboard.

"Joe?" The word was an ice pick shoved into my ear canal.

I grunted something.

"Joe?" she repeated, the ice pick pushing deeper. "You don't look well. What's wrong?"

"I'm fine."

"No, you're not." She came closer, just a blur, her features scrubbed away with a wet eraser. Her footsteps on the stone thundered like war drums. "Migraine?" her voice boomed. "I get them too sometimes."

Not like mine you don't.

"Joe? Can you hear me?"

Stop talking!

"Joe?"

"*What?*"

"How bad is it?"

"It'll go 'way."

Helen started telling me all about migraines, the science behind them, shit like that, when the only thing I wanted was for her to shut the hell up. I would have covered my ears with my hands, but I knew from experience that the maggots didn't like movement. Even the slightest nod would fatten them into furious flies, buzzing every which way with wings made of razor blades.

"Too bad we don't have any water," she said.

Water and a shotgun so I could shove the barrel against the roof of my mouth and pull the trigger and splatter my brains against the wall, and that would be something only slightly less painful than the infestation eating them from the inside out now . . .

"What can I do to help?"

The ice pick struck raw nerve endings, turning everything sheets of raging white.

I hissed.

"Joe! You're scaring me!"

More ice picks, these ones hammered through my eyes. Blood flowed.

"Joe!"

"Stop!"

My right hand dropped the torch; my left one rubbed my eyes, coming away wet not with blood but tears.

Eels swam in my stomach, their solid, slimy bodies churning faster and faster, and I knew they were going to squeeze up my throat and shoot out my mouth and slap Helen right in her fucking face—and maybe that would shut her up.

"Why don't you lie down?" She'd picked up the torch, and it was so bright I had to close my eyes—yet there was no sanctuary there, only more blinding white light. "I'll stay right here beside you until . . ."

I lurched away from her, retched, but nothing came up.

However, the sudden movement made the flies berserk, and they tunneled with their razor wings in a thousand new directions, leaving trails of lava in their wake that wouldn't stop burning.

A pair of very strong hands peeled open the top of my skull, and the fingernails went digging and clawing and hunting through my brain for the ungodly little insects . . .

I passed out.

Like everybody, I'd had my share of bad dreams in my life. But since Jen's death, they went from a handful a year to a handful every week—and this was one of the worst yet.

It began benignly enough. I was trekking along the Madera Canyon Nature Trail near Green Valley, Arizona. I didn't pass anybody on my ascent, which was unusual, as I'd typically see birders, couples, a young family, dog walkers, or lone hikers like myself.

Today, however, nobody.

Until I rounded a bend and spotted a little girl coming down the shaded dirt trail. She wore a wool hat with bouncing pom-poms (even though the weather felt like late summer), as well as a pink ski jacket, unzipped. It did get cooler at the higher elevations, but her attire seemed excessive.

As we passed each other, she said, "Hi, mister," and I nodded, and that was that. I didn't give her much more thought until I looked back at some point and found her following me, along with seven or eight little girls her age.

Now, one little girl wearing a hat with pom-poms was the antithesis of menacing . . . yet a gaggle of them, all with angry faces and wicked-looking hatchets in their hands, was a frightening sight to behold.

I picked up my pace and kept looking over my shoulder but could never seem to put any distance between me and the frightful girls.

So I began to run. Although I was going uphill, the gradient wasn't steep, and the run shouldn't have been difficult. Only in the dream, it was. My legs protested and my shins ached until I resorted to crawling on my hands and knees.

Suddenly I found myself at the top of the mountain, where I could walk again. I went to the lookout spot that offered views of the desert all the way to the distant horizon. This was one of my favorite places in the world. I couldn't count how many times I had been before, simply to sit and gaze out over the tiny landscape and breathe the fresh air and clear my mind and soul.

I decided it would be a fine time to have a snack and some water—I had become incredibly thirsty on the hike—and was about to shrug off my backpack when I heard the throttling of a chainsaw behind me.

I turned—and there was Jen, alongside the little girl with the pom-poms. Jen, too, was dressed in winter clothes, and she was the one holding the chainsaw. They were standing before a small pine tree. I called them over—the little girl no longer looked menacing; in fact, laughing and hopping about in excitement, she now appeared innocent as little children should—yet neither of them paid me any attention. And then a goblin of a man emerged from the trees. His shrunken head sat atop his decrepit body, and tufts of fur sprouted from the scabby, splotchy skull. His eyes were small and beady, and his chin was twice the length it should have been. Despite all this, I recognized him immediately.

Blake Brown didn't look like a goblin in real life. He was tall and fit with blond hair and a square chin and all-American looks. Yet he was a goblin in my dream, because what type of man fucked another man's wife behind his back?

I despised him to this day. He almost destroyed my marriage.

Almost. Because Jen came clean with me. She didn't have to. I had no idea what had been going on while I was at work. And I believe had I discovered her infidelity on my own, I would have ended our marriage right then and there.

But she came clean, and so I heard her out.

The affair had been unplanned and, according to Jen, the stupidest thing she'd ever done. She'd met Blake at the local library one day in December. She went often to browse the selection of magazines. Blake Brown was working on his laptop at one of the communal tables. He was there the next few times she went, as well, and on their third or fourth encounter, he finally came over to introduce himself (this had really pissed me off—not so much that Blake had come over to talk to Jen, but that she had used the word "finally" in her retelling of events, as though she had been waiting for him to do just that). In any event, they continued to "bump" into each other at the library over the next few weeks, and each time, they went for coffee afterward. And then one day when I was out of town, they had drinks together and returned to his place. I was furious by this point. I was yelling, Jen was hushing me, worried the neighbors could hear us fighting. She reiterated how stupid she'd been, how much she regretted what she'd done. She'd been lonely. I was spending so much time at work. She had just turned thirty-nine and was feeling *old*.

I stormed out of the house and checked into a Comfort Inn a short drive away. When I returned home a few days later, Jen was as apologetic as ever. What could she do to make it up to me? What could she do to make me trust her again? I asked her if it had only been the one time. She said yes. She'd deleted Blake's number the next day and never went back to the library.

And so I forgave her.

It would never be the same between us again, but I loved her, I couldn't imagine her with anybody else, and so I forgave her.

The affair—the apex of it, at any rate—had been roughly a week before Christmas, and standing at the lookout point now, watching Jen and Blake and the little girl, I wondered with renewed fury if Jen had ever gone into the woods with Blake Brown to cut down a Christmas tree. Had he stood it proudly in his living room? Had one of the presents beneath it been for Jen? Had one of them been from Jen for *him* . . . ?

They began kissing, Jen nonchalantly holding the rumbling chainsaw at her side while Blake's hands smoothed over her back and buttocks. Jen reached between his legs and fondled his genitals while the little girl danced around them in a circle, throwing fistfuls of charred grass into the air like confetti—

And then Jen was lying on the tarmac at the airport, bleeding out. And I was there, too, kneeling next to her, holding her hand. She was trying to say something. Only gurgles accompanied the river of blood gushing from her mangled mouth. And what made the dream so god-awful terrible, what made it one of the worst I'd ever had, was that I was happy to see Jen like this, happy she no longer had any lips with which to kiss Blake Brown, even though she had promised me she would never see him again . . . happy that, by a twisted turn of fate, she had gotten exactly what she'd deserved.

When I opened my eyes, Helen said, "Joe!"

It took a moment to collect myself and remember what had happened. The dream was fresh and hot in my head, the memories of it almost as excruciating as the migraine that had previously occupied that space. Self-loathing and revulsion scissored through me for my awful thoughts, even though they'd only been dream-thoughts, and I missed Jen right then more than I had ever missed anybody or anything in my life.

"Joe?" Helen repeated, looking concerned.

Despite wanting nothing more than to close my eyes again, find my way back into the dream, make things right, I sat up with a moan.

"God," I mumbled, and found that my mouth was bone dry.

"Do you feel . . . okay?"

Working my tongue around my gums, I nodded before I thought better of it. However, the fire was out; the maggots were gone—until they came again, and they would come again.

I exhaled deeply, almost a sigh.

Helen said, "You were white as a sheet. I was so scared."

I said, "And now?"

"I'm still scared. You just—you literally fell over and passed out."

"I mean, I'm still white?"

"No, you look fine. Well, you look okay. What happened?"

"Migraine."

"It was like you were dying."

"Felt a lot worse than that."

"Do you get them often?"

"Once every month or two."

"Don't you have meds . . . ?"

"Nothing works. I've tried everything. So I just . . . deal with them." I sighed again. "I don't suppose the midget came by when I was out and told you the way to the next room?"

Helen shook her head. "No, but I've been thinking about it."

"And . . . ?"

"It's gotta be the mirrors . . ."

"Huh?" I said, my head clearing.

"You know the Hot and Cold game, right . . . ? Are you sure you're better? Fine, fine, I'll stop nagging. Did you play it at school?"

"When the teacher hides something . . ."

"And you have to go around the classroom looking for it, and your classmates yell out *hot* or *cold* depending on whether you're getting closer or farther from it. So . . . I think the mirrors are our classmates. Back around the midget, the mirrors covered every inch of the walls. We were hot. Now they're super spread out. We're getting cold."

"I'm with you," I said, adjusting my position on the ground. "So like I said earlier, we follow the crumbs back and find the actor."

Helen's lips tightened. "But if he lays one finger on me . . ."

"He won't, Helen. You could sue him—and Izzy—if he touches you. But whatever. If he does . . . fuck, he comes up to my waist. He won't."

She folded her arms across her chest. "This game sucks."

I grunted. "You're telling me."

"Impossible!" Helen said. She was on her hands and knees, searching the ground. "Still no crumbs!"

"Maybe we stepped on them?" I said, checking the soles of each of my shoes.

"Don't be silly! I dropped them *behind* us, all down this tunnel, one crumb every ten or so yards."

"So where did they go?"

Her eyes narrowed. "*The midget*," she said quietly.

"Huh?" Then I shook my head. "No . . . you think?"

She stood up. "Has to be. He's the only other person down here with us."

"*Prick*," I muttered, knowing I was jumping to conclusions, but jumping to conclusions about people I didn't like was all right in my books. I raised my voice: "Hey, asshole!" The taunt echoed satisfyingly down the passageway.

"Joe, stop it!"

"Stop it? We're lost down here because of him, Helen. Maybe he's waiting for our torch to go out. Maybe that's the big fucking scare."

"Joe, take it easy. I'm angry, too, but making *him* angry won't help us."

"I'm going to kick his little ass to the moon."

"Joe!" She squeezed my forearm and held my eyes with hers. "Just . . . calm down."

I swallowed my frustration. Unlike Helen, my feet didn't hurt (they'd already walked halfway around the planet, after all, and were well-conditioned to finish the other half), but my head was still heavy, I was getting sick of the dampness and chill of the tunnels, and the place I really wanted to be was back outside, in the fresh air and sunshine . . . and that was not going to happen anytime soon.

"This is bullshit," I said.

"Hello?" Helen called pleasantly. "Hello? Mr. Nazi?" She listened for a reply. None came. "We know you're somewhere nearby. We know you took our muffin crumbs. We also know the exit to the next room is close to where we started. So could you please help us get back there so we can complete this challenge?"

Crickets.

Helen said, "He can't just ignore us . . ."

I said, "He seems to be doing a pretty good job of it."

"Mister Notttttt-ziiiiii!"

"Fuck him." I went to the nearest mirror, cocked my elbow, and drove it into the concave glass. Large, jagged pieces shattered against the stone floor.

"Joe!"

I raised my voice again and said, "I'm going to break another mirror every five seconds until you show yourself!"

"Joe!"

"One!"

"Joe!"

"Two!"

"*Joe!*"

"I'm not sitting around here until—"

"No—*look!*"

I turned and saw that she was staring at the mirror I had broken. Frowning, I held the torch up to the hollowed frame.

"Hol-ee shit," I said.

The arrow painted on the stone behind where the mirror had been pointed in the direction from which we had originally come.

"I *knew* the challenge had something to do with the mirrors!" Helen said triumphantly.

"You think Izzy wants us to break all her mirrors?" I said skeptically.

"A tunnel only goes two ways. So assuming there's an arrow painted behind each mirror, we only have to break one in each tunnel to find the way out of here."

It sounded logical to me, so off we went, leaving destruction in our wake. Sure enough, behind each smashed mirror was a hastily painted black arrow pointing (presumably) to the exit.

We were momentarily stumped the first time one of those arrows sent us backtracking to an intersection of passageways we had previously passed through. Nevertheless, after breaking a mirror in each of the branching tunnels, we realized the arrows in the redundant tunnels pointed back to the intersection—effectively canceling themselves out—while the arrow in the correct tunnel pointed in the opposite direction and (presumably again) to the exit.

It was a rudimentary but ingenious system, and Helen and I hurried quickly through the labyrinth, both of us eager to finally be free of it.

Maybe ten minutes later—time was proving surprisingly hard to judge while cocooned in underground darkness—we found ourselves back where the mirrors covered almost every inch of the stone walls. A few minutes after that, the tunnel we were following abruptly ended. Like all the others, the dead-end wall was a jigsaw of different-sized mirrors . . . yet it also featured the largest and most opulent mirror we had come across yet. The beveled central glass was wrapped in a frame of layered glass bordered with scalloped edges and topped with an etched panel of flowers and leaves. Floor-to-ceiling in height and half that in width, it probably weighed more than all the other mirrors on the wall combined.

Helen grinned at me. "Are you thinking what I'm thinking?"

"That's the exit?" I said.

"It's gotta be!"

"It's gotta cost a fortune."

"Good thing Izzy has money coming out of her wazoo. Now go on, go break it."

I handed Helen the torch and stepped closer to the imposing mirror. I knew Helen was right; it had to be the exit. The arrows led us to it. Not only that, but unlike the thousands of other mirrors down here, this one reflected our images without exaggeration. That seemed like a pretty big tell in itself. Yet destroying something so expensive seemed wrong in my mind. . . .

"What are you waiting for, Joe? Bruce Lee the thing!"

And then I noticed the fleurs-de-lis etched into the top panel alongside the flowers and leaves.

They were just like the ones on Lard-Ass's ivory cards. More to the point, there were *three* of them.

Raising my knee nearly to my chest, I drove my foot into the mirror. The beveled glass spiderwebbed away from my heel. I leaped backward a moment before large, sharp panels fell to the stone floor.

Revealing what else but a doorway.

Chapter 8

"One's age is the most consequential of numbers."
—The Book of Nine

The short hallway led to another small, shadowed room. It was just like Lard-Ass's chamber—vaulted ceiling, stout columns, medieval chandelier—minus the stagecoach and the fat man himself. Instead, against the far wall, a slim figure stood behind some kind of carnival booth that appeared to be built from sticks.

"Looks like we're back beneath the palace," I said, surprised—and relieved—by the turn of events. Until then, it hadn't struck me that we might have circled back through the maze to Izzy's cellar.

"Makes sense," Helen said. "It's called The No-End House challenge, after all. Not the Barcelona sewer challenge. Hi!" She waved at the figure in the booth.

The person raised an arm. I thought they were about to wave back. Instead, they took a drag from a cigarette. A red dot smoldered in the darkness.

We continued to the kiosk, which, it turned out, wasn't

made from sticks, but rather the bones of large animals lashed together with old rope. I had never seen anything like it, and I was both impressed and unsettled.

"Izzy's got one sick fetish . . ." Helen said, holding the bone torch close to the bone booth to appreciate all its ghoulish detail.

The actor behind the counter of tightly packed tibias and femurs and ribs was a very pale woman. She wore a simple black trench coat buttoned to the neck and cinched tightly around an hourglass waist. It was something you might see a businessperson wearing in downtown Manhattan on a rainy day or maybe a model on a Paris fashion runway. Her ghost-white skin and silver hair, braided into a tall bun on top of her head, stood in stark contrast to the coat. Her blue eyes watched us coolly from beneath hooded lids. They were set so deep in her sockets, they bled shadows across the rest of her face. Given her sallow complexion and sunken cheeks, I had difficulty deciding if she was supposed to be a strung-out junkie or some noir fiction vixen.

She took a drag on the cigarette, pursed her lips as she blew the smoke out of the side of her mouth, and said, "You two certainly took your time getting here." Each word was spoken deliberately and sounded Eastern European.

"We got lost on the way, thanks to one horrible little midget," Helen said tartly, not tempering her annoyance at the runaround we'd been put through. "You might know him, I'm sure? But we made it in the end, didn't we?"

Another drag. "It seems you did; you are here."

"Nice costume, by the way."

"Costume?"

"The *Matrix* thing you got going on. Really original. Are these supposed to be human bones?"

"They are the remains of people like you," said the woman, without expression.

"Like us?" I said, amused by her callow humor.

"People who play games they do not fully understand." She studied me while she took another leisurely drag on the cigarette. She might have been undressing me with her eyes or planning my murder, I had no idea. Either way, I decided she was the sexiest creepy woman I'd ever met.

She flicked the cigarette away into the dark and then parted a red velvet curtain behind her with an extravagant gesture.

Four silver serving dishes sat on top of a tall table draped in the same material as the curtain.

"Another food game . . . ?" Helen grumbled, clearly not impressed.

The enigmatic woman removed the lid of the first serving dish, revealing a human head on the platter. My insides jumped before I realized the obvious: a person stood beneath the table with their head sticking through a hole—artfully concealed by a fake platter—in the tabletop.

"Is that a real head?" Helen asked, leaning forward with the torch to scrutinize it.

"As opposed to . . . ?"

"It could be a wax replica, Joe. Ever hear of Madame Tussauds—oh, she blinked!"

The woman's head was middle-aged, Asian, with auburn hair teased into something unreal. Her eyes were blank, her face slack. The empty expression was doll-like and disconcerting. But she was definitely a living, breathing person.

"What's the game, ma'am?" I asked the Eastern European woman.

"Ma'am?" She smiled thinly at me. "I like that. You have much better manners, Joe Hadfield, than your friend. And since I know your name, you shall know mine. I am Carmilla."

"Like the vampire?"

"Like her, yes."

Helen said, "She was a lesbian vampire, wasn't she? And my manners are just fine, thank you, Vampmilla."

Carmilla held her with a slim gaze. "You are . . . forty-three, dear?"

Helen frowned. "How'd you know that? Most people think I'm younger than I am."

"Forty-two, easy," I said.

"Thanks, Joe."

"I *did* think you were a lot younger. Forty-three—really?"

"Don't sound so horrified. And yes, forty-three. *Just* forty-three. My birthday was last month." To Carmilla, she added, "So are you going to explain the game or what? Do we eat her brains?"

"One of you shall guess the ages of each of my four pets—"

Helen said, "There are *more* heads under those other lids? Are you sure the poor people can breathe? And did you just call them . . . your *pets*?"

"They are soulless husks, mindless beasts, that exist only because it pleases me that they do. Pets, yes. Would you like to volunteer for this challenge, dear? I would very much like it to be you."

"Don't get all hot and horny over me. You're going to make Joe jealous." Helen looked at me. "You played the last game. I guess I'll play this one?"

I shrugged. "Be my guest."

"All right, Vampmilla," she said, "I volunteer. But what's the catch? I know there's gotta be one. Joe lost an organ in the first game we played."

Carmilla's indolent eyes brightened. "The catch, dearie, is that for each age you guess incorrectly, the negative-sum years will be subtracted from *your* life."

Helen scoffed. "Dearie . . . okay. And what if my guesses are like a hundred years off? I'll owe you a raincheck in . . . sixty-seven years when I turn one hundred?"

"Transactions within The No-End House are processed promptly, and you will more than likely die from old age within the hour. So if I were you, *dearie*, I would not enter into this arrangement so cavalierly."

The tension (and condescension) between Carmilla and Helen had been present from the get-go, but it had ratcheted up quickly during the last few exchanges. Before one of them took things too far, I intervened with, "And after my friend plays the game, you'll show us the way to the next room, right?"

"Absolutely, Mr. Hadfield."

"How about this, *Vampy*," Helen said conspiratorially, "let's not play this ridiculous game and just say we did. Point us in the right direction, and you can take all the years you want from me."

"I would like that very much," replied Carmilla, with the same dose of whispered venom. "Oh, so very, very much. Unfortunately, however, that is not how it works."

Helen rolled her eyes. "Let's make this quick."

The Asian woman's age, written on a card inside an ivory envelope identical to the envelopes in the obese lord's game, was forty. Helen guessed forty-five, which Carmilla marked on a small chalkboard she'd produced from beneath the bone counter. The ages of the subsequent three actors—an olive-complected man with a receding hairline; a young blonde girl with watery hazel eyes; and an equally young man with arrogant features and an especially aggressive scowl (all of whom did a great job playing mindless, soulless pets)—were forty-nine, twenty-one, and twenty-three, respectively. Pursuing expediency over accuracy, Helen guessed forty-five, twenty-five, and twenty-five. That meant she was indebted a total of fifteen years of her life to Carmilla, who seemed delighted by the result.

At the conclusion, Helen said, "Wow, that was fun. Thanks, Vampy, for wasting the last ten minutes of my life."

"Ten? No, dear, there are closer to eight million minutes in the years you have given me."

"Staying in character to the very end—I guess I have to give you credit for that."

I said, "You told us you'd show us the way to the next room?"

Carmilla nodded. "Of course, Mr. Hadfield." She parted the curtain that covered the table.

The actors behind it were buck naked.

"Whoa," I said, looking away.

Helen laughed. "Is that necessary? And is that another hole in the wall?"

I looked again—this time past all the bare skin and brazen genitalia on display—and saw what appeared to be a hole in the stone wall.

"How are we supposed to reach that without . . . ?"

"Singeing off their pubes with the torch?" Helen offered helpfully.

Carmilla removed the fake platters from around the actors' necks; they lowered their heads through the holes in the tabletop, stepped out from beneath the table, and marched in single file off to the side of it. Breasts jiggled and penises swung.

Helen seemed about to bust a gut.

I felt giddy, too—this was all too bizarre—but I wasn't going to laugh at these folks, who were simply doing their jobs and performing their roles.

I told Helen in a reasonable voice, "You have the torch, you go first. I'll be right behind you—"

She began to titter uncontrollably.

Chapter 9

"The best explorers know not what they seek."
—The Book of Nine

I crawled through the hole in the wall behind Helen. When I stood up, I discovered there was only about an inch to spare between the top of my head and the rock above. Helen was mumbling and wiping her face with the back of her hand.

"What's wrong?" I asked her.

She scrunched her nose. "I . . . ate a spiderweb." She blew air through her lips and kept wiping her face. "Gross."

"Did you eat the spider, too?"

"You can go first from now on," she said, and thrust the torch at me.

Since there was no room to hold it above me, I held it directly ahead—and discovered we were in an egg-shaped shaft that might have been chiseled through the earth with pick-axes.

"Oh, great," Helen said. "It's not even a proper tunnel."

"It might lead back up to the surface."

"Or down to the center of the Earth . . ."

"It was probably an escape tunnel if the palace was under siege."

"So we're going to pop up in some other part of Barcelona?"

"Maybe another palace owned by Izzy?"

"Anywhere would be better than these shitty tunnels." She squinted into the darkness. "I mean—is this even safe? There aren't any struts or supports."

"At least there aren't any mirrors."

"Or midget Nazis."

"Not yet . . ."

She slapped me on the shoulder.

"I hope I don't have to start crouch-walking," I said as I started down the crude passageway. I added over my shoulder, "We probably should have asked Carmilla for a new torch." The flame still burned brightly, but it wouldn't last forever.

"Bitch," Helen muttered.

"What was the deal with the two of you? Don't you think you were a bit rough on her?"

"*Me?*" she said churlishly. "You saw the way she looked at us. Like we weren't worthy enough to lick her boots."

"It was part of her character, Helen. She was playing a snooty femme fatale."

"I don't think playing that kind of character was any stretch of the imagination for her."

"You haven't liked any of the characters down here . . ."

"They're all such a lovely bunch . . ."

"The fat guy was kind of cheery."

"Did *you* like Vampmilla?"

"That's what really ticked her off, I think, that nickname."

She caught up to me so we were walking abreast. "Did you, Joe?"

"I don't know . . ." I shrugged. "I thought she was fun . . . kinda sexy . . ."

Helen whacked my shoulder again. "Joe!"

"I can't think someone's sexy?"

"Not someone twenty years older than you!"

"What are you talking about? She wasn't any older than you."

"Please, Joe. She was in her sixties."

I glanced at Helen in the flickering torchlight. She didn't appear to be kidding. "Forty-five tops, Helen."

"You're crazy! I suppose you were blinded by lust . . ."

"You're not exactly an expert on ages . . ."

"I wasn't trying in that game. I just wanted to get it over with."

I shook my head. "Carmilla definitely wasn't in her sixties."

"She definitely wasn't in her forties."

"How old do you think I am?"

"Forty-five?"

"Thank God," I said with a chuckle. "With your track record, I thought you might have thought I was seventy-five or eighty."

"How old *are* you?"

"Forty-four."

"See!" she said proudly. "I know what I'm talking about. Hey, look at those."

A short distance ahead two life-size marble statues flanked the passageway. The semi-naked figures were painted with flesh tones and a mix of bright colors.

"They look Greek," I said, running my hand over the smooth stone of the one closest to me. "Except for the paint."

"The Greeks painted their sculptures, Joe."

I frowned at her. "I have a hard time picturing that."

"Pigments don't last as long as stone."

"Michelangelo's *David* was painted?"

"Michelangelo wasn't Greek, silly."

"I know that, Helen. But Renaissance art was based on classical art."

"Renaissance artists didn't know any better. They thought Greek statues were plain white marble, so that became all the rage. But *David* unpainted would have been considered unfinished by the Greeks and Romans."

"So what are you saying? These are original Greek statues?"

"If that were the case, they would have needed to be moved here two thousand years ago to be this well preserved. Barcelona probably wasn't even around then. Or if it was, it was a tiny village."

With a final look at the curious statues, I continued onward, keeping the licking flames of the torch at arm's length so I didn't get any embers or ash floating back in my face.

After less than fifty feet, the passage emptied into a giant cavern—and suddenly the two statues were the last thing on my mind.

Dozens of fifty-foot-tall pillars carved to resemble naked men and women soared up to a vast ceiling lost in darkness. The torch cast enough light to make out a shadowy bas-relief frieze resting atop the pillars' capitals and linking the perimeter of the room. The figures it depicted were also without clothes and engaged in all sorts of sexual antics. Perched atop the entablature, gargoyles and other demonic creatures looked down at us with monstrous expressions.

"Holy shit!" Helen exclaimed, latching onto my forearm with force.

"What the fuck . . . ?"

"It's like the Pantheon—designed by the Marquis de Sade!"

"What the *fuck*?" I repeated, shuffling in a slow circle

and craning my neck to see the entirety of the architectural marvel.

Helen released my forearm. "I feel like we're on the set of an Indiana Jones movie."

"Seriously, Helen . . ." Spots of yellow-orange torchlight danced in her wide eyes. "Something like this beneath the streets of Barcelona would be huge for tourism. How could the city not know about it?"

"Guess Izzy has been keeping it a secret."

"It can't be hers. I mean, there's no way her ancestors built it when they built the palace."

"It's gotta be at least as *old* as the palace . . ."

"It's not part of the palace," I insisted.

"Semantics, Joe. Whether it's part of the palace or not, does that matter? It's *linked* to the palace, and that says to me whoever built the palace built this place, too."

"Look at the *size* of the fucking statues, Helen! They dwarf the palace."

"Who built all this then, Joe? Aliens? And it's not like whoever built it dug out the room. It's not even a room. Look at the walls. It's a natural cavern."

I'd been so fixated on the statues that I hadn't noticed the walls behind them. Helen was right: we were in a giant cavern.

"I bet when Izzy's ancestors were building the palace," Helen went on, "they came across this cavern and decided it would make a good spot for a secret . . . temple, or whatever it is."

"You think it's a temple?"

"Or a mausoleum. Yeah, maybe Izzy's ancestors are all buried in here somewhere."

"Technically speaking, an underground cemetery isn't called a mausoleum—"

"*Catacomb*, sorry. I forgot you're an expert on this kind of stuff. Let's see if we can find some tombs."

I shook my head. "I don't think we should. I feel . . . I don't know . . . like we're getting in over our heads."

"Getting in over our heads? What are you talking about? We're practically halfway through the challenge!"

"This isn't some haunted house, Helen. This is . . . or should be . . . a national treasure. How's it possible that nobody knows about it? The people who took the challenge before us . . . they've never said to anyone, 'Oh, hey, by the way, there's a giant cave below Barcelona filled with statues rivaling the biggest finds from ancient Egypt?' I sure as hell know I'm going to tell somebody when we get out of here."

"Maybe nobody else has gotten this far. We have no idea how many people have even taken the challenge."

"The actors have to know."

"Izzy might have made them sign nondisclosure—"

"Oh, come on, Helen," I snapped.

"No, *you* come on, Joe! This is so cool. It's like the coolest thing I've ever seen. And you want to—what do you even want to do? Backtrack out of here? Give up the ten grand? And why? Because you don't know who built the place? Or why? Who cares! Why did the emperor of India build the Taj Mahal? Don't—don't tell me it was a tomb for his wife. I know that. I was being rhetorical. He built it *because he could*. Whoever built this built it *because they could*. Why doesn't anybody know about it? Maybe it was forgotten like so many other things from the past until they're dug up. Maybe Izzy only recently discovered it. Maybe it gave her the idea for the challenge. I don't have any of those answers, Joe. You don't, either. But that doesn't mean we're involved in something somehow nefarious."

My jaw had tightened while I listened to her rant. But it

made some sense and pushed back at my gut reaction that we
shouldn't be down here.

Lifting the torch high, I marveled once more at the statues
and bas-relief carvings and gargoyles, and I was about to con-
cede to explore the mysterious cavern when Helen screamed.

I thought it was another of her scare tactics—the scream
had been more of a squeal—until I swept the torch low and
saw what had frightened her: a carpet of shrunken skulls
spread away from us for as far as I could see.

"Jesus!" I said, stumbling backward a step.

"Wait a sec . . ." Helen said, crouching and extending a
hand. "Are they . . . ?" She let out a brittle laugh. "Mushrooms! I thought I'd stepped on a dead mouse!"

I crouched next to her. What I had mistaken for miniature
skulls were indeed bulbous, brown mushrooms. "What the
hell are *mushrooms* doing down here?"

"They grow well in the dark and the damp."

"This many? It's like someone's farming them."

"Maybe one of Izzy's ancestors used to farm them, and
when he or she died, they went wild."

"*Bats*," I said, looking up at the cavern's roof—I could see
only witch-hat blackness. "The mushrooms have to be growing in something . . ."

"Bat guano?" Helen sniffed. "I don't smell any."

I didn't, either, so I picked a mushroom, revealing a patch
of rich soil. I dug my fingers into the dirt to my knuckles and
didn't reach the stone ground beneath. "This is so fucking
weird . . ."

"Of course!" Helen said, standing up. "This is the challenge, Joe!"

I stood up, as well, and brushed my hand on my jeans.
"What is?"

"If this is Room Four—and it's gotta be, right—then what's the challenge? I'll go out on a limb and say it has something to do with *mushrooms*. They might be covering a staircase out of here, just like the fancy mirror covered the doorway out of the maze." She steepled her fingers together in front of her chin. "Please, please, please don't wimp out on me now."

"I'm not wimping out," I told her. "Before you screamed, I was about to tell you I was okay with looking around a little—"

"Great!" She planted a kiss on my cheek and started into the field of mushrooms. "Keep your eyes open for any sort of clue. I wouldn't put anything past Izzy at this point."

The mushrooms felt squishy beneath my feet. It was an altogether unpleasant experience, and I changed my path to follow Helen's trail of flattened fungi.

The cavern was about the size of two school gymnasiums, and we spent the better part of half an hour crisscrossing it every which way and finally walking around the circumference. We came across a good number of wet stalagmites rising like inverted icicles from the ground, a few deep puddles that oozed like leaking pustules in the forest of mushrooms—and most importantly of all, a dozen unlit torches. They jutted from sconces attached to the rocky walls at evenly spaced intervals. We agreed to light a few of them, so that whether we figured out the room's puzzle or not, we'd have some unlit ones in reserve.

"Let's take a break," I said when we came to a knee-high boulder free of fungi.

I sat on the edge of it, and Helen sank beside me with a loud sigh. "This is ridiculous," she said.

"Yup," I said.

"It's not even fun anymore."

"Nope."

"I wonder how Izzy's keeping track of our progress."

"Night-vision cameras?"

"Probably. I bet she's sitting somewhere in her palace now on a plush sofa, sipping champagne, getting a pedicure, and having a grand old time watching us walk around in circles."

"So what do you want to do?"

"I'm not giving up."

I knew she would say that, and I didn't reply.

My silence spoke for me, and she said, "We can't give up, Joe. We can't let her win."

"Do you really care, Helen? Money aside, do you really care if Izzy beats us, or her game beats us, or whatever?"

"We have spare torches now. We don't have to worry about losing light anymore. So what does it matter if we're down here for a few more hours?"

"It's going to be a lot longer than a few more hours."

"So what! What are you going to do instead? Go back to the hostel and read a book? Seriously? After this, you're just going to sit down and read a book?"

It did sound fantastically mundane, but that was probably exactly what I would do. I began massaging my temples. Nothing like another nascent migraine coming on; more like the flat sides of two spoons pressing against them from the inside out.

"Mushrooms," I said. "How are they the key . . . ?"

"The answer's gotta be obvious, like the mirrors."

"What do you do with mushrooms?"

"You grow them?"

"What else?"

"Cook them?"

"What else?"

"I don't know . . . eat them?"

"What else—?"

"No, wait, Joe! You *eat* them."

I stopped rubbing my temples and frowned. "How is eating them going to show us the way out of this room?"

"Maybe they're magic mushrooms?"

"*Magic* magic, or psychedelic?"

"Psychedelic, Joe! Come on."

"And maybe they're poisonous . . ."

Even so, I was intrigued enough by her suggestion that I picked a mushroom next to my feet and examined it in the torchlight. The cap was the diameter of a baseball, the golden brown in the middle lightening toward the edges.

I sniffed it.

"What does it smell like?" Helen asked.

"A mushroom," I said. "But not a poisonous one."

"How do you know that?"

"Poisonous mushrooms usually have a bad smell."

"What kind of bad smell?"

"Chemical . . . like ammonia or iodine."

"And you know this because . . . ?"

"I eat them when I'm walking."

"Around the world?"

"Sometimes when I'm out of food and I'm hungry and I'm far from anywhere, I keep an eye out for berries, mushrooms, things like that." I turned the mushroom over. The gills were purplish, a good sign. I pointed to them and said, "The poisonous ones usually have white gills. Hold it for a sec." I gave the mushroom to her, then bent over to probe the soil around what remained of the stalk. I was looking for a sack-like base, another indicator the mushroom might be poisonous. I didn't find one. "I don't think it's poisonous."

"Is it a magic one?"

"I don't know. Magic ones look just like normal ones. You've never taken them?"

"When I was younger. But they were dried and shriveled up and everything."

"Turn it over."

She did this, and I flicked the stem with the nail of my index finger.

"Don't torture the poor thing."

"It's a mushroom, Helen. And look at the flesh."

"What am I looking for?"

"The color."

"It's bluish where you bruised it . . ."

"That indicates it has the psychedelic stuff in it . . . I think."

"You *think*?"

"Whenever I find mushrooms, I always research them on my phone before I eat them to make sure they're not poisonous. I've only come across magic mushrooms a few times, and I'm pretty sure I read they had bluish stems when bruised."

"Oh my God, Joe!" she said, suddenly keyed up. "This must be it! The solution to this room!"

I scoffed. "Getting high?"

"Why else would Izzy be growing thousands of magic mushrooms down here? Think about it! The Doors! 'Break on through . . .' " She looked at me expectantly.

" 'To the other side . . . '?"

"Yes, Joe! Why did Jim Morrison name the band that? He was inspired by William Blake's poem about doors of perception. Seeing things clearly. And all the acid and drugs and everything he took helped him do that!"

"You sure you haven't nibbled on the mushrooms when I wasn't looking?"

"It's gotta be the answer, Joe. I can *feel* it. And even if all the Morrison stuff is BS, the mushrooms aren't. They're here, thousands of them, and they're here for a reason, and the only reason I can think of is for us to eat them. They're gonna show us the way."

She chomped a bite out of the mushroom cap in her hand.

"Holy shit, Helen!" I said, grabbing the mushroom from her.

She smiled at me as she chewed. "You know I'm right."

"Even if you are, that was a huge bite."

"Mushrooms are mostly water," she said around her full mouth. "So if we want a good trip, we're going to need to eat a bunch."

Chapter 10

"Some believe mushrooms are the flesh of gods, others believe they are the food of gods. What cannot be debated is that they allow mortals to communicate with the gods."

—The Book of Nine

"Do you feel them yet?"

"You keep asking me that."

"I feel them," Helen said. "I feel them tickling my stomach."

I did, too. Tickling my stomach, my groin, my fingers, everywhere.

My thoughts, as well. Everything seemed mildly amusing. Amusing and mind-blowing. After all, Helen and I were sitting in a mushroom field in some underground temple that the world didn't know about. *And don't forget about the maze with about ten thousand expensive mirrors.* Yeah, that also. And one of those mirrors held a midget inside it. I felt a little bad for Helen. She had looked terrified when he shouted that he was coming after her. Admittedly, I'd been frightened, too. It didn't matter that the guy was four feet tall; he'd sounded mad as a hatter. And he'd been following us around in the tunnels, picking up our muffin crumbs . . . ? That was fucked up—but now everything was fucked up in a good way. I didn't know why I had been so glum before. I'd pay to do this challenge. It had to be the best escape room in the world. Izzy could make gobs of cash if she didn't keep it such a secret. From a business standpoint, she was doing everything backward: keeping it a secret, paying *us* to compete. But I suppose it wouldn't be the same if everybody knew about it.

"What?" Helen said. She was grinning at me.

"What?" I asked.

"You're smiling. What's so funny?"

"Nothing. I was just thinking about Izzy."

"Fucking Izzy!"

"Do you think she ever leaves her house?"

"She must. Nobody just sits in their house all day."

"I think she might."

"Maybe. She lives in a palace, after all. And she'd definitely make a scene in public with how she dresses." Helen shook her head. "They're so weird . . ."

"Who?"

"Not who. Mushrooms. They're not plants. They're not animals. They're just . . . *fungi* . . ." She giggled. "What a silly word. It sounds like a dance move. Do the *fungi*. Hey, Joe, are you a fun-guy?"

"If I'm fungi, you're cacti."

"Ouch. What's another one?"

"Another what?"

"Word that ends in *i*."

"I think that's all there are."

"No way, Joe! There are way more . . . wait . . . oh! Hippopotami!"

"I think it's hippopotamuses."

"No, it's hippopotami . . . definitely . . . or at least it's both."

"It can't be both."

"Sure it can—alumni! That's two-to-one for me."

"We're keeping score?"

"You don't want to because you're losing."

I thought hard for a few seconds and said, "Octopi."

"Nope."

"Why?"

"English plurals ending in *i* are from Latin. Octopus comes from Greek."

"Do you read the dictionary for fun?"

"I don't know where I read that . . ." She giggled again. "Holy shit, I'm totally fucked."

"You should be. You ate those mushrooms like candy."

"You had just as many."

"I'm bigger than you."

"I don't think that matters. But I feel *good*. Do you?"

I felt great.

Helen changed her position. We had been seated side by side, cross-legged, on the ground. Now she was in front of me, facing me like we were at a table. However, the fact there was no table between us made the arrangement oddly intimate.

"We can see each other better this way," she said, apparently feeling an explanation was necessary for what had seemed like a big production. "Why don't you put the torch down?"

"Where?"

"Lean it against the rock."

"What if it falls over?"

"Why would it fall over?"

I didn't have an answer to that, so I placed the torch carefully against the boulder we had been sitting on. I made some small adjustments to ensure the stave was lodged securely and wouldn't topple.

Helen was watching me with an amused expression. She asked, "Are you okay?"

"Why?"

"You're moving really slowly."

"Oh," I said, relieved. *Are you okay?* wasn't something you wanted to hear when you were stoned out of your mind. "Yeah, I'm fine."

"When was the first time you had mushrooms?"

My freshman year in college. I was living in a dorm on the campus of the University of Arizona in central Tucson. Someone had told me they were doing shrooms that night in a friend's room, and did I want to come. I said sure. I didn't know anything about shrooms then, except they were a drug I'd never tried before. The room was on the third floor of my residence building, and there were about thirty people already there when I showed up, everybody wearing a costume. Someone explained to me that we were going to a Halloween party at the Delta Chi frat house later (which, in retrospect, explained why so many people were doing shrooms together).

A lot of pizzas arrived shortly, and the guy who shared the room with his roommate—I'd only known him as the campus pot dealer—loaded them with magic mushrooms and handed out slices. The high kicked in after about half an hour, and I had a blast. But I learned that night that you couldn't simply eat magic mushrooms with people and then go off and do something like read a book on your own, or go and hang out with people who weren't on mushrooms. You became part of a clan, and you stuck with that clan. So when someone ordered several cabs, and everyone started getting ready to leave, I panicked, because I wasn't wearing a costume, and apparently I wouldn't be allowed into the frat house without one. My solution was to strip the sheet off one of the beds in the room and wear it over my boxers as a toga.

It got me into the frat house, and the party kept rolling, until a group of Delta Chi assholes kicked me out. At the time, I had no idea what I'd done to piss them off, but the next day a friend told me I had been spending too much time with the girlfriend of the frat's president.

Anyway, something else I learned that night was that you could have a bad trip on magic mushrooms. I'd left my wallet with my clothes back in the residence, I didn't have money for a taxi, and I began heading in what I thought was the direction of the university campus. And while getting kicked out of a party and walking around an unfamiliar part of the city in a bedsheet with no money was a pretty big buzzkill, it wasn't until I was sitting on a park bench, trying to get my bearings, and somebody asked me if I was okay, that the bad trip really set in. I remember thinking, *That's what you ask a homeless person.* And right then, I was suddenly convinced I *was* a homeless person. Of course, I wasn't. I would eventually find my way back to the dorm, I would wake up the next day feeling like crap, but everything else in my life would be as it should. Yet none of that mattered right then. The shrooms had fucked with my head, and there was no way to get it unfucked until the effects wore off.

I didn't want to get into all of this with Helen, so in response to her question, I fudged the truth and mentioned the second time I did shrooms, which had been six or seven years ago.

"Where'd you do them?" she asked me.

"Some nightclub. I'd sold a house, and the buyer wanted to celebrate by taking me out for a couple of drinks. He had some mushrooms and asked me if I wanted any."

Helen laughed. "So you and this dude just did mushrooms together in the middle of the dance floor?"

"We weren't dancing. We were in a booth."

She frowned. "A booth?"

"Yeah, a booth."

"What do you mean, a *booth*?"

"A booth! It had a round table with round benches—kinda like a pod."

"I know what a booth is, Joe! But why was there one in the middle of the dance floor?"

"There wasn't just one. There was a bunch."

"On the *dance floor*?"

"Are you fucking with me?"

"I don't get what you're saying! Why would there be a bunch of booths on the dance floor?"

"What's with you and the dance floor? There might have been a small dance floor off in the corner. But most of the nightclub was *booths*. Like, that's what you did. You sat in a booth and ordered drinks and food."

"So it was a *restaurant*?"

"No. It was a nightclub. You couldn't order a steak. You could order . . . bar food."

She exhaled. "Jesus . . . okay, I get it now."

I laughed. "I don't know what there is to get."

"I was thinking you were at . . . a rave or something. You know, like when you're in a huge open space and everyone is dancing and there's a DJ at the front."

"Why would I be at a rave? It was probably six-thirty in the evening, and I was with a guy I'd sold a house to."

"It *sounded* like you were at a rave. And you never said it was six-thirty. Whatever . . . so are you like some big shot in real estate?"

"I've taken a break from it."

"I know that. You can't sell houses and walk around the world at the same time. But you had clients that took you out to fancy clubs? You must have been selling some expensive homes?"

"That was the first time someone took me out."

THE NO-END HOUSE   101

"So are you rich and famous, or what? Walking around the world can't be cheap. And you're barely interested in the ten grand from Izzy."

"I'm not broke."

"You *are* rich!"

"I'm not rich."

"I bet you are."

"Why are we talking about this?"

"I'm getting to *know* you, Joe. This is how you do that."

"It feels more like an interrogation to me."

"An interrogation—that's so rude!"

"An interrogation by someone who speaks a different language and doesn't know what a booth is."

She slapped my knee.

"Anyway," she added, "you don't look like you sell houses."

"I didn't know there was a look."

"You wore suits and ties and everything? I can't see it."

"Because you've never seen me wear a suit."

"You're just the guy from the hostel."

"Thanks."

"There's nothing wrong with that. You're kinda cute in just jeans and a shirt . . ."

"Thanks . . . I think." To change the topic, I said, "You don't look like you work for UNICEF."

"Oh, jeez, we're doing this again?"

"Doing what?"

"Like when we first met. I said you didn't look like a Joe, you said I didn't look like a Helen."

"Maybe you do look like you work for UNICEF. I have no idea what someone who works for UNICEF looks like."

"Me!"

"Does UNICEF still give out those little orange boxes to kids on Halloween to collect money?"

"Yeah, but now most people donate online."

"So why'd you decide to work for UNICEF?"

"Because they help kids . . . vulnerable kids. I think it's . . . one of the most important organizations in the world." Her voice had changed. Suddenly the silliness was gone; she sounded somber and introspective. "Do you want to hear something crazy? I've never talked about it to anyone. Well, except the police."

I wasn't sure I wanted to hear her secret, but I couldn't articulate that politely before she said, "I was kidnapped."

I blinked. "Kidnapped? Who kidnapped you?"

"A kidnapper, obviously."

"But like . . . your neighbor?"

"No, Joe! This was serious shit. I was seven years old and walking home from school. This asshole pulled up in a car beside me—don't say anything, I know what you're going to say, but don't— and he pulled up and told me he was going to take me home." She shook her head. "Anyway, I got in the front seat next to him, and he kidnapped me."

I was quiet while I absorbed that. I wasn't going to make the mistake of saying anything flippant. Helen was right: it was some serious shit. And I was sort of bummed she brought it up. We'd been having fun—goofy fun—but this was dark and heavy, and it might put her on the road to a bad trip.

Helen plucked a mushroom from the ground in front of her and idly turned it over in her hands. Shadows moved across her face, and the whites of her eyes were very bright. She seemed indecisive about whether she would keep going but eventually said, "He drove me to a big Tudor-style house and told me that my mom would be coming by soon. But I was barely listening. I was so impressed by the fancy house. He even had a remote garage opener. This was the mid-eighties, and those things had just been invented, and I thought it was magic when he pushed a button and his garage door opened. Inside, he took me to the kitchen and made me an ice cream cone. Then he gave me a tour of the house, showing me all the rooms. As crazy as it sounds, I didn't feel like I was being kidnapped—yet."

"He never locked you up?"

She nodded. "He locked me in the basement. But it was finished and decorated just as nicely as the rest of the house."

"Were there windows?"

Another nod. "Ventilation windows. They had bars on them, but I didn't even notice them at first. And then he told me I had to stay down there. I asked him when my mom was coming, and he told me she changed her mind. He said I was a 'bad little girl'—those were his exact words—and my mother never wanted to see me again. But he would take care of me." She drew a finger down the side of her nose to wipe away a tear. "I started to cry—and he slapped me across the face. Hard. He told me he never wanted to see me cry again. And for the rest of the time I was there, I never cried in front of him. I cried most nights in bed, usually when I woke up from a nightmare, or when I thought about my mom, and the reality that I was never going to see her again—and that was my reality. That's what I truly believed. I never thought I was ever going to leave that basement."

"How long were you there for?"

"About a year."

"A *year*? Holy shit, Helen! And he never had any visitors?"

"A few times, not many. And no, I didn't yell for help. He told me if I ever did something like that, he would hurt me, and I believed him. In a way, I was more scared of the visitors than him. Because for all I knew, they might have been just as bad as him—or worse. At least I knew him. I knew nothing about the visitors. And in my head, a kidnapper probably had other kidnappers or at least some bad people as friends."

"Did he tell you his name?"

"Yeah, I know his name . . ."

"How did you get away?"

Helen had stopped turning the mushroom over in her hands. Now she was breaking it into small pieces and letting the bits fall to the ground. I didn't think she even realized she was doing it. She'd gone into a kind of trance. But now her eyes cleared, and she smiled when she said, "I killed the mother-fucker."

"Whoa . . . !" I was watching her closely, waiting for her to tell me she was messing with me, but she never did. "How . . . did you kill him?" It was a question I'd never asked anyone else in my life, and to speak those words felt surreal.

"There was a big TV in the basement, along with a VCR. The TV didn't get any channels. He wouldn't have wanted me to see myself on the news, I suppose. But there was a bookcase filled with VHS tapes. I must have watched *The Goonies* and *The Never Ending Story* twenty times each. All those movies were what kept me sane. Anyway, every Friday was pizza night. He'd bring down a pepperoni pizza—it was the only pizza he liked—and a new movie that he'd purchased. He never rented them. He always bought a new one and left it on the bookshelf afterward. We'd eat the pizza and watch the movie sitting next to each other on the sofa. I think . . . I think he might have done stuff . . . I don't know. I don't remember it happening, but I think he did. Mostly because for years after I escaped, I hated it when people touched me."

She wiped away another tear.

"But during the movies, near the end, he would sometimes fall asleep. He was often away for a full day and night at a time. And I guess living a double life messed with his sleeping patterns or whatever." She shrugged. "Anyway . . . on one of the movie nights, when he had fallen asleep next to me and was snoring, I took a mirror off the wall. It was oval and not that big, but it had a super heavy frame. It was almost too heavy for me to carry. But I carried it over to behind the sofa and lifted it in the air." She demonstrated, thrusting her arms high. Tears streaked her cheeks, but her voice remained even and strong. "And I brought it down on the motherfucker's head. *Wham!*" She slammed her hands against the ground, obliterating a few mushrooms. "I don't think I meant to kill him. Or maybe I did. I hated him. But mostly I just wanted to get out of the basement and see my mom again. So I drove the mirror down on his head with all my strength, because I was so scared that if I didn't at least knock him out, he was probably going to kill me. And I ended up killing him. I didn't know it then. I just took the key to the basement door from around his neck and got out of the house as fast as I could. I ran down the street and kept on running. I guess I ran for three or four blocks before I saw a girl about my age walking with her father, and I asked them for help."

I shook my head. The idiom *at a loss for words* had never seemed as appropriate as it did right then. I mean, not only had Helen been held as a prisoner for a year, it sounded as though she'd been molested, too. And on top of that, she'd been forced to kill someone in cold blood. All that . . . and she was only seven?

"I'm sorry, Helen," I said. "I don't know what else to say . . ."

"You don't need to say anything, Joe. I don't even know why I brought all this up. You probably think I'm a psychopath."

"Of course I don't. I would have done the same thing in that situation. Actually—no, that's not true. I don't think I would have had the guts to do what you did."

She smiled faintly. "Thanks, Joe . . . you're . . . sweet. And

I *do* know why I told you all that. Because when you said you knew me earlier, and I got all mad at you . . . that just . . . I don't know . . . I can get touchy sometimes . . . but I want to apologize for that. How I reacted. Because we're friends. I . . . like you. I guess I just wanted to explain to you why I acted how I did."

I gave her leg a reassuring squeeze above the knee, and then my thumb rubbed back and forth. It was meant to be a gesture of comfort and support, but it quickly felt like more than that. I enjoyed hearing her say she liked me, the *way* she said it. Because there had been more to that, too.

Helen cupped my hand with hers and held it tightly. I thought for a moment she was telling me to stop, but then she was leaning forward, and we were kissing.

The kissing, as kissing tends to do, led to touching and exploring and undressing. Helen unclasped her bra. I pushed her snug jeans down her thighs. She unbuttoned and unzipped my jeans, pushed them down, as well. I was on top of her, my lips buried in her neck, but I was in no rush to do more adult things. I was enjoying the moment.

Abruptly and with surprising strength, Helen rolled on top of me.

She guided my hands to her breasts and teased me with kisses, alternating between my lips and earlobes. Her hair smelled like lemons and had come loose from her ponytail. Her kinky orange bangs dangled in front of her brown eyes, which shone bright and intense, almost as if lit from within. She had always been pretty, but right then she was sexy—powerfully and seductively sexy—and enjoying the moment was no longer enough. I moved my hands from her breasts to the waistband of her panties. I was about to tug them down when she froze.

I also froze. "What?"

She was looking ahead at something. I couldn't tell what from where I was lying. I eased her off me and flipped onto my stomach.

A mushroom the size of a small house stood in the center of the cavern.

And in fact, it *was* a house. There was a wooden door in the center of the fat white stem. Windows blazed on either side of the door with warm yellow light.

"Where did *that* come from?" I said, half-convinced I was imagining it.

"You see it, too . . . ?" Helen whispered.

"It's a Smurf house," I said, though that wasn't quite right. Smurf houses had colorful, polka-dotted roofs. The torches that lined the cavern illuminated this mushroom house enough that I could see the roof was the same brown-gold as the magic mushrooms that carpeted the ground. That detail almost convinced me that I was indeed imagining the fucking thing—except for the inconvenient fact that Helen could see it, as well.

I stared and squinted, waiting for my eyes to quit playing tricks and for the giant mushroom to revert to what it must be: a collection of deceptive shadows.

Helen got to her feet and said, "Where did it come from?"

I got to my feet, too—and the mushroom house stubbornly remained a mushroom house. I rubbed my eyes. That changed nothing. I pulled up my jeans and fastened them.

"You can see it, right?" Helen said. "It's a *house*. It just sprouted from the *ground*. What the hell, Joe? Are we hallucinating?"

I felt like smacking my forehead when she mentioned the house had sprouted from the ground. While that was impossible, it wasn't impossible that it had been lowered from above.

I waved at the roof of the cavern, even though it was too

dark to see the catwalks and accompanying rigging system of ropes and pulleys and weights that must be installed up there. "Hey! Hello?"

"Who are you talking to?"

"You might want to get dressed. They can probably see you."

"*Who?*" But she was already pulling up her pants. I collected her bra and sweater. "What's *going on*, Joe?" she demanded.

"They *lowered* the mushroom house," I told her, yanking my shirt over my head. "Like they do in a theater production when they turn off the lights and push one set off stage and lower another one from the rafters. That's what they did here once we were high and distracted."

"Oh . . . my . . . God . . ."

"Can you believe that shit? And I'll bet you my half of the ten grand that that mushroom house is the way out of here."

Chapter 11

"There is that which is real, that which is unreal,
and that which exists in the space between."
—The Book of Nine

"I don't see any ropes or wires attached to the top of it,"
Helen said.

"Guess they unfastened them."

"It *does* look like a Smurf house."

"It's even got a chimney," I said.

"But no rickety attic window. Should we knock on the
door?"

"You go knock."

She frowned. "Why just me?"

"It was your idea." The truth, however, was that I felt apprehensive. Despite my theory about the house's origin, its
sudden appearance bothered me. I was probably just having
some kind of magic mushroom anxiety, making a bigger deal
about the house than was justified . . . except . . . the house
was a big deal. It underscored just how elaborate The No-
End House challenge was, and if lowering something so large
from the roof of a giant cavern was fair game, what else

might be in store for us? How far would Izzy push the envelope to scare us into quitting the contest?

"Why don't we knock together?" Helen suggested.

I nodded, and we approached the door. It was made from plain wood that looked neither new nor old. There was no knocker, so I rapped my knuckles against the wood.

"Who is it . . . ?" called a wispy female voice.

"It's Joe . . . and Helen."

I looked at Helen and shrugged. She gave me a thumbs-up.

The door opened a moment later. The woman who stood on the threshold was about our age, with a riot of tangled blonde hair and lively blue eyes. She wore a simple white slip that was frayed and dirty in places. The lace hemline stopped above her knees. Her feet were bare, her toenails long and broken. She was both stunningly beautiful and frighteningly feral.

"Hello, Joe and Helen," she said, pleasantly enough. She cocked her head to one side. "Are you lost?"

"Lost—no," Helen said. "I think we're supposed to be here . . . ?"

"Supposed to be here?" said the woman. "No, nobody is ever supposed to be here except for my godmother and me." She gave us a curious smile.

And then I realized we likely needed to unravel some riddle to enter the house. That, however, seemed far beyond my current mental capabilities, so I asked simply, "Can we come inside?"

"If you must," she said after a hesitant pause. "But you cannot stay for very long . . ."

She stepped aside, and I followed Helen inside.

White candles filled the room—they were perched atop chests and chairs and most of the chunky wood furniture— and their combined glow spared no haven for shadows, re-

vealing an interior every bit deserving of a mysterious mushroom house.

Intertwined flowers and leaves festooned the high-gilled
ceiling. Framed portraits of noble-looking men and women
decorated the fleshy white walls, alongside thousands of taxi-
dermized animals (but only the sort found in caves, it seemed,
such as rats, bats, spindly spiders, fish, beetles, salamanders,
snakes, and a variety of birds).

Mushrooms spilled out of an assortment of glazed vases
almost as numerous as the candles, and not only the plain
brown-gold variety growing outside. Some were orange, some
indigo, some as white as bone and oozing a gooey red liquid,
and some resembling chunks of rotted meat.

Two beds with threadbare sheets were tucked out of the
way against one wall, next to a very basic kitchen that contained little more than cupboards and a sink (currently overflowing with dirty dishes). Most of the large room appeared
dedicated to scholarly pursuits. To our left, a huge bookcase
was stuffed full of old scrolls and battered tomes, many secured with weighty locks, others as thick as dictionaries.
More books were stacked high on an adjacent desk, leaving
just enough space for a crystal ball and an imposing, leather-
bound grimoire. The book of spells stood open on a bronze
stand, the aged pages revealing a kaleidoscope of hand-
drawn magical sigils.

Nearby was another desk, this one larger and crowded with
antiquated scientific instruments such as gourd-shaped glass
vessels with beaked heads, a clay crucible, a balance scale,
numerous containers holding who-knew-what, and a complex distilling apparatus of the sort you might need to turn
lead into gold. On the wall behind the desk, dozens of colorful ceramic jars lined a wooden shelf. Hanging beneath the
shelf from hooks were iron tongs, small bellows, and a pair
of leather-and-brass steampunk goggles.

An alchemist's workshop would be useless without fire, which explained the huge cast-iron stove with a flue that connected to the chimney stack we'd seen from outside. Izzy's eye for details went so far as to include crates stuffed with timber, coal, and other sources of fuel for the stove.

"Hol-ee jeez," Helen said in awe, like a kid who'd just stepped inside the world's greatest curio shop. "This place is *nuts.*"

"Reminds me of Disneyland," I said.

"Way too dark for Disneyland, Joe. The walls are covered with dead stuff."

"What is Disneyland?" asked the woman.

"The happiest place on Earth," Helen told her. "Um, do you have anything to drink here? My mouth is really dry."

"I can make tea. Please sit down and rest."

The only chairs not already occupied by books or other miscellaneous items were at a small round table.

Helen and I sat beside each other while the woman busied herself in the kitchen.

"This is totally weird," Helen whispered to me.

I nodded. It would have been weird even if we weren't tripping out. Now it was weird to the extent that I was having a hard time deciphering between what was real or not. Was Izzy's challenge even real? Or was it cover for some big-budget, candid-camera TV show? Was a host going to spring out from somewhere at any moment and point to hidden cameras and laugh at us? Or was this all a dream I would wake up from back in the hostel? At this point, I wasn't ruling anything out.

"*She's* so weird," Helen added.

I nodded again.

"Can't you talk?"

I swallowed. "My mouth is really dry, too."

"That's why I asked for something to drink. Did you see her toenails?"

I glanced at the kitchen, where the woman was fetching teacups and saucers from a cupboard. "Can she hear us?"

"Not way over here."

I continued watching the woman. The material of her slip was thin enough, and the candlelight bright enough, that I could see the silhouette of her naked body.

Helen said, "Don't tell me you have a crush on her, too?"

"Too?"

"First Vampmilla, now this feral thing. And that's sort of gross if you do. She looks like she was raised by wolves—"

"Shhh," I said, convinced we were speaking loud enough to be overheard. "She's coming over."

The woman set a silver platter in the center of the round table. She poured water from a silver pot into three delicate ceramic cups. There was no milk or sugar on offer, so Helen and I picked up our cups. Dried flowers floated inside mine. I held the cup up to my nose and sniffed. The tea smelled like floral tea should.

Helen sniffed hers, as well. "There's just normal stuff in this, right? I can't do any more drugs. I'll be sick."

"Drugs?" The woman furrowed her brow, as if confused by the word. "If you mean medicine, no, there is no medicine in the tea, only flowers that I picked yesterday."

"Flowers that grow underground?" I asked.

She shook her head. "I've never found any flowers that grow underground."

I didn't know whether she realized she was veering off-script—her character, after all, was supposed to be a cave-dwelling recluse, wasn't it?—but I didn't care. I sipped the tea. It was diluted but soothed my throat.

"It's good," I told Helen.

She sipped. "It's cold!"

"We heat our water on the stove, but I'm forbidden to use it when my godmother is away—"

"Whatever," Helen said. "It tastes fine. Are you going to tell us where the next door is?"

"The next door?"

"To the next room. Joe . . . what room are we in?"

I counted in my head. "Four, going on five."

"The door to Room Five," Helen said.

"Room Five? I'm not sure where Room Five is. This is the only room in this house."

I set my tea down and said, "Look, as you can probably guess, we ate a lot of the mushrooms outside, and we're probably not going to be doing much of anything for another few hours . . ."

The woman was staring at us in shock. "You *ate* the mushrooms?"

"Weren't we supposed to?" Helen said.

"Not those mushrooms! They're poisonous!"

"Come on . . ." Helen said.

"Don't fuck with us like that right now," I said.

"But they are. My godmother told me never to—"

"Who's this godmother you keep mentioning? Are we supposed to talk with her to find the next room?"

"She went to Merchant Belmont to purchase his truffles—*those* are the only mushrooms we eat."

"Is Merchant Belmont by chance a really fat guy who lives in a stagecoach?"

"I would not know. I never stray far from this house—"

"Except when you pick flowers," I said.

She looked at me freshly, and I sensed a crack in her righteous-naïve-girl act. Izzy's actors, it seemed, didn't like being called out.

"Now that I think about it," the woman continued, unruffled, "my godmother must be on her way back as we speak. You both must leave. You cannot be here when she arrives."

Helen folded her arms across her chest. "There's no way I'm going anywhere for a while."

Wild Child began stroking her hair in an agitated manner. "But she does not tolerate visitors."

I said, "Doesn't tolerate them?"

"We do not get many strangers out this way, but those who do find themselves at our house when my godmother is home always meet an unfortunate end."

Helen said, "Does she turn them into toads?"

"She turns them into compost."

I frowned. "Did you say *compost*?"

She nodded. "Which she uses to fertilize her mushrooms. Although we do not eat the mushrooms outside, she loves them so very much and treats them like her children."

"How exactly does she turn people into compost?"

"She slits them open from here to here." She pointed to her neck and navel. "Scoops out everything inside and fills them with manure she gets from—"

"Okay, I can't do this right now," Helen said, standing abruptly. The legs of her chair dragged loudly on the floor. "This is way too fucked up."

I stood, too. "Are you okay?"

"No, Joe, I'm not. Why the hell is she talking about turning people into compost?" She glared at the woman. "Are you for real?"

Wild Child shook her head. "You must leave immediately—"

"You know we're tripping out, right? And the shit you're saying is really fucked up. That's not cool."

"Hey," I said, resting my hand on the small of her back. "Why don't you lie down for a bit?"

"I can't lie down, Joe! I'm wired. And this bitch is fucking crazy! She knows what she's doing."

"Let's go sit on our own then. It'll just be . . . us. We'll chat." My heart started to race. If Helen's trip went south, so would mine. In fact, that was already inevitable, wasn't it? Because as soon as you start thinking you're going to have a bad trip, you're going to have one. Regardless, I saw no other option than to find our own space and said, "Come with me."

I guided Helen toward the beds.

Wild Child shouted, "But you cannot be here when Mother returns!"

"Enough with that shit!" I snapped over my shoulder.

And stiffened.

Someone was looking through one of the front windows at us.

The woman in the window wore a golden crown over a skintight black cowl that framed a face as ageless and cool as ice. Furious eyes and a cruel mouth accentuated, rather than diminished, her regal beauty.

"Who's *that*?" I blurted, although I knew it must be the god-mother.

Wild Child spun around and gasped. "She is here! You must hide!"

"*Hide?*" Helen said, her eyes as wide as golf balls. "*Where?*"

The godmother's face vanished from the window. Wild Child rushed to the door and slammed it shut a moment after it had bumped open a few inches.

"Hide! Quickly!" she shrieked. "Or she will get you!"

Fear motivates our behavior to protect us from immediate danger. If you're about to cross a set of train tracks and see a train coming in your direction, you will perceive danger, get anxious, and more likely than not, wait until the train passes before trying to cross the tracks.

And while waiting those five or ten minutes might seem like an inconvenience, it's a much better alternative than the worst outcome of deciding to cross the tracks: getting run over by the train.

Fear, however, is also an emotion. It's ruled by feelings and often functions irrationally, which can make you act irrationally in certain situations.

Not too long after I set out from Arizona on my walk around the world, I was passing through Zacatecas in north-central Mexico when a local approached me on the road and told me I should not be there. His English was decent, and he explained that over the last year, several tourists had been attacked, robbed, and left for dead by members of a local cartel. At that point in my journey, I was still green around the gills and hadn't been keeping up to date with US Department of State travel advisories. It was a sobering moment for me, and the first time—and there have been many more times since—that I'd considered turning around and going home.

Nevertheless, I decided to press on, and later that night made camp in a rocky field of brown grass and small shrubs. I was sitting at a fire and thinking about going to bed when a black car zipped past on the nearby four-lane highway. I thought nothing of it until it returned a minute later, driving at a crawl. It pulled over to the shoulder, fifty yards away from my camp. The sky was overcast with few stars visible, but I thought the car was a vintage model Cadillac with tinted windows. And although I couldn't see inside the vehicle, I knew the occupants could surely see me.

I remained at the fire, trying to be inconspicuous. An impossibility, of course. The cartel had discovered me, they had come for me, and I was to be their latest victim.

But then the car abruptly drove off.

I packed up camp quickly and spent the rest of the night hiking offroad through fields and forests. This was illogical. I could very easily have followed the highway and, at the first sight of headlights, flattened myself in tall grass or crouched behind a tree. But fear was in the driver's seat, and it drove me through the unforgiving terrain. Along the way, thorny shrubs sliced up my arms and legs, a tree branch nearly poked out my eye (it left a three-inch-long cut from my nose to ear), smelly marshes bogged me down, and hungry mosquitoes stole at least a pint of my blood. Yet I never once stopped or returned to the road until around midmorning, when I spotted buildings in the distance.

They belonged to a colonial-style town with colorfully painted adobe houses and narrow streets. While looking for a bus station where I could catch a ride to the closest big city, I spotted the black Cadillac parked outside a central plaza. Well, I *thought* it was the same one because, although it seemed to be the same vintage model, it had perfectly unthreatening non-tinted windows and an elderly couple seated inside it.

As they were getting out of the car, I crossed the street and confronted them. After some back and forth in Spanish and English, I worked out it had indeed been them on the highway the previous night. They were visiting friends and became lost. While across the highway from my camp, they had been consulting their GPS.

So, sure, fear can save your life . . . but it can make you do some crazy shit, too.

"Hide! Quickly!" Wild Child shrieked. "Or she will get you!"

To my horror, Helen had dropped to her knees and was rocking back and forth with her hands pressed against her ears. She was mumbling that she wanted to go home.

I looked back at the front door—and if I was shocked and frightened by the woman in the window, I was petrified now. Not because of the mask of terror on Wild Child's face as she braced her back against the door to keep it closed, but because the door had punched open with a loud bang, and an arm had reached in through the gap.

An arm not remotely human.

It was thin and long and nearly translucent—a naturalist might have described it as *insectoid*—yet there was no mistaking that it wasn't an arm, because it terminated in a hand, similarly slender and translucent, but a hand nonetheless, with a thumb and four needle-like fingers.

The nightmarish limb bent at the elbow, and the hand slapped against the inside of the door. It tried again and this time found the blonde woman's hair, which it seized in a fist.

Wild Child screamed and batted at it with her hands, even as the door thumped again and again at her back, threatening to open farther and let more of the horrible creature inside.

Wild Child pointed past me and yelled, "Hide!"

I simply stood there paralyzed with fear, watching the impossible spectacle as if I were a bystander in someone else's dream.

"There!" she said, pointing. "There!"

Finally I turned around—thinking slowly and calmly, *She's lost her mind*, and then just as slowly but much less calmly, *No, Joe, it's you who's lost your mind*—and realized she had been pointing to the big black stove.

It took me a torpid moment to understand the significance of what I saw. But as soon as I did, I returned to my senses.

I yanked Helen to her feet and pulled her after me toward the stove.

The witch at the front door—I'd always thought of a witch as wearing a pointed black hat and black dress, but I was convinced that whatever that thing was, it was first and fore-most a witch—shrieked in a cackly and very hag-like voice, "You ate my mushrooms, you filthy little rats! You had no right! You had no right!"

When we reached the stove, I yanked open the heavy door—it was pentagonal—and looked inside the iron belly.

A shaft at the back of it descended into inky blackness.

"Get in it!" I told Helen.

Eyes squeezed shut, hands on her ears again, she shook her head violently.

"The door's a pentagon! *Five* sides! *Five!*" She kept shaking her head.

"There's a tunnel—"

The front door crashed open. I didn't look. I didn't want to see what had just burst inside the house.

"*Go, Helen—*"

"I'm not crawling inside a stove!" she wailed. "She'll turn it on! She'll cook us alive!"

Fear can save your life, but it can make you do some crazy shit, too.

Damn right, it can.

Snagging Helen by the scruff of her neck and the seat of her jeans, I tossed her headfirst into the stove.

I was right behind her, shoving her butt to make her crawl down the shaft faster.

Behind us, I heard furniture tumbling and dishes shattering. Then the witch's voice boomed: "You can't get away from me, you filthy thieves! I'm going to eat your eyeballs for dinner and your tongues for breakfast and dine on the rest of your bits and pieces all week! Look at me! LOOK AT WHAT I AM!"

I didn't look, because I knew the witch was no longer the woman I had seen in the window. She was a horror not from this world, and if she caught us, she was going to devour us just as she'd promised—

Something snaked around my ankle, something thin yet terribly strong, something like a ghastly, elongated hand.

I shouted, and then Helen shouted . . . and then she was no longer in front of me.

In the next frenzied moment, my hands sank into the ground. I dropped through thin air before jerking to a halt, upside down, in perfect blackness.

An eternity or a second passed before the alien hand around my ankle relinquished its grip, and I fell and fell and fell.

Chapter 12

"Are dreams born of the mind, or is it the very
opposite?"
—The Book of Nine

Not long after Jen and I met, we did what many young and
in-love people do: we went to Disneyland. It was the end
of a long, hot summer, and we booked a room for two nights
at the Courtyard Anaheim Resort, less than a mile from the
park. On the first day, we arrived at the gates at 7:40 a.m.,
twenty minutes early, and hung out on Main Street until the
rides opened. After studying our map, we decided to head west.
We spent most of the sweltering morning checking out some
of the main attractions like the Indiana Jones simulator and
Tarzan's Treehouse. We were lucky enough to stroll up to the
Enchanted Tiki Room just before an audio-animatronics
show began, led by four talking macaws. After lunch in New
Orleans Square, we poked around the shops and went on a few
more rides. We finished the day in Frontierland with a leisurely
river cruise onboard the Mark Twain. Back at the hotel, we ordered pizza in our room, got in the Jacuzzi, watched the fire-
works from our window, and had an early night.

We started the second day in Fantasyland, and the attraction that stuck with me most from the entire weekend was Snow White and Her Adventures. Not because it was all that interesting or exciting, but because the morning's rain meant there was no line at the turnstiles, and the operators let us remain in our mine cart for three consecutive whirls through the slow ride.

I was on that ride now in my dream, with both Jen and Helen squeezed next to me and giggling like sisters in the front seat of Sleepy's mine cart (or perhaps it was supposed to be Sleepy's bed, and wouldn't that be some Freudian shit). The mine cart's first stop was the Seven Dwarfs' cottage, and despite the happy music and yodeling of Doc, Grumpy, Bashful, and the rest of the gang, I felt only dread. The cutesy, fairy-tale charm of the cottage reminded me of somewhere I had been recently, although I couldn't say for certain where.

Until I discovered the Evil Queen standing outside next to the window—and everything returned in a rush of horrible memories: the mushroom house, the witch, the chase through the stove.

The mine cart passed beneath a tree branch with two vultures leering down at us, and then a pair of huge doors swung inward, and we were inside a castle. Not just any castle; it was the Evil Queen's castle, and that meant it was the *witch's* castle, the witch who wanted to eat my eyeballs for dinner and my tongue for breakfast.

My dread quickly metastasized into terror.

I would have leaped out of the mine cart except for a rigid bar across my lap. Jen and Helen were pointing and laughing at the skeletons we passed, oblivious to the danger we were in. Jen wouldn't have had any reason to fear the witch masquerading as the Evil Queen, but Helen definitely would. I wanted to warn her, to shake some sense into her orange head, but I was so afraid, I couldn't move.

The mine cart approached a laboratory flooded with green lights. The Evil Queen stood at a bubbling cauldron, holding not the apple she used to poison Snow White, but instead a brown, bulbous mushroom. Although her back was to us, the shadow she cast on the stone wall behind her was impossible and monstrous, a nightmare creature that resembled a praying mantis with long thin arms in place of pincers.

I closed my eyes and tried to wake up. That didn't work, and the next thing I knew, we were in a forest where the trees had human faces and reached for us with their anthropomorphic branches. My paralysis broke, and I rattled the bar across my waist in a mad attempt at escape—and to my astonishment, it lifted easily. I turned to Jen and Helen, to tell them to follow me, and found them happily stuffing their mouths with mushrooms.

I fled, leaving them behind. Logs lying across my path became crocodiles that snapped at my heels as I jumped over them. Bats swooped down from the purplish sky and obscured my vision.

Sinister eyes watched me from the dark. Moans rose from a place unseen, wretched sounds that made me think of the damned whom God condemned to suffer eternal punishment in hell.

I never slowed or stopped. I was a man possessed, running for my life—and maybe for my soul, as well. Yet no matter how hard I pushed myself, I couldn't escape the witch's cackle, which followed me through the menacing forest.

And then ahead: hope. The Seven Dwarfs' cottage. As I approached it, my legs threatening to give out beneath me, the door swung open, and the witch stood silhouetted in a green light, her arms filled with mushrooms, cackling at me . . .

*   *   *

My eyes cracked open. The pain that greeted me was everywhere and so intense that I drifted back into unconsciousness.

My mind rose from the abyss. The pain was still there, vaguely, in my head and neck and shoulders. There was a light nearby, maybe a torch. I heard someone speaking. To me? I didn't know. Thinking hurt too much . . .

Sharp, ferocious pain in my side. My eyes snapped open.

I was seated upright in a chair. The light stung my eyes.

"Ah! You are finally awake, my friend," a deep, familiar voice said.

I blinked until I could finally see. The obese lord stood before me, his green jacket open to reveal the ginormous girth of his belly.

I tried to speak, but my tongue felt glued to the roof of my mouth. More jolting pain in my side.

I jumped in the chair.

"If you do not stop zat, my darlink, I am going to make a bigger mess zan I already have."

I stared in horror at the midget Nazi crouched next to me. He'd removed his black greatcoat and rolled up the sleeves of his tan shirt. Blood covered his hairy forearms and hands. *My* blood. My shirt was gone, and a brutal, messy incision extended from my navel around my right side.

With a wild cry, I tried getting to my feet but found that my wrists were bound behind me to the chair. I tried again and again but got nowhere. The chair was bolted to the ground.

"*What . . . ?*" My voice was unrecognizable, like the rasp of a rusty wood saw. "Fuck!"

"You must sit still, my friend," Lard-Ass said, placing a meaty hand on my shoulder. "Let Moritz finish his work. You'll feel as good as new in no time."

I glanced again at the midget Nazi with the Hitler mustache. He held a pair of toothed forceps in one hand and a needle dangling a thread in the other.

I jerked and squirmed. "Don't . . . fucking . . . touch me."

"I have already taken what was owed, my darlink. Now it is time to patch you up."

I kicked and strained my wrists against the rope. "Get away from me!"

The midget Nazi sighed as he set down the forceps and needle and stood. He withdrew a black baton from a holster on his belt and raised it above his head.

"Zere are two ways but to do zis, *die Schlampe*. You have chosen ze hard way."

He swung the baton.

Lard-Ass and the Nazi were gone. The electric light above me remained on, carving out an inverted yellow cone in the blackness. My head throbbed where the baton had struck me, and I would consider myself lucky if my skull wasn't fractured.

I didn't want to look at my side, but I couldn't help myself.

The sutures were a mess. A Frankenstein zigzag of ripped flesh and black thread. For a moment, I thought I might vomit, but I kept it down.

They took a kidney, I thought, filled with a dizzying combination of sadness, revulsion, and rage. *They took one of my fucking kidneys.*

And I knew they did. This wasn't some sick prank where they cut me open only to stitch me back up again, none the worse for wear. Severe pain radiated from beneath my ribs down to my abdomen and groin, and where my kidney was supposed to be was only a constant, heavy aching.

I felt like crying. I couldn't remember the last time I had done that, but tears welled in my eyes.

I blinked them back. I wasn't going to wallow in self-pity. I was going to hunt down Lard-Ass and that little fucking Nazi, and I was going to beat the living shit out of both of them.

I rattled my wrists against the back of the chair. I twisted and contorted my body.

I blocked out the pain this resurrected until I became numb to it.

Sometime later, I gave up trying to free myself—all I had to show for it was a dangerously fragile psyche and skin abraded nearly to my wrist bones—and I closed my eyes.

As darkness claimed me once again, I found myself not caring if it would be for the final time.

Someone was calling my name. Over and over again.

I tried ignoring the voice. It was from a lost corner inside my mind, a siren call luring me into another nightmare.

I preferred the nothingness.

"Joe . . ."

Was it in my head?

"Joe . . ."

Was it Helen?

"Joe . . ."

I might have kept ignoring her . . . except she sounded scared. Had something happened to her, as well?

Did she need my help?

"Joe . . ."

Although I was drifting beneath consciousness in what felt like an infinitely heavy suit, somehow I rose to the surface.

"Joe . . ." She sounded faraway and frightened.

"Helen!" Someone standing next to me would have had a hard time hearing that. I cleared my throat, worked my jaw and tongue. Tried again. "Helen!"

"Joe . . . ?"

"Helen!" I coughed. "Helen! I'm here!"

"Joe!"

"Helen!"

We kept this up—her name, my name, her name, my name—and it was working. She was getting louder and closer. And then she was before me, in the light, yet there was no smile to greet me. Her expression was one of shock and dismay.

"Oh, Joe . . ." she said, and if she were a flower, she might have wilted right then. "What happened . . . ?" Her lower lip began to tremble. She bit down on it while shaking her head. Tears streaked her cheeks. "You need help . . ."

"Can you untie me?"

Still shaking her head—she couldn't seem to stop herself—she went behind me. I heard her inhale sharply, likely at the sight of my wrists, but she said nothing. I felt her working on the rope, and eventually it dropped free. I sagged forward and almost fell out of the chair when my arms failed to work. Helen, however, gripped me by the shoulders.

"Who did this?" she asked gently.

I didn't tell her. She didn't need to know the midget Nazi had returned. It would only get her more worked up—regardless of the fact the little asshole had been after me, not her, all along.

"Joe?"

"Doesn't matter."

"Who . . . cut you?"

I was surprised she hadn't made the connection. Maybe it was too bizarre to believe. Or maybe, like me, she was already one step over the line to madness.

I simply shook my head.

Gradually the pins and needles left my arms and hands. I tried to stand.

On the second attempt, with Helen's assistance, I suc-
ceeded.

"I don't know the way out," she said, as we surveyed the
enormous darkness that imprisoned us. "I've been walking
for hours—"

"Isabella!" I bellowed, and I was surprised by the strength
in my voice. "Isabella! We quit! We're finished! Game over!"

Suddenly, numerous overhead lights flicked on. We were
back in the palace, in the center of a room every bit as opulent as the entrance hall where this nightmare began.

Doña Isabella stood next to a door, her hand still on the
light switch.

"No need to yell, señor," she said. "I am right here."

Chapter 13

"There are animals, there are human beings, and there are gods. Which is which is a question for the ages."

—The Book of Nine

With her luxurious black hair and sooty black eyes, Doña Isabella looked just as she had before, although in place of the slinky red dress, she was now clad from neck to ankles in skintight blue leather. A gold belt shaped like a snake was cinched low on her hips, while similar serpent bangles wreathed her wrists. Gold earrings, a pearl choker, and gold empress-strap heels that almost had her standing vertically on her toes finished the Cleopatra-chic look.

I didn't hold back. "What the *fuck* are you running here? What the FUCK are you running?"

"You signed up for The No-End House challenge of your own volition—"

I pointed at the scar on my side. "I didn't sign up for this! They took my kidney!"

Helen gasped, but my focus remained squarely on Doña Isabella.

She said, "I have no control over any side hustles made within the challenge, señor. That"—her eyes flicked to the scar—"is between you and Merchant Belmont. And you are lucky you fared so well in his game. Had you made many more mistakes, I doubt you would be standing before me right now."

Helen gasped again—only this gasp was so much higher-pitched, almost a yelp, it drew my attention.

She was exploring her face with her fingers as a burn victim might do fresh out of surgery. Since we had reunited, I hadn't looked closely at her. Even so, I was shocked I hadn't noticed the change in her appearance until now.

She was older. Much older.

"What have you done to me?" she wailed at Doña Isabella. "*What have you done?*" She turned to me, her eyes pleading. "Joe, what's wrong with me? I feel different, my skin feels different. Don't tell me I'm old. Please don't tell me I'm old. It was just a game. *It was just a game.*"

I clenched my jaw. Helen had lost fifteen years in Carmilla's "game" . . . only it had been much more than a game.

Helen appeared to be roughly sixty years old.

When she saw the truth of this in my eyes, she let out an anguished cry, more animal than human. She rushed toward Doña Isabella.

The woman didn't back away or flinch. Her hand moved with lightning speed, her palm striking Helen across the cheek with enough force to send her into a pirouette that ended with her crumpled on the ground, sobbing.

I knelt next to her and stroked her back, feeling helpless at my inability to do anything more. Tears gushed from her eyes, and blood spit from her mouth with each wheezing breath.

I glared up with hatred at the mastermind of our suffering.

"We're out. We're done. The contract said we could leave before Room Nine. It said we could leave any time. *It said that.*"

I was expecting lies and excuses. She said simply, "Indeed it did, señor."

I blinked and thought, *It can't be that easy. We've been through too much. We're never leaving. She'll never let us leave.*

I had never in my life wanted to be so wrong.

Doña Isabella indicated the door she stood before. "This leads back to the palace courtyard." She pointed to a different door on the other side of the room that I hadn't noticed until then. It was identical to the door in the antechamber with the elaborate black hinges and the equally elaborate *1* carved into the wood—only here, the hinges encircled the number *6*. "That leads to the next room. As it has always been, Señor Joe, the choice is yours to make."

I held Helen in my arms until she was all cried out, and then I said, "Are you ready?"

She lifted her head from my shoulder and wiped her eyes and nose with her knuckles. She sniffed and said, "We can't leave, Joe."

I stared at her, haunted by her prematurely aged face. "Can't leave?" I had no idea what she meant.

"You think Izzy will let us walk right on out of here?"

Doña Isabella had disappeared while I had been comforting Helen, just as inexplicably as she had appeared.

"The door's right there," I said. "This is over."

"It's not over, Joe! Look at me! I'm *old*! How is this ever going to be *over*?"

I was getting worried. Partly by her state of mind . . . but mostly because I knew she was right. It couldn't—

shouldn't—be this easy to leave the challenge. "How's Izzy going to stop us?"

"How?" Helen scoffed. "However she wants! She's not human, Joe!"

I was shaking my head. That wasn't what I wanted to hear.

Was it possible we'd both gone mad? Would we know if we had? Do the mad even know they're mad?

My stubbornness persisted. "If she's not human, Helen, then what is she?"

She seemed on the verge of tears again and simply shook her head.

"The thing in the Smurf house," I said, "the thing that chased us, it was some sort of special effects—"

"Stop it, Joe—"

"Lights and mirrors and—"

"Stop it, Joe—"

"Like a magic show, Helen! If they can make an elephant disappear on stage in front of a thousand people—"

"Stop it!" she shouted. "Stop it! Stop it! Stop it! Look at me, Joe. *Look at me.*" She stuck out her hands and splayed her fingers. Her knuckles were bony, her veins pronounced and bluish. "Is this lights and mirrors?"

I had no answer to that.

She tucked her hands away beneath her thighs, as if embarrassed by them. A few moments later, in a careful voice, she said, "I was walking for hours in this room, Joe. *Hours*, looking for you. There wasn't a single door or wall. There wasn't any of *this*." She waved an arm at the antique furnishings that filled the room.

"What was there?"

"Nothing! Absolutely nothing! When I fell through the tunnel . . . I don't even remember hitting the ground, but I must have. I felt *crushed* when I came to. And I found myself here. Not *here*. A big empty black place that went on forever. I thought I was dead. I thought I was in hell. And then Izzy turns on the light and we're *here*? That's not magic—not David Copperfield magic. It's not mirrors and lights. It's not special effects. It's *real* magic."

"That's impossible, Helen."

"Yes, impossible! Exactly! All of this is impossible!"

"Helen . . ."

"I don't know what's going on, but we fucked up, Joe. We fucked up so badly. We should never have come here."

In the most reasonable voice I could muster, I said, "We don't know what's going on, you're right. So how about we get up and go over to that door and see if it leads to the courtyard? What's the harm in doing that?"

"The contract."

"What about it?"

"If we withdraw from the challenge before exiting Room Nine, we forfeit the prize."

I was incredulous. "Who cares about the money!"

"I'm not talking about the money! *The stuff about our souls.*"

Frowning, I tried to recall the specifics of the clause.

"If we forfeit the prize," Helen said, "we forfeit our souls. That was in the footnote with the tiny letters. And the funny language—withdrawing from the challenge before exiting Room Nine, not exiting Room Nine, it sounded redundant—Izzy said it was just silly lawyer legalese. Bullshit, Joe! It's to cover all the bases. It means that if we *die* before exiting Room Nine, she gets our souls. But it also means that if we *leave the challenge* before exiting Room Nine, she gets our souls. Don't you see? Don't you see how screwed we are? The only way out of here is to *win*, and the only way to do that is to exit Room Nine."

* * *

I had never before felt true despair. The closest I had come to that was in the days and weeks after the neurologist took Jen off life support. But in retrospect, the seemingly bottomless hole that had opened in my chest had been the result of loss and grief, and not despair. I might have confused the emotions at the time, but now I knew the full enormity of despair. It was like watching an extinction-level asteroid flaming through the sky and knowing not only you and your loved ones, but the entire human race, had only minutes left to live. And maybe even that wasn't doing despair justice because, upon death, you became free. Yet for Helen and me, death might not be the end. If we had signed away our souls—if souls exist and such a transaction is possible—then we might never be free. Ever.

Eternal damnation, just like the Bible said. Eternal. Damnation.

I couldn't get my head around that. I couldn't conceptualize how that could be possible or what that might entail. It was beyond the realm of reason.

But not emotion.

I could comprehend "eternal damnation" on a visceral level, and the reaction those two words inspired in me was greater than grief, greater than loss, greater than fear of death itself.

So despair—true despair: it was the only description I had for my mindset right then.

We didn't speak for what felt like a very long time. Were we in shock? Maybe. I was done self-analyzing. I went over everything that Helen had put forth. I tried poking holes in her argument. I couldn't find any. Nothing else explained the footnote in the contract. It had been written to trap us, and we had stepped right into it.

If only I'd never woken up last night and overheard the Kiwis. . . . If only I'd never met Helen on the hostel's patio. . . .

If only I hadn't gone with her for coffee in the morning. . . .

I frowned, backing up.

Helen staring at me to get my attention.

Staring at me so I would strike up a conversation. Randomly showing up on the patio again in the morning. Insisting we go to The No-End House. *Leading* me to The No-End House . . .

I shrank away from her. She jerked upright and opened her eyes, looking dazed, like she might have been asleep.

"You're in on this," I said, my voice half accusatory, half wondering.

She rubbed her eyes. "In on what?"

"*This!* All this! You work for her!"

"For who?"

"Izzy!"

"What!"

"What were you doing at the hostel last night?"

"Are you serious, Joe?"

"Tell me!"

"I already told you! It looked pleasant. It wasn't filled with backpackers at the time. So I sat down for a drink."

"And in the morning?"

"I'm not doing this, Joe."

"Jesus Christ, Helen, you work for her!" I shot to my feet, ignoring the reawakened pain in my side. "*Why?* Why are you doing this? This is costing a hell of a lot more money than you can get for a kidney on the black market."

"You're crazy, Joe!" She got up, too, and stepped toward me.

I backed away. "It was your idea to come here."

"Mine? *You* told *me* about it. At the Starbucks. *You* told *me*."

"The Kiwis—they were planted, too. They were talking loudly on purpose. So I'd hear them."

"Oh, my God, Joe. Right, everybody in Barcelona is in on this!"

"Why are you doing it?"

"Please don't flake out on mé, Joe. I can't get through this without you."

"*Why, Helen?*"

"I'm not doing anything!" she cried. "I swear! You're acting crazy!"

"*Why me?*"

"I'm not doing anything! Stop it! *Please?*"

"Is that makeup?" I reached for her face.

She slapped my hand. "Don't! Don't touch me!"

"I'm outta here." I strode toward the unmarked door.

"Joe! Don't leave me here! You can't leave me here!"

I gripped the door handle.

"Joe . . ."

It was only one word, my name, but it was filled with so much sorrow that it broke my heart.

I looked back.

Helen was on her knees, her face buried in her hands, her shoulders shuddering as she shed tears.

"Goddammit," I said.

A few minutes later, after she had composed herself, we stood before the door with the elaborate 6 carved into it.

"Four more rooms," I said solemnly.

Helen nodded. Tears hadn't smudged her old-age makeup. She wasn't wearing any, never had been.

This was all real.

Bloody God, it was all real.

"We can do this," I said.

She nodded again.

"We stick together, no matter what."

"No matter what."

"Ready?"

She nodded again.

Steeling my nerves, I opened the door.

Chapter 14

"Adventure is often found in the unlikeliest of
places."
—The Book of Nine

The tunnel on the other side of the door engraved with the
number 6 was graveyard black when the door closed behind us. Since we no longer had a torch, we pressed ahead,
with our hands trailing along the rocky wall.

"What if we get lost?" Helen said from behind me, her voice
disembodied.

"I think there would have been a torch for us in that room
if we needed one. That's how things seem to work."

"Do you think people do this challenge alone?"

"Izzy said we were an exception . . ."

"I couldn't do it alone."

"Me either."

"I think you could."

"I would have taken the door to the courtyard if it wasn't
for you. And if you're right about the contract . . ."

"I don't want to be right . . ."

I couldn't help but smile. It felt unfamiliar and wrong

under the circumstances, but also good. "I bet that's the first time in your life you've said that."

"You think I'm snooty."

"Confident."

"The thing is . . . I usually *am* right."

"Arrogant."

She whacked my back, which triggered the pain in my side. I grunted and nearly stumbled.

"Oh!" she said. "I wasn't thinking!"

"I'm okay," I told her, my hand finding the wall again. "Just a bit unsteady."

"I'm really sorry, Joe. I didn't know an old granny would have so much strength in her."

She said that in jest, or at least she tried to, but some things you couldn't make light of, regardless of how much you might want to.

Aging fifteen or so years in a matter of hours was one of those things.

We continued without speaking. The only sound was our footsteps on the dusty ground. The air, I thought, was becoming warmer, and I wondered if this meant we were getting closer to the surface.

Then, ahead, the darkness appeared to lighten.

"Do you see that?" Helen said.

"Is it getting lighter?"

"I think so."

We soon found ourselves in a cave the size of a small movie theater. Sunlight filtered through a fissure in one wall that was only a couple of feet wide but fourteen or fifteen feet high.

"Where do you think we are?" Helen asked.

"No idea. But if that's the sun out there, it's better than where we are."

"What's that?" She indicated a lumpy pile of shadows in the corner of the cave.

Cautiously we approached what turned out to be the skeleton of some large animal.

"Is that a snake?" I said, disgusted by its size.

"It's too fat to be a snake," Helen said. "It looks like . . . a centipede."

"It's as big as I am!" Even so, the disarticulated bones could very well have been the pieces of a giant exoskeleton.

"It definitely looks like a centipede."

"A centipede that big would have gone extinct millions of years ago."

"More like hundreds of millions of years ago."

"It's not fossilized," I pointed out. "So it hasn't been dead for anywhere close to that long."

Helen folded her arms across her chest and shuddered. "Whatever it is, it's gross. I hate bugs."

"Calling that thing a bug is like—"

"I mean, I *really* hate bugs. I have a phobia. Spiders, beetles—especially centipedes and millipedes. How does Izzy know that?"

I hated bugs, too, and said, "She doesn't. She's just trying to scare us."

"She could have put anything there to scare us. And she chooses my biggest fear?"

"It's a coincidence."

Helen shook her head several times but didn't say anything more.

"Screw Izzy," I said, hooking my arm around her waist and turning her toward the light spilling through the crevice in the wall. "Let's get some sunshine."

Whatever I had expected to find on the other side of the crevice, it wasn't what awaited us. Stepping out from the rocky slit, we found ourselves on the side of a low mountain that jutted from a sea of verdant forest.

Helen didn't seem bothered by the fact we were no longer

in Barcelona and maybe not even Spain. She tilted her face up to the sky, closed her eyes, and stretched out her arms as if to absorb the light.

"This is impossible," I told her bluntly.

"Impossible is the new possible, Joe."

"Where the hell are we?"

She dropped her arms and looked at me. The many new lines and creases in her skin were even more apparent outdoors.

I did my best to keep my eyes on hers.

"Does it matter where we are at this point?" she said. "Wherever it is, I'm just relieved we're no longer in those god-awful tunnels."

She had a point.

"So this is Room Six? A forest that stretches to the horizon? Finding a door is going to be like finding a needle in a haystack."

Helen surveyed the seemingly infinite vegetation for a long while. Then she pointed. "Is that smoke?"

It took me a few seconds to see what she was talking about.

Indeed, a misty gray curlicue rose from the forest two, perhaps three, miles from our location.

"You think that's where we need to go?"

"It looks like a smoke signal to me, and smoke signals are one of the oldest forms of communication."

"Who's trying to communicate with us?"

"I guess that's what we have to go find out."

The trek down the side of the mountain was precarious. Loose rocks and soil shifted beneath our feet, causing us to pause often and recalculate our route. My throbbing side added to the difficulty of the descent. Helen appeared to be having an equally unpleasant time. Her agility wasn't what it used to be; she seemed stiffer in the knees and hips. I was worried she might break a bone or two if she took a tumble. So all in all, it was a slow and careful slog, during which I had plenty of time to process our bizarre new reality. And if truth be told, I was worried about how easily both of us were taking that new reality in stride. We agreed that Doña Isabella was not human. That made her . . . I had no fucking idea. But we agreed she wasn't human . . . and we were fine with that? At least, we were accepting of that? Did this make us crazy?

I didn't believe it did. After all, most people accept the concept that everything in the universe came from something smaller than an electron, and if you can accept that . . . well, believing in a nonhuman intelligent being isn't exactly beyond the realm of possibility, is it?

We're all naïve when it comes to things we know little about. And in that vein, perhaps naïveté serves a purpose greater than making one a target for mockery; perhaps it's an evolutionary trait necessary for survival, a mental off-ramp that allows a cynical and rational species a way to believe in the unbelievable, to accept situations that on first glance seem inconceivable. In other words, maybe it helps keep us sane in an insane universe.

"What are you thinking?" Helen asked me, when we'd stopped on a rocky plateau to survey the foothills rolling into the forest below.

"We should make it to the bottom in another half hour or so."

"I mean, what are you *thinking*? You haven't said much since we ended up here."

I shrugged. "What's there to say?"

"Do you think Izzy's a god?"

I scoffed. "More like a devil."

"Same thing. A devil's just a bad god the same way an asshole's just a bad person."

"Do you believe in gods and asshole gods?"

"Not until recently," she said. "But now that she's stolen more than a decade of my life and transported us to God knows where, I don't know what I believe anymore."

I was surprised. "Transported? As in teleportation?"

"Look around, Joe. We're not in Kansas anymore. And we certainly didn't walk here."

I considered that and said, "I was unconscious for a while. You said you were, too. Izzy could have driven us outside of Barcelona."

"To a palace-like room built inside a mountain?"

"At least she'd still be human."

"You want her to be human?"

I shrugged. "I can get my head around that."

"Well, she's not. She's not human, Joe. You know that, and I know that. She's a god, whatever that means, and like the Greek ones, she's into mischief. This is all a game to her. She's playing with us, and she's playing at being human, as well."

I didn't want to go down that rabbit hole and said, "We need to get to the fire before dark."

We resumed our descent.

While walking in Central and South America during what seemed like a lifetime ago, I'd passed through my share of tropical rainforests. They were all very dark, very green, and very dense.

The forest that Helen and I found ourselves in at the bottom of the mountain checked each of those boxes plus one more. It was very, very old. The largest trees—needle-leaved conifers and other broad-leaved evergreens—soared maybe two hundred feet or more into the air, rivaling the giant redwoods on the West Coast of the US. The canopy of interwoven branches blocked out not only much of the sky, but

THE NO-END HOUSE   145

also the sunlight and wind, creating a shadowed, quiet, and still world below. An assortment of smaller tropical flora fought for space, including tree ferns, palm tree-like plants, and woody-stemmed cycads with feathered emerald crowns. Felled trees and rotting deadwood and a variety of shrubs and ferns populated the leaf-littered ground, creating a near-impassable barricade into the forest's murky depths.

"What do we do now?" I said, fighting a wave of futility and frustration. From our bird's-eye view earlier, the forest hadn't seemed so daunting.

"We find the fire," Helen said, craning her neck to look up at the pine tree next to us. Its trunk had to be at least ten feet in diameter.

"We can't see the smoke anymore," I pointed out.

"It's that way," she said, waving in what seemed to me to be an arbitrary direction.

I frowned. "Are you sure about that?"

"I have a good sense of direction."

"We still must be two miles away from it. And with all this undergrowth, we won't be able to walk in a straight line."

"Follow me," she said simply, and forged a path into the snarl of vegetation.

Chapter 15

"Time is both a voyage and an illusion."
—The Book of Nine

The dark and damp rainforest swallowed us rapidly and completely. It was so dense, it seemed to dull sound, making it feel like we were trudging through the leafy vegetation in a bubble. The sharp, pungent smell of rotting deadfall soon became overwhelming; there was no escape from it. After ten minutes of arduous hiking (I fell twice on the slippery ground), we stopped to rest. I flopped down on a mossy rock to catch my breath. Muddy mushrooms sprouted from the decomposing leaf litter, and I happily crushed them beneath my sneakered feet. When I drew my arm across my forehead, it came away slicked with sweat. Not only was it as hot as an Arizona summer, but it was also extremely humid. The air seemed stuffy, almost drippy, and I heard more than felt the drumbeat of a mild headache rallying behind my temples—no migraine, thankfully. I knew the difference between the two as surely as I knew the difference between air and water.

Helen appeared to be equally exhausted. Her sweater clung

like a wet rag to her shoulders and breasts. We hadn't spoken more than a few words since first entering the antediluvian forest—it had taken intense effort and concentration to navigate the vegetation—but now she said, "I was right."

"Of course you were," I said, examining a shallow cut on my arm where I had bumped up against something. It was nothing compared to the mess that was my wrists. "About what?"

"Izzy teleported us."

"I'm not doubting that anymore. There aren't any rainforests like this in Spain. I wouldn't be surprised if we're somewhere in the middle of the Amazon."

"I don't think so," Helen said. "I think we're still in Spain—or what's going to become Spain."

I glanced at her. "Going to become?"

"She teleported us back in time, Joe."

I blinked. "Don't go loony on me, Helen."

"This isn't the present," she stated.

"Just because we haven't seen any roads or—"

"Epiphytes," she stated, in that self-assured way of hers when she knew she was right about something. "Have you seen any? Bromeliads, orchids, elkhorns? In a normal rainforest, there are dozens, if not hundreds, on a single tree."

I looked up at the trees surrounding us. I didn't see any of the plants she mentioned.

"And strangler figs? Every modern-day rainforest is dominated by strangler figs."

Now that she mentioned that, I realized I hadn't seen any of them, either. And they were hard to miss. I'd always thought it fascinating how their aerial roots choked a host tree to death and assumed its shape with a hollow latticework shell.

"And vines?" Helen pressed.

The lack of ubiquitous ropey vines was something I *had* noticed; I simply hadn't given their absence much thought.

I asked, "Why does any of that mean we've gone back in time?"

"Because they're all flowering plants, and flowering plants didn't appear until the Cretaceous Period."

A hot flash zapped me, and it took a couple of seconds to clear my head. I'd figured she'd been talking about time travel measured in hundreds or thousands of years, and as crazy as that would be, it wasn't half as crazy as pre-Cretaceous time travel. "You think we've gone back in time *millions* of years?"

"At least a hundred million," she said.

"Don't fuck with me, Helen."

"Where are the birds, Joe? That's what got me thinking about it. Screeching macaws? Toucans? Parrots? I haven't heard any, have you?"

I hadn't. The forest was preternaturally quiet.

Helen said, "Birds evolved from small carnivorous dinosaurs during the Late Jurassic, and those weren't even anything like modern birds. They still had teeth."

She tilted her head back and made a monkey call. The absurd howl echoed eerily in the stillness and went unanswered.

"No primates around, either," she said. "And that's not surprising, since they didn't appear on the evolutionary scene until after the dinosaurs vanished."

Belief and denial at what Helen was saying collided head-on inside my chest, and belief was the only one to walk away. I felt sick.

"So if I had to guess," she went on blithely, "I'd say we're in the Early to Middle Jurassic Period. I don't think it would have been this lush in the Triassic. And as I mentioned, there

would have been flowers and bees and birds and all that stuff
you would take for granted if we were in the Cretaceous or
later."

I cupped my head in my hands and rubbed my temples.
Impossible. I repeated that word over and over. Yet it no
longer held any meaning. Impossible was the new possible;
impossible was dead.

I glanced at Helen. Waited for her to smile, to let me in on
the joke, to say something that would suddenly make everything make sense.

She simply stared back at me without expression.

I swallowed tightly and looked around the hushed, pri-
meval Jurassic forest. And it was definitely that: Jurassic.
How I hadn't recognized that on my own, I didn't know. I'd
had blinders on, I suppose. I didn't want to see what was
right in front of me, and so I didn't.

Helen held out her hand and helped me to my feet.

"We better keep moving," she said. "We're running out of
daylight."

I took the lead, watching where I stepped, parting big wet
ferns with my hands, pushing branches with glossy green
leaves out of my way, careful they didn't snap back and whack
Helen in the face.

Soon I was moving on autopilot through the wet tropical
forest, distracted by the array of thoughts racing within my
head. I was terrified, certainly; I was a hundred million years
away from home, which made flying to Mars seem like nothing more than a hop, skip, and jump in comparison. I was
mystified, justifiably; I wasn't exactly in a strange new world
but a strange new *time*, and I don't think any amount of ther-
apy will ever make me fully copacetic with that. But also—
and surprisingly—I was in awe, and not entirely in a bad

way. I was in awe that time travel existed. Time didn't only move in one direction. It could be wound backward like the film on a movie reel.

Which meant we don't die; we're always present, on the reel, ready to replay our lives over and over again.

Not only was I in awe of all that, but I was also in awe on a more practical level: time travel existed, yes, but more, Helen and I *had experienced it*. We were somewhere no other human being had ever set foot. It was an almost religious reconciliation that couldn't be put into words—

"I wish I had my phone," Helen said abruptly.

I slowed to allow her to move up beside me. Her phone had been in her handbag, and the last time I'd seen her with that had been inside the mushroom house.

Even so, I asked, "What happened to it?"

"I didn't think to grab my bag when that stick monster came after us."

"You would've had a tough time getting reception out here."

"The compass app would've come in handy."

"No satellites above us . . ."

"It would likely use a magnetometer, not GPS."

"In this time period, Helen, the North Pole is probably somewhere around northern Africa, so I don't know how much any compass would help you." I glanced sidelong at her. "Are we lost?"

She shook her head. "I'm pretty sure we're still heading in the right direction."

I cocked an eyebrow. "Pretty sure? What happened to your great direction?"

"We're still going in the right direction, Joe. Don't worry about that. I just would have liked to confirm it, that's all."

I decided to finally address the elephant in the room: "You know there are probably dinosaurs in this forest, right?"

"Not probably. Definitely. You've seen *Jurassic Park*. It's named that because the Jurassic was the peak era of the dinosaur's reign. They were everywhere then."

"You sound like you're an expert on dinosaurs."

"I'm an expert on many things. Don't you know that by now?"

She certainly knew more than I did about a lot of things. And one of those things I didn't know much about was dinosaurs. I said, "Where did dinosaurs come from? They're just evolved reptiles, aren't they?"

"Very large evolved reptiles."

"Because there was a lot more oxygen in the atmosphere back then?"

Helen shrugged. "I've heard people say that. But I think their gigantism had more to do with the fact they laid eggs."

"Gigantism?"

"It means—"

"I know what it means. You just sound like a bit of an ass when you speak like that."

"An ass! You're vocabulary-shaming me now, Joe? The reason dinosaurs *got so big* was likely because they laid eggs. That let them develop and grow outside of their mothers' bodies. With us, it's the opposite. We grow inside a uterus, which limits our size."

"Birds lay eggs," I said, "and they're not giants."

"They don't need to be giants. They're doing fine how they are. But back in the day, it was like an evolutionary arms war. The bigger you got, the bigger the ecological advantage you had. Dinosaurs with longer necks could reach higher food. Larger carnivores could eat larger prey, which gave them an energy advantage over smaller carnivores."

"I guess bigger isn't always better, given how things worked out for them."

"Big dinosaurs weren't the only losers. Three quarters of Earth's animals vanished after the asteroid impact. The small guys, it turned out, were the winners. Mammals and birds, which now dominate the planet."

We ducked beneath a low branch, then pushed through a patch of ferns taller than me.

On the other side, Helen said, "That asteroid would have been traveling for millions of years, and if it hit Earth only a few minutes later—*a few minutes*—it probably would have landed in a lot deeper water. There would have been less rock to vaporize, less heat generated, less crap in the sky to block out the sun's light and warmth. There probably wouldn't have been a mass extinction. Non-bird dinosaurs would have survived, and we wouldn't be here today. All because of a few minutes."

I said, "Did dinosaurs have good hearing?"

"I imagine so."

I ducked beneath another branch and held it up for Helen to pass under. "Then maybe we should stop talking so much . . ."

"I think we're okay," she said, stretching her arms out for balance as we trudged through a muddy puddle. "As a general rule, animals can hear the sounds they produce. So big dinosaurs could probably hear the heavy footsteps of other big dinosaurs well but not the higher-frequency sounds of smaller things like us."

"I don't know if we should leave that to chance—"

Ahead of us, in a relatively shrub-free patch of land, a five-foot strip of dark loam marred the forest floor. I crouched next to the strange track. It was about three inches in depth and double that in width.

"Almost like someone plowed the ground with a hoe," I said. "Except hoes won't be invented for a hundred million years."

Helen said, "So a better description would be *scratched*. Like what a chicken does to find food."

"One hell of a big chicken."

"Chickens, like all birds, are theropods, Joe—two-legged dinosaurs."

I frowned, feeling uneasy. When I thought of two-legged dinosaurs, T-Rexes and velociraptors came to mind. I stood and said, "Let's get out of here."

Helen nodded, and we continued in the direction we'd been heading, with a renewed urgency in our steps. That scratch in the ground might not have been a dinosaur's footprint, but I couldn't imagine anything else but a pair of very large claws that could have made it.

And it had looked fresh.

Helen remained in front of me, leading the way. I hoped she knew where she was going. I had lost most sense of direction, and what sky I could glimpse through the canopy was already turning twilight shades of yellow and orange. It would be night within half an hour.

"We're not going to make it to the campfire," I told her.

"We still have light," she replied.

"We should start looking for somewhere to spend the night. We'll continue in the morning."

"We still have light," she repeated.

I frowned. I didn't think it would be a good idea to be wandering around the forest in the dark. I didn't know if dinosaurs were nocturnal, but I suspected some were. We'd passed several fallen trees that had rotted away in the middle. Those trunks would offer shelter . . . but who knew what might already call them home? The last thing I wanted was to wake up to find a giant centipede like the one up in the cave trying to share a bed with us—

In front of me, Helen froze.

Coming to an abrupt halt is a universal sign of danger, and

so I froze, too. I looked in the direction Helen was looking and almost sagged with relief.

A wide river meandered through the jungle thicket ahead of us. The slow-moving water was clear and deep and frothing where it splashed against protruding stones covered in rusty-colored lichen.

"Jesus, Helen, you scared the—"

"*Shhh*," she said sharply.

And then I saw it. I'd been looking right at it the whole time, yet it blended perfectly with the surrounding foliage.

A dinosaur.

A *big* dinosaur.

And it was staring back at us.

The scaly green head was low, as though it had been drinking from the river. A bony crest shaped like a boomerang rose from the top of it. Bumpy ridges circled jaundiced, unblinking eyes. The front of its face protruded like a snout, but was laterally stretched, and ended in what appeared to be a beak.

"Back away slowly," I heard myself saying under my breath.

"It's okay, I think," Helen said, and stepped forward. She raised one hand, as if she thought the fucking thing would recognize a wave.

"*Helen*," I hissed.

With a fluidity of motion that seemed all too elegant for something so large, the dinosaur disappeared into the forest.

"What the fuck were you doing!" I whispered, spinning her toward me.

She was grinning from ear to ear. "That was a dinosaur, Joe. A *dinosaur*. We just saw a living, breathing dinosaur!"

"*Keep it down.*"

"What are you so worried about?"

"We were fifty feet away from something that could have eaten us for dinner!"

She laughed. "It was a herbivore! It had a beak."

"So did pterodactyls, and I'm pretty sure they were carnivores."

"They didn't have beaks, Joe. They had long thin jaws with teeth. Didn't you learn any of this in school?"

"I don't care if that thing we saw had a beak or not. It was the size of a minibus. It could have—"

"It stood on four legs. It was a sauropod. Ergo, a herbivore."

"Jesus Christ, Helen," I said. I was happy that she knew what she was talking about—or at least *sounded* like she knew what she was talking about—but her cavalier attitude was infuriating. "So what if it was a herbivore? What do we really know about dinosaurs? What do paleontologists know? All they have are bones to go by. They don't know anything about behavior—"

"They do, too."

"Nothing for certain. They definitely don't know how a dinosaur would react to the presence of a human in its territory—"

"Herbivores aren't territorial—"

"But they can be aggressive! Elephants charge people all the time. Imagine if that thing charged us? We'd be as flat as pancakes in seconds."

Helen was shaking her head. "Listen to you, Joe! Yes, we're in a super shitty situation. But it's also a once-in-a-lifetime situation. A once in an *all-of-human-civilization* situation. Let's try to keep that in perspective and not be such grumpy bums."

"Grumpy bums?" I laughed curtly. "I'm a *grumpy bum*? I just want to get through this alive, all right?" I shook my head. Arguing wasn't accomplishing anything except wasting what little light remained in the sky. "Anyway, whatever. It's going to be dark soon. We need to decide where we're going to sleep."

She shrugged. "In a tree."

I scanned the understory. The tree ferns and cycads didn't have any branches for us to climb or shelter within. And the conifer trunks rose dozens of feet in the air before the first boughs appeared.

"A small tree," Helen clarified, "that we can climb up." She surveyed the trees around us and pointed to a miserable-looking one that seemed doomed to perish in the shadows of its much larger brethren. "That one looks good to me."

It was certainly climbable, and the trunk diverged about twenty feet up, providing us a crook to settle into for the night. Even so, it was far from ideal. We'd be visible to anything that strolled past.

"Well?" Helen said.

"Guess it will have to do."

After some experimentation, we decided the best seating arrangement would be to straddle the crook with our backs to each other. Despite the tree being as high as a two-story building, the view of the forest hadn't changed much. We were still dwarfed by the much larger trees surrounding us. However, twilight had leached the vibrancy from the vegetation. The greens had turned sepia-toned, and the pooling shadows had lengthened and darkened to impenetrable blacks. What little I could see of the sky through the canopy blazed orange and crimson, although those colors were purpling by the second.

From somewhere not too far away, a foghorn pierced the humid stillness.

Helen stiffened against me. Neither of us spoke.

Another honk—and that was probably a better description of the sound. A honk like a goose makes, only much deeper and louder.

A distant honk answered it, then two more. Then nothing.

"Herbivores?" I whispered.

"Sounded like it," Helen whispered back.

"Better than carnivores."

"Better than them."

It was going to be a long night.

Helen woke me. She needed to pee. I told her to hold off until morning. She said she couldn't and began descending the tree.

It was sometime in the middle of the night. Stars filled the sky. Their light filtered through the canopy like silver dust, allowing me to see surprisingly well. When Helen reached the ground, she started away from the tree.

"Where are you going?" I called to her quietly.

"I'm not going to pee on our tree!"

She stepped behind a nearby conifer, and I didn't see her reappear.

I leaned back against the trunk, enjoying the reprieve of relative comfort. Falling asleep in economy class on a flight was rough business; falling asleep in a tree was damn near impossible. No matter how I adjusted myself, my butt would start hurting after a few minutes. Just as often, I'd switch from wrapping my arms around the trunk to folding them on it. The latter was more comfortable, as I could rest my head on my forearms instead of the furrowed bark, but there was also a much greater chance I might fall out of the tree, so it wasn't a permanent option.

We hadn't heard any more honks. No roars, either, thank God. Helen, being the encyclopedia she is, had suggested at one point that dinosaurs didn't roar. The only animals that roar today—bears, big cats, and so forth—are all mammals. Birds don't roar. Reptiles don't roar. And because birds and reptiles are both descendants of dinosaurs, dinosaurs likely didn't roar, either . . .

When I realized I was drifting off to sleep, I sat up and saw Helen coming back toward our tree.

Something huge and dark was moving right behind her.

I tried to yell, but my throat was so tight, I couldn't make a sound. Helen either heard or sensed the danger and whirled around.

She managed a short, glassy scream that was cut off the moment the T-Rex's jaws snapped closed over her. The creature raised its massive head, chewed twice, and swallowed. Helen's legs fell from the side of its bloody mouth to the ground. It tilted its head to look with one eye at the severed limbs. Then it scooped them up with its teeth and disappeared into the night as silently as it had appeared.

I shot awake with a breathless gasp. I knew exactly where I was.

Disorientation came only with deep sleep, and I had been barely dozing. Throughout the dream, I'd known I was dreaming, yet that hadn't changed the cold horror of it. I felt Helen's tailbone pressed snugly against mine. Even so, I turned to ensure she—or more specifically, *all of her*—was there. She was, of course. She was leaning forward against her trunk, her arms hanging sloth-like from either side of it.

"What?" she asked, without opening her eyes.

She would have felt me turning, the same way I felt her every time she shifted positions.

"Just checking on you," I said. "What time is it?"

"No idea."

"I'm so uncomfortable."

"Might only be a few more hours until morning."

"I want my bed."

"Me, too," I said.

She opened one eye. "You want my bed?"

I turned back to my trunk. "My bed."

"You don't have a bed. You're walking around the world, remember?"

"I have a sleeping bag."

"You can stay in my bed when we get back."

"Thanks."

"I'm serious," she said.

I sighed. "This is crazy."

"What is?"

"We're sitting in a tree, and there are dinosaurs honking in the night around us."

" 'There are more things in heaven and earth, Horatio . . . ' "

"Ghosts would be easy to believe in compared to . . . all this shit. Have you considered the possibility that we might be crazy?"

"Nope," she said.

"Why not?"

"The chance that we're both crazy—and more, that we're both the same kind of crazy to be imagining all of this—would be astronomical."

"We wouldn't have to both be crazy. Just one of us. All of this could be inside one of our heads."

"That would mean I'm the crazy one," she said. "Because I sure as hell know this is all happening."

"Maybe I'm just imagining you saying that?"

She groaned. "Maybe you need to get some sleep, Joe. We're not crazy, okay? And even if we are, we wouldn't know it. The crazy don't know they're crazy. If they did, they wouldn't be crazy."

She was quiet for a little, and I figured she'd dozed off. I thought about what it might be like to sleep next to Helen (in a proper bed, at least). To wake up next to her. To make her breakfast and to kiss her off to work. And I was surprised that none of that sounded impossibly far-fetched or unpleasant. In fact, it sounded like something within reach—and something I might give up walking around the world for . . .

I patted my pocket that held the pill bottle, and I did my best to take it out without disturbing Helen too much. I looked at it for a long moment and had a wild urge to twist off the cap and dump the lot into my mouth. Instead, I threw the bottle away into the night and felt rather proud of myself. That had been something I'd wanted to do for a long time now but could never muster the courage.

"What's happening?" Helen asked me sleepily.

"Nothing," I said, as I imagined the surprise on the face of the archeologist who might dig up the bottle in the far future, and I thought, *It's for good, too. I'm never going back on them. Whatever I have to deal with, I'll deal with. If something positive is going to come from all this shit we've been through, let it be that.*

Sometime later—I might have been sleeping—I heard Helen ask me a question.

"Mmmm?" I said.

"Are we dating, Joe . . . ?"

"What?"

"Because, you know, we were fooling around earlier."

"Feels like a hundred million years ago."

"Are we?"

"If we are," I said, "this has been one hell of a first date."

"You could have just bought me flowers."

"I'll buy you some when we get back."

"No, you won't."

"Sure, I will."

"No, you won't, Joe. I'm old. I'm like sixty."

I swallowed tightly. I'd almost forgotten that—almost. "Maybe when we finish this thing, when we exit Room Nine, everything goes back to normal. Like it was before."

"Do you really think so?"

"Probably," I said, with more conviction than I felt. "I wish—"

I felt Helen jerk upright. I started to turn again to ask what was wrong—and I saw it, too.

A T-Rex was stalking through the undergrowth directly below us. The same one from my dream.

Chapter 16

"The natural evolution of understanding is
action."
—The Book of Nine

To the best of my limited knowledge, there are two broad
interpretations of what Tyrannosaurus Rex looked like.
The first is the popular culture green/gray/brown lizard-like
T-Rex from the *Jurassic Park* movies. The second is a mullet-
sporting, feather-tailed, multicolored T-Rex favored by aca-
demia.

The one below us fell somewhere in between.

It had no feathers that I could see, but in the starlight, it
was bright green with vibrant yellow stripes across its back
and flanks.

Yet what surprised me most was how quiet it was. For
the few seconds it was visible, it made hardly any sound—
definitely no booming footsteps that could ripple the water
in a glass. Then branches rustled, and it was gone.

Helen's hand gripped my thigh. I wanted to take it in my
hand, but I couldn't move. I felt both terrified and brazenly

lucky, as though Death had just crossed my path but had been looking in the other direction.

My heart pounded madly in my chest. I willed it to slow down, half-convinced the T-Rex could detect heartbeats the way sharks could detect blood in the water from miles away.

Helen spoke so quietly, I almost didn't hear her: "It's gone."

I said, "It could come back."

"We're safe up here."

"Was it . . . real?" I knew it had to be. But the experience had been so brief and surreal, I wasn't ruling anything out.

"We both saw it."

"It barely made any noise."

"What successful predators do?"

"I had a dream about it, Helen."

"A T-Rex?"

"No, *that* T-Rex. A bright green one with yellow stripes."

"When?"

"A few minutes ago, right before I woke up."

"*Shit, Joe.* It must have been by earlier." A shrill edge had crept into her voice, likely mirroring the shrillness in mine. "You must have seen it when you were sleeping or thought you were sleeping. What did it do in your dream?"

I didn't think she would appreciate the graphic truth, so I said, "It just walked by."

"I wonder why it came back. Do you think it can smell us?"

"No idea. But like you said, we're safe up here."

"But in the morning. . . . We can't stay up here forever."

"It will be long gone by then—"

The T-Rex reemerged stealthily from the foliage, and this time, it looked right up at us.

The next few seconds seemed to last hours. High in a tree or not, I was convinced we were going to die—and worse, be devoured in the same gruesome manner that Helen had suffered in my dream.

Different scenarios of how this might come to pass flashed through my mind, yet the one that lingered (only slightly less absurd than the others) was the T-Rex ramming its head against the tree until we either fell out of it or the whole thing uprooted and toppled over.

Amazingly, however, the T-Rex simply lowered itself to its knees, wrapped its tail around its torso, closed its eyes, and tucked its chin, assuming a roosting position similar to modern birds.

Helen and I watched it breathlessly for several minutes. It remained crocodile-still.

I whispered, "It's sleeping."

Helen said, "Why *here*?"

Suddenly my head cleared. My thoughts became reasonable and reliable again.

"It's the *game*, Helen!" I exclaimed. "It's the *goddamn game*."

"What d'you mean?" she asked, sounding confused yet hopeful.

"The clues to the next room are always right in front of us. The mirrors, the mushrooms. Now *this*."

"The T-Rex? What! What are we supposed to do with a T-Rex?"

"I have no idea," I said. "But I doubt it's going to be easy."

We spent the remainder of the night in the tree, whispering back and forth like a couple of burglars on a stakeout. It had been very easy to agree that the T-Rex was part of the game. It had come looking for us, after all, and we weren't its natural prey. We were so small, we wouldn't even be a satisfying snack; certainly, we were no reason for it to camp out at the base of our tree. Nevertheless, deciding *how* it was part of the game was a different matter altogether. This had stumped us for the last three hours, and even now, as the sun rose in the distant east and the forest shed its assassin's cloak, we still were no closer to an answer.

"I hate it," Helen stated suddenly, after we had been silent for a while. We had changed our position earlier so we were sitting side by side, facing the sleeping dinosaur. "What if it never leaves? We're going to starve to death up here."

More accurately, we would die from thirst first, and dehydration was something that had been worrying me. A coffee in the Starbucks and a tea in the mushroom house were all we'd had to drink in the last . . . I wasn't sure how many hours. Twelve? Twenty-four? Forty-eight? It was impossible to judge, since I had no idea how long I'd been blacked out in the last room. We should have drunk from the nearby river before climbing the tree. Yet to be fair, we hadn't thought we would end up under siege by the most ferocious land creature of all time.

I said, "Maybe we should try waking it up?"

Helen chuckled. "Yeah, right."

"I mean it. If it's part of the game, maybe it's waiting for us to make the first move."

"You can go tickle its nose with a feather. I'll keep watch from up here."

"You know what's a crazy coincidence? I used to have a toy dinosaur, a small plastic thing I got for Christmas one year. It was my favorite toy for ages, even though it was just a hunk of plastic. You couldn't even pose its legs or arms or anything. But it looked just like that T-Rex. Bright green with yellow stripes. Who would have thought a toymaker's vision would have been more historically accurate than all the experts'?"

"Are you serious, Joe?"

Helen was staring at me with wide, frightened eyes.

"What's wrong?" I asked, concerned.

"Are you really serious?"

"About my toy?"

"It looked just like that T-Rex?"

"Pretty much."

"Oh . . . my . . . God . . ."

"What?"

"Ooooooh . . . my God . . ."

I realized she wasn't frightened. Completely the opposite: she was having some sort of sublime epiphany. "What is it, Helen? You're freaking me out."

She looked down at her toes for several long seconds, and I let her gather her thoughts. The suspense was agonizing.

Finally she looked back at me and asked, "Have you ever had an eating disorder?"

I blinked. "What? No."

"But mushrooms . . . you've done magic mushrooms before the cavern, right?"

I told her I had, hoping she wasn't having some sort of mental breakdown.

"Me, too," she said. "That's one."

I shook my head. "What's one?"

"That's one thing we have in common, one thing that helped us escape one of these rooms."

"What the hell are you talking about, Helen?"

"This game!" she said, loud enough that I glanced apprehensively at the T-Rex; it remained asleep. "I think it's tailored to us," she added more softly. "I mean . . . the mirrors. All those mirrors . . . breaking them, the way out. When I was a kid, that's how I escaped the kidnapper's house. I bashed the asshole with a mirror! Shattered it right over his head! And that Nazi . . . I'm Jewish. My grandparents were rounded up during the Holocaust. My grandfather died, but my grandmother survived. She was pregnant with my mother. I've been hearing stories about the horrors of the Holocaust ever since I was a little kid. And this dinosaur—it's just like a toy you had?"

I was getting caught up in Helen's excitement, yet at the same time, I knew she was going off on a flight of fancy. She was ignoring a fatal non sequitur that I reluctantly pointed out: "How would Izzy know all our private thoughts to tailor her game around them?"

"Because she's a god, Joe! I don't know how she knows what she knows. But who cares about *how* right now! After what we've experienced, *how* is a moot point. What's way more important is *why*."

"Shit, Helen," I said, getting eagerly onboard, maybe too eagerly. "You really think everything's been coming from us?"

She counted on her fingers. "Magic mushrooms . . . we've both done them before. And I bet you've had a bad trip. Right? Me, too. And what happened in that mushroom house was the bad trip to end all bad trips. So if we dreamt up the mushrooms, we probably dreamt up the bad trip, too."

"The mushroom house reminded me of the Seven Dwarfs' house."

"I remember you saying it reminded you of Disneyland."

I nodded. "There was a ride there . . . I went on it with my wife. It went through the Seven Dwarfs' house—and the Evil Queen was spying on them through a window."

Helen was frowning.

I said, "The godmother that arrived—"

"The stick monster."

"Before she was that, when she was looking through the window, she wore a black cowl and a golden crown—"

"Like the Evil Witch!" she exclaimed victoriously. "See! It's *us*, Joe. All of this, it's *us*."

I believed that. My God, I *wanted* to believe that. I didn't know why it was important; I didn't see how it helped us in any way.

However, it was something.

"When I had a bad trip back in college," I said, "I wanted to knock myself out to end it. I almost ended up trying that. I'd never done mushrooms before and didn't know what else to do. And then inside the stove . . . well, we did knock ourselves out to end it, didn't we?"

"By falling?" She nodded. "I don't remember hitting the ground. But we must have. I ached all over for hours."

"Jesus, Helen . . ." My mind kicked into high gear. "So . . . if we're making everything up, then The No-End House must be different for everybody who enters it. Because it's *our* fears, *our* insecurities that we're experiencing—it steals them from us and makes them real."

"Yes, Joe! My God, yes! That explains everything!"

Did it? I said, "Let's start at the beginning. The fat merchant—"

"No, the first things we saw were the animatronic skeletons."

"How do they fit?"

"What were you thinking when you entered the challenge?"

I shrugged. "Nothing. I wasn't expecting much at all."

"Me neither. I thought it would be corny, like all the other haunted houses out there. Dry ice, cheesy animatronics—"

"Jason," I said.

"Actors in scary costumes, right! An unexplained picture of us in the courtyard. Total run-of-the-mill stuff."

"And the fat merchant?"

"That was all about food. That's why I asked if you've ever had an eating disorder or something along those lines."

"I haven't," I said, shaking my head even as I realized that wasn't true. "Well, I struggled with my weight."

"You were fat?"

"The majority of my life, no. But after my wife died, I began to overeat. A lot. It was all I did—that and drink beer. I became huge. It made my depression even worse. I knew I was self-destructing . . . which was a big factor in my decision to walk around the world. It wasn't just for my mental health, but my physical health, too."

"So the mirrors and the Nazi—they came from me. The fat dude came from you."

"What about Carmilla?"

"That one's easy," she said. "I'm forty-three." After a heavy pause, she added, "At least I *was* forty-three. I've been thinking too much about getting old ever since I turned thirty. And that bitch. That fucking bitch—"

"Forget about her right now," I said. We were on a roll and needed to stay focused; grievances could come later. "So the fat merchant and the mirrors and Carmilla—things weren't so cheesy anymore. They were getting more complex and darker. The game was evolving, so we started to evolve along with it."

"We were starting to genuinely scare ourselves, so we conjured up scarier and scarier scenarios."

I closed my eyes briefly. "I don't know, Helen. I really don't. This is too fucking weird . . ."

She gripped my arm. "It's the truth, Joe! This house is a parasite—or maybe Izzy is the parasite—and they're using us. They're not just stealing our fears and insecurities—they're *feeding* off them, they're *feeding off us*. The more we scare ourselves, the better it is for them."

My hand went to my side, the dull pain, the stitches. Feeding off us—figuratively . . . or literally?

Helen said, "Do you remember what you said before we started the challenge?" Her voice was sober. "When we were in the palace, before signing the contract, you said—"

"I didn't want to wake up in a bathtub missing an organ." I shook my head. "Jesus Christ. Jesus fucking Christ, Helen."

"And now this?" she said, swinging her arms wide. "You made all this, Joe! You brought us here! This is all from your mind!"

"No, it's not," I said. "It can't be. I know jack-all about dinosaurs. My world would have come straight from the movies, roaring dinosaurs and all. I didn't know that Jurassic forests were mostly coniferous. I didn't know there were no flowering plants. I wouldn't have thought dinosaurs could be so silent—"

"But I did," Helen stated. "I knew all that. So I'm wrong then. This room is a *combination* of our minds. The more accurate details are from me, the less accurate ones are from you."

"Like the centipede . . ."

"And that thing," she said, nodding at the T-Rex.

I frowned at it. "But why?" I said, mostly to myself. Why would I conjure a dinosaur to scare us? It was based on my favorite toy. I was never afraid of it. I was never scared of dinosaurs in general. I used to love all the old movies and comics about them—

"I was *me*, Joe," Helen said abruptly. "Oh, shit, Joe. Oh, shit. It was *me*. I'd forgotten all about it. Maybe I'd blocked it out."

"Blocked what out?"

She steepled her hands over her mouth. "One of the movies I watched when I was locked in the kidnapper's basement—it was Japanese but dubbed in English. What was the name? Come on—what was the name?" She shook her head. "I don't know. But it was about dinosaurs. A woman wandered into a forest by Mt. Fuji—Suicide Forest, where people go to kill themselves—and she fell into a cavern full of large eggs. Oh, my God, Joe, that movie was so scary—at least it was for me then. People disappeared, animals disappeared. There's this one scene of a headless horse on the road. Anyway, the movie was about dinosaurs—*The Legend of Dinosaurs*—that was it! That's what it was called. It was a horror movie. I don't know why it was with all the other kiddy movies. Maybe the kidnapper watched it one day and forgot to take it back upstairs. Anyway, *I* watched it. It scared the bejesus out of me. I mean, when I was a kid, I probably had just as many nightmares about that movie as I did of the kidnapper." She looked at me. Sadness filled her eyes—for the past or present, I didn't know. "It wasn't you, then, Joe. This room—this one's on me."

I slipped my arm around her back. "It doesn't matter who's more responsible for whichever room," I told her. "We're in this together. And what matters is that we find a way out together. Besides, even if going back in time to the Jurassic era was your idea, I brought *that* here, and it's our biggest problem."

We both contemplated the sleeping Tyrannosaurus Rex.

Helen cocked her head curiously. "It doesn't look how a T-Rex should look. I know it looks like your toy. What I mean is, it doesn't look like a T-Rex, and it doesn't act like one, either."

"The roosting is definitely from your mind. I would have had it sleeping on its side."

"Like it could push itself to its feet with those tiny little arms. But what I *really* mean is, once you get used to it, it's almost not scary at all. So maybe it's not supposed to be." She sat a little straighter, as if struck by an idea. "You said it was your favorite toy, right? You said you were never scared of it, right? Well, that sort of means you wouldn't— or shouldn't—be scared of it if it came to life . . . right?"

I furrowed my brow. "I'm not following . . ."

"Maybe it's not here to *eat* us, Joe. Maybe it's here to *help* us."

Chapter 17

"Friends can be enemies, and enemies can be friends. It depends very much on the moment."
—The Book of Nine

When I'd suggested waking the T-Rex earlier, I hadn't anticipated strolling up to it and patting it on the snout. But that was exactly what I planned to do. It might just be the stupidest thing I've ever done in my life, but my gut was telling me Helen was right: The big guy was here to help us.

"Are you sure you don't want me to come with you?"

I shook my head. "It only takes one of us to test this theory. And if we're wrong . . . it'll only take one of us to learn that lesson."

"If it eats you, I'm as good as dead anyway. I'll starve to death or go crazy or both."

"It might leave you alone when it realizes I'm mostly bones. So just stay here. I'm going to lose my nerve if we keep talking about me getting eaten."

I climbed down the tree and dropped from the lowest branch to the ground.

"It's awake!" Helen said from far above me.

I looked at the T-Rex. Indeed it was. Still in the roosting position, but its yellow eyes were open and looking directly at me.

A bolt of fear pierced my lungs, and a voice inside my head screamed at me to scamper back up the tree. I might have done this, too, had I been able to move. Yet I was rooted to the ground, petrified.

However, the immobilizing fright ebbed quickly. The dinosaur wasn't getting up to come after me. It wasn't roaring or growling.

It was simply looking at me. Waiting for me?

I started forward.

And stopped when I was about ten feet away.

Its eyes watched my every move, unblinking, emotionless, reptilian.

Standing before the most infamous predator of all time, I should have been trembling like a leaf. I should have been incapacitated and terror-stricken, unable to breathe, move, think. Yet I was only humbled. By its sheer size. By its power. By its majesty. By its beauty. It was the most amazing creature I had ever seen.

Large, flat scales like those of a crocodile covered its craggy face. Bumpy, dome-shaped protrusions rounded its yellow eyes and merged in the center of its surprisingly narrow snout, forming a ridge that divided its nostrils. Robust teeth, more like lethal bananas than hunting daggers, poked out from its lipless, smirking mouth. Its powerful hind legs, bent at the knees so its belly could rest on the ground, ended in three black-clawed toes—claws that could very well have left that furrow in the ground we came across earlier. Its ill-proportioned forelimbs had only two hooked fingers, which it held vertically, as if it had paused mid-clap.

"Hi," I said dumbly, raising my hand. It was the same

thing I would have said if I had been abducted by aliens and taken to their leader. In some situations, no words were appropriate.

A low thrumming rumbled up from deep within the T-Rex's throat.

Like a loud bass note, I felt it as much as heard it. A haunting and portentous—but nonthreatening—sound. I smelled it, too: a stench of rot and death.

The T-Rex unwrapped its tail from around its legs, a slow and almost serpent-like movement, until it was extended straight back. The tip rose in the air and slapped the ground once. Then the T-Rex lowered its head to my height and snorted loudly, spraying me with a fine mist of mucus.

I stepped audaciously toward the creature and placed my hand on its cheek. The scales were neither warm nor cold. I continued past its huge head. Its eye—the size of a baseball—followed me. I stopped behind its short, stubby neck.

I was contemplating how to mount the beast—I was pretty sure it had lowered its head so I could climb up onto it—when Helen appeared beside me.

I had been so mesmerized by the T-Rex that I hadn't even noticed her descend the tree.

"I think it wants us to climb it," I said.

Helen nodded her head without taking her eyes off the dinosaur.

"I'll help you up first, and then you can help me."

She nodded again.

"Helen?" I said, touching her shoulder. "Are you all right?"

She shook her head. "Not really. Are you?"

The T-Rex rose easily to its feet. The swift rise in altitude was exhilarating. Then it turned and carried us away into the forest.

* * *

We sat tandem on its neck. Helen was in front of me, her hands placed firmly on the back of the T-Rex's skull. I was behind her, my arms around her waist. With each of the animal's steps, we rose rhythmically up and down. Palm fronds parted around us like waxy green curtains. Leafy tree branches shook and snapped, many crashing to the ground in our wake. The T-Rex didn't run. It walked at a pace only slightly faster than mine. Given its size, this made it feel ponderously slow, like a bus crawling along at five miles an hour. I wondered if it was walking so slowly because of us. Was it being considerate? Careful that it didn't toss us off its back? I probably should have slapped myself. A considerate T-Rex—nobody was going to believe this shit when we got back home. And maybe this was its top speed. After all, it was a huge animal. It likely needed one leg to always remain in contact with the ground to support its substantial weight. Yet if this were the case, how did it feed? Was it a scavenger, as some scientists hypothesized? Or was it simply a persistent hunter, tirelessly following its prey until the prey collapsed from exhaustion?

These thoughts came and went in a back-of-the-mind way, as thoughts tend to do in extraordinary circumstances: fleeting, a little dopey, inconsequential. I wasn't concerned with them. I certainly wasn't anticipating answers. Demanding my full attention right then was a much more impressive and tactile matter: Helen and I were riding a living and breathing Tyrannosaurus Rex.

I'm not sure how best to describe my feelings as we marched through the jungle upon the back of my favorite childhood toy come to life, but I suppose *wonder* would do. And I realized what an underrated and intoxicating sensation wonder was. Unadulterated, uninhibited, profound, blissful. It was something I hadn't fully experienced since I was a child, and something I hadn't even known had been absent from my life all the years since.

"I smell smoke," Helen said abruptly.

My nose twitched, and I smelled it, too, an acrid yet rich smell.

The T-Rex pushed through a final curtain of rustling palm fronds and protesting tree branches, and we emerged in a large clearing dominated by a towering, burning tree.

And what I could only assume was its guardian.

I had my first crush when I was in grade two.

The girl's name was Beth. I might have known her surname then, but I certainly didn't now. Yet I never forgot how she looked: short black hair, hazel eyes, always wearing silly-looking dresses of the sort you might dress a doll in. During "playtime" one morning, I'd been lounging on a collection of cushions in a corner of the classroom, mashing my plastic T-Rex toy against a rubbery Hulk Hogan figure. Beth came over and sat down on the cushion next to mine. She held a rainbow-haired My Little Pony in one hand and a triceratops in the other. She began speaking for each of them (a high-pitched, squeaky voice for the My Little Pony; a deep, gruff voice for the triceratops), offering greetings, niceties, inviting each other to tea.

Growling loudly, I bashed her triceratops with my T-Rex.

I guess I hit it too hard, because it flew out of her hand. She had some harsh seven-year-old words for me before getting up, collecting the triceratops from where it had landed beneath a desk, and retreating to another part of the room. That wasn't the reaction I'd wanted, of course, and I was left confused, especially because a T-Rex battling a triceratops made much more sense to me than a triceratops having tea with a My Little Pony.

Regardless, while we were waiting outside behind the

classroom for our moms to pick us up after school, I approached Beth when she was by herself and apologized for beating up her triceratops. She told me I hurt her hand, and so I apologized for that, as well. She frowned but nodded, and the grudge was forgotten, as only childhood grudges could be instantly and irrevocably forgotten.

As all our moms (and a few dads) began to show up, our teacher organized us into a single line against the brick wall, and because I was still next to Beth, I asked her where she got her triceratops. She said she didn't know; she simply found it in the toy room in her basement. I asked her if she wanted to trade it for one of my toys.

After some negotiations—they'd gone nowhere with my GoBots and Transformers until I began offering my little sister's toys—she finally agreed to trade the triceratops (she called it a "trisarrytop") for a Strawberry Shortcake doll, as long as the doll came with her pink cat. We made the swap first thing the following morning, and while the T-Rex would remain my favorite toy, the triceratops, as its perfect foil, became a close second.

In the end, I'm not sure what fate befell that triceratops . . . but it was back now, only living and breathing, the size of a city bus.

It lowered its gigantic head as if to charge.

Behind the frill of bone that rose from the back of its skull, the triceratops's patchy-brown body resembled that of a rhinoceros, only one on a steady diet of growth hormones and steroids. The two wicked horns protruding from above the beady eyes glinted threateningly in the dappled morning light.

The triceratops made a low, bleating noise, not unlike the foghorn we had heard the day before.

The T-Rex raised its head and returned a deep, booming call. It sounded like a challenge.

"Are they going to fight?" Helen asked, panicked.

"Hold on tight," I said, holding *her* tight.

"I want to get off!" she said. "Joe! We need to get off—"

The T-Rex lumbered forward.

The triceratops bobbed its head up and down, as if egging on the larger dinosaur.

"Let us off!" Helen cried.

If she was speaking to the T-Rex, it wasn't listening to her.

I glanced down at the ground. We couldn't have been any more than fifteen feet above it, but it still looked pretty far away.

Could we jump?

Helen screamed.

The T-Rex was snapping its jaws in a show of strength, its putrid breath wafting back at us. When it was almost on top of the triceratops, it pivoted laterally. The triceratops's upward-thrusting horns sailed through the air next to its throat. The T-Rex swiveled its head. Its jaws clamped onto the bony frill. The triceratops bellowed and shook its head, which shook the T-Rex, though the carnivore didn't let go.

Helen was still screaming.

I didn't know how she managed to hold on, because I felt as though I was going to plunk to the ground at any moment.

Suddenly the T-Rex reared up on one leg. Its raised foot stepped on the triceratops's exposed flank. Its clawed toes split the brown scales, exposing three lines of bleeding pink flesh.

With a wounded bleat and vicious jerk, the triceratops tore its frill free from the T-Rex's jaws, then swung its head with the force of a wrecking ball at the T-Rex's side.

The T-Rex reared up again, this time with a ferocious grunt.

I lost my grip on Helen and slid backward down the dinosaur's curved spine, my hands grasping for some sort of purchase, finding none. The impact against the ground blasted the air from my lungs. Everything went black. Bright white. I rolled onto my side, blinked stars from my vision, and tried not to throw up.

Ignoring the eruptions of pain in my back and legs and eardrums, I wobbled to my feet and looked up at the two dinosaurs locked in a fight to the death. For a moment, I thought one of the triceratops's horns had snapped off, until I realized it was buried in the chest of the T-Rex. Blood gushed from the wound, painting the T-Rex's side crimson and staining the grass beneath its feet.

Helen remained atop the enraged carnivore, her body flattened against its neck as she struggled to hold on.

"Jump!" I told her.

"I can't!"

"If it falls, it's gonna crush you!"

She looked my way but made no move to jump.

The T-Rex clamped its jaws over the back of the triceratops's neck. The triceratops's long tail slammed into the side of the T-Rex, knocking it unsteady.

Shrieking, Helen flew off its back and struck the ground with a flat *thud*.

"Helen!"

She didn't move.

One of the T-Rex's feet punched the earth next to her. I dashed to her side.

She appeared to be hyperventilating. Fear, shock, pain, I didn't know.

I grabbed her wrists and began dragging her. She screamed.

I didn't care. If she remained where she was, she would be trampled.

When we were out of immediate danger, I knelt beside her.

Her eyes were wide and wet. She didn't seem to see me. Yet she surprised me by saying in a brittle voice, "We need to get to that tree."

I nodded. "Can you stand?"

She could with my help.

Giving the battling dinosaurs a wide berth, we made for the towering, burning tree.

Chapter 18

"Adversity is a great teacher; it is also a killer."
—The Book of Nine

It must have been two hundred feet tall, and the trunk was wide enough to drive a car through. A huge crevice split the furrowed bark at ground level, leading into a hollow of inky blackness. Helen slipped inside it first, and I followed. The air smelled damp, peaty. Strangely, I could see nothing, not even my hands when I raised them in front of my face.

When I turned back to the crevice, it was gone. We were cocooned within the tree.

Helen said, "Shit! What happened to the door?"

"Guess it closed on us."

"Shit," she repeated softly, and where there should have been pragmatic outrage in her voice was only resignation and exasperation. Then, "I can't hear them anymore."

I assumed she meant the dinosaurs; I couldn't hear them, either. "We've moved on," I said. "This is the next room, or the path leading to it. They're in the past now."

"Are you sure?"

"Ow—sorry."

She'd stopped walking, and I'd bumped into her.

"Are you okay?" I asked.

"Yeah."

"I mean . . . from before. You hit the ground pretty hard."

"I hurt everywhere, but I don't think anything is broken. What about you?"

I shrugged before realizing she couldn't see me. "Same. But I'm really thirsty."

"Me, too," she said, and then went quiet for a few moments. She added, "How do you know this tree is the next room? I get that we were supposed to follow the smoke to it, but maybe it was just a halfway point or something. Maybe we were supposed to keep going to another tree or somewhere else. All the other doors were numbered."

"So was this one," I told her. "The triceratops had seven horns."

"Seven?" She sounded doubtful. "It had three horns, Joe. Two above its eyes, and one on its nose."

"And two smaller ones on each cheek."

"Are you sure?"

"Are you going to keep asking me that? Yes, I'm sure. I conjured that triceratops just like I did the T-Rex—it was identical to a toy I had as a kid—except it had two horns on each cheek. Seven horns in total. I can't believe that's coincidental."

I heard her moving, maybe turning in a circle. "So where are we?" she asked.

"On our way to Room Seven?"

"But it's pitch-black. How do we know which way to go?"

"I doubt it matters which way we go. We'll get to wherever we're going in the end."

"Deep, Joe. But I'd prefer a lighted pathway."

"I think the way through The No-End House is more linear than it appears to be. We always end up going in the right direction, don't we?"

"I'd say we've taken some pretty damn big detours."

"But there seems to be only one way forward," I said. "As long as we keep moving—keep playing—we always seem to end up in the next room. Where's your hand?"

"Here," she said.

"Where?"

"*Here.*"

I felt it brush my belly. I took it in my hand.

We didn't have to walk for long in the blackness before, in the impossible distance (impossible because we were still inside the tree), a light appeared. The closer we got to it, the more the stark white light resembled a doorway.

I stopped.

"What's wrong?" Helen said.

"That's it. That's the door." I was suddenly apprehensive. "We're conjuring everything, right?"

"We've been through this, Joe. Yes, we're conjuring the rooms. And everything inside the rooms. Carmilla and Izzy's gang of other freaks included."

"And everything, eventually, turns against us."

"Your T-Rex was on our side."

"Because we were lost. We needed help. I somehow conjured it to get us to the smoke signal."

"What are you getting at?"

"When we go through that door ahead, Helen, whatever we're thinking, even if we're not aware we're thinking anything . . . something in one of our subconsciouses is going to come to life. My previous weight issues were manifested with Merchant Belmont. Your obsession with aging was manifested with Carmilla."

"It wasn't really an obsession . . ."

"The Nazi was manifested because of your family history, the mirrors because of the kidnapper. Or maybe the mirrors were also because of your obsession with aging."

"It wasn't an *obsession*, Joe."

"The magic mushrooms," I pressed on, "manifested by

both of us. The Evil Queen, me. One hundred million years BC, you, because of that horror movie you watched."

"More like two hundred million years BC. And yes, I get it. So you're saying we should think of something . . . *good* . . . when we walk through that door?"

"Good or . . . maybe nothing."

"Nothing?"

I heard the surprise in her voice. "Good memories can turn bad," I explained. "I've had nightmares about good people and good events. The subconscious can warp things however it wants."

"Like in *Ghostbusters* with Dan Aykroyd and the Marshmallow Man."

"I'm serious, Helen. If we clear our minds, think of nothing, maybe we won't manifest anything at all. Maybe we'll just end up in an ordinary, boring room."

"Do you meditate? Because part of meditating is thinking about nothing. Another part is breathing properly. You need to take deep, even breaths. It calms you. Try it."

I inhaled deeply before exhaling just as deeply. I repeated this several times while thinking only about those breaths.

"Well?" Helen said.

"The breathing helps," I admitted.

"So we walk and meditate," she said.

"Think of nothing," I said.

"Until we're through the door."

"How will we know that?"

"We'll just know," she said.

That was good enough for me.

Closing our eyes, emptying our minds, we started forward.

I knew the moment we passed through the doorway because the darkness on the other side of my eyelids lightened to fleshy, pink tones. Also, the air changed. It was no longer damp and peaty; it was . . . maybe not fresh . . . but *clean.*

"We're through," Helen said. "Should we open our eyes?"

"I think we better before we think of something we shouldn't."

We opened our eyes.

A cloudy, slate-gray sky stretched to the horizon. It was a vast, uninspiring roof over an equally vast and flat desert landscape.

There were no trees before us, no shrubs, nothing but a barren ocean of undulating sand dunes as far as the eye could see.

"Oh," Helen said, clearly not impressed.

I looked behind us. The two-hundred-foot smoldering Jurassic tree was now only a fraction of its previous height, a burnt-out husk, branchless, dead, the charred bark a silvered black.

I shaded my eyes with my hand. Despite the raft of clouds between the sun and us, the light was unusually bright and harsh, causing me to squint. Facing forward again, I was un-sure what to make of the situation. Certainly there were worse places where we could have ended up. Yet a desolate wasteland was not ideal. Helen and I were both parched. We weren't likely to find a drop of water anytime soon. And de-pending on how long we were stuck here, that could prove extremely problematic.

"Where the hell is *this*?" I muttered, frustrated.

"We wanted nothing," Helen said, opening her arms with a flourish. "We got nothing."

I squeezed my eyes shut.

"What are you doing?" she said.

"Trying to conjure a lake."

"That's what we *should* have been thinking about. A lush, tropical lagoon. With one of those tiki bars that you can swim up to and order a cocktail."

I opened my eyes. "I'm sorry. I wasn't expecting this."

"It doesn't matter, Joe," she said with a sigh. "Whatever

we thought of instead would have turned out bad. The tiki bar cocktails probably would have been made with third-world water. We would have gotten diarrhea, maybe bacterial infections, too. Besides, this isn't so bad. No dinosaurs to worry about, at least."

"Have you ever seen *Tremors*?" I shook my head, not wanting to conjure giant worms. "Where are we supposed to go?"

"Does it matter?" She quoted me: " 'We'll get to wherever we're going in the end.' "

"So we just walk in a random direction?"

Helen shrugged. "Sounds good to me."

We walked. And walked. And walked.

Nothing changed except for the zigzagging line of sloppy footprints we left in the burnt-yellow sand behind us. The sky remained apocalyptically gray and bleak. The sun stayed behind the veil of listless clouds, a shimmering, washed-out disc following our every step. Its harsh light not only seared my eyes but also reflected off the sand, turning the desert into a never-ending frying pan that was slowly cooking us alive.

Every so often, I looked up from my feet and scanned the horizon. *Something should have been happening by now*, I thought. When we stepped through the first door with the elaborate *1*, we came to the room with Merchant Belmont in short order. When we crouched through his wagon, we came to the mirrors almost immediately.

When we passed through the big opulent mirror, Carmilla was not far away. Even when we crawled beneath her table and through the hole in the wall, it had not been very long before we reached the cavern with the magic mushrooms and the mushroom house.

The exception to this pattern was the previous room. It had taken us a day and a night—and a morning jaunt atop the T-Rex—to reach its exit. Which raised the question: was it an outlier, or a foreshadow of the remaining rooms to come? Would it take us more than a day to reach this room's exit? Or, if events were accelerating exponentially, would it take us several days? A week? Longer?

I didn't want to think about that. Without water, we wouldn't last a week or longer.

We likely wouldn't last another day.

I stopped walking and worked my dry mouth, trying to generate saliva. My skin felt itchy and dusty. My legs and feet ached. How long had we been walking? A few hours? More? Less?

Helen caught up and stopped next to me. She doubled over, bracing her hands on her knees.

I said, "What if we're going the wrong way?"

"There is no wrong way. Straight from the horse's mouth." She stood straight and tilted her head to the sky and said nothing more.

"Helen?"

"Mmmm?"

"What are you doing?"

"I'm tired. And thirsty. *Really* thirsty."

I swallowed. The back of my throat burned painfully.

Helen finally looked at me. A sheen of perspiration slicked her face. Her cheeks were ruddy, her lips cracked. Her eyes looked faded, their once-vibrant brown now a drab black. "We're not going in the wrong direction, Joe," she said. "If there were one way and one way only, there would have been a clue. There would have been something to point us in that direction. That's how this stupid game works. But there was nothing. Absolutely nothing. So there's no correct way. Not yet. We just need to keep walking until the nothing becomes something."

I suspected she might be right, but I wasn't sure how much

longer I could keep walking. Like her, I was tired and thirsty. I felt lightheaded and nauseous, as well. Maybe it was the onset of dehydration, maybe heatstroke. Whatever it was, my symptoms would only get worse the longer we remained exposed to the unforgiving environment.

I wanted to tell Helen that we needed to start looking for shelter and water. Yet what would be the point? There was nowhere to look. There was nothing around us but sand. There was nothing for us to do but walk.

And walk.

And walk.

And when night fell? It would be cold. Maybe freezing. We had nothing but the clothes on our backs. We would likely develop hypothermia. And what would we do then? What could we do?

But walk. And walk. And walk.

This was despair, I realized. What I was thinking, what I was feeling. *How* I was thinking and feeling. Despair— maybe not *true* despair—but despair nonetheless. My thoughts were on a hamster wheel, going nowhere. Because there was nowhere for them to go.

There was no way out for us.

No solution to our situation, however distant. No hope, however faint.

There was nothing.

We were fucked. We were done. We were going to die out here—

"Joe! There!" Helen said suddenly and excitedly, pointing past me. "There! Look!"

Blinking in confusion, dazed by the abrasive light and scorching heat, I turned and looked.

In the distance, I made out a black speck moving along the ridge of a dune.

It appeared to be a person coming our way.

Reinvigorated, we started toward the person. Helen was giddy, peppering me with *I-told-you-so*s. I imagined tilting a waterskin to my lips, the cool water spilling over my tongue, down my bone-dry throat. Whether this stranger would have a waterskin, I didn't know. How he or she would help us—I didn't know that, either. But help us they would, I was sure of that. As Helen had observed, that was how the stupid game worked. Something always came of nothing, pointing the way forward, moving us from point A to point B—

Stopping abruptly, Helen made a sound that very well could have come from a fairy who'd just had her wings plucked off.

Dread surged inside me even before I understood why.

"It's *him*," Helen said, those two words soaked in repugnant terror. A moment later, I realized the distant silhouette was a large man, and he was wearing a burlap sack over his head.

"It's Jason," I said unnecessarily.

Helen, of course, knew that; she'd recognized him first. Now she turned around and was gripping my arm, pulling me to follow her.

"Come *on*, Joe!" she said. "He's going to catch us!"

I stubbornly held my ground. I wasn't going to run. This was neither an act of bravery nor resignation; it was one of exhaustion. I couldn't muster the strength to move. I would have to fight Jason. He was bigger than me, and he was armed with hatchets, but maybe if I could get the jump on him—

"Joe!" Helen yelled. "He's *coming*!"

"You go," I told her.

"Stop it, Joe! He's going to kill you! *Please?*" She tugged my arm so hard, I nearly fell over.

"There's nowhere to go, Helen. He'll get us no matter what we do. Maybe we're supposed to confront him."

"Please, Joe. Don't do this. Come with me. *Please?*"

Each word was a plea, pulling my eyes to hers. What I saw in them was sheer panic and desperation—as well as a wild will to survive. And I realized that wouldn't be reflected in my eyes; they would be flat, empty . . . and maybe I was giving up, after all.

I let Helen lead me away.

We kept up a brisk pace. This wasn't easy. The sand was loose and deep. We were walking through it rather than on top of it. We continuously glanced over our shoulders. Although we had put a little more distance between us and Jason—he was roughly fifty yards behind us—he didn't appear to have any issue with the sand. He might not be fast, but his step was unfaltering, and I couldn't help but think ominously of the tortoise and the hare.

A dune rose before us. Halfway up it, Helen and I resorted to crawling on our hands and knees. At the top, I squinted back again.

Jason was at the dune's base.

"I need to take off my shoes," Helen said.

"There's no time," I said.

"They're full of sand. They're slowing me down."

"There's no time, Helen." I drew my wrist across my forehead. It came away drenched with sweat. "He's right behind us."

We started down the leeward side of the dune. Our controlled descent quickly became an uncoordinated run and then a full-on tumble.

At the bottom, we got to our feet, shook the sand from our clothes, and kept going.

For a while I told myself I couldn't do it. With each step, I contemplated collapsing to my knees and not getting back up. If I were by myself, I surely would have. My head, my back, my legs, my feet, the hollow cavity where my right kidney had once been, even my goddamned hands throbbed—a culmination of two days and one sleepless night of unrelenting physical hardships. Continuous walking, psychedelic drugs, a concussion, surgery at the hands of a maniac, trekking through a brutal jungle, hours in a tree, and now this, a scorching, inhospitable desert.

I was worn down. Weary to my bones.

Nevertheless, I kept going. Helen's grim perseverance inspired me to keep up with her, to fight and survive . . . and at some point, I got a second wind. My mind detached itself from my body, and all my thoughts, all my pain, all my worries, stepped off stage. They were still there, in the shadowed wings, waiting to make an encore. But for the moment, they were no longer in the spotlight, and that was probably the best I could ask for.

While plodding forward on autopilot, I wasn't aware of how much time might have passed—I had long ago stopped monitoring the sun's position in the sky—only that it must have been hours.

Then, very quickly, night fell.

There was no spectacular sunset, no celestial streaks of vermilion or cotton-candy pink. The light simply leached out of the air. Everything turned ashen and gloomy. And then black. Thankfully, Helen and I could still see. The moon, round and swollen, shared the sky with an abundance of stars. But the temperature plummeted, too. Shivering, my teeth chattering, I soon found myself longing for what before had been anathema: the blistering daytime heat.

"C-cold," I mumbled, folding my arms across my chest. That provided some warmth, but it also upset my balance and made trudging through the sand more difficult than it already was.

For the first time in a long time, I glanced back over my shoulder.

"How . . . far?" Helen asked.

"I can't . . . go much farther."

"You c-can't stop."

Arguing with her would not change the inevitable out-come. When it came to the point that I could no longer con-tinue, I would no longer continue.

Instead I said, "How can it be so hot . . . then so cold?"

"The sand."

I hadn't expected an answer, although knowing Helen, I probably should have. I surprised myself by laughing. It sounded like a bad smoker's cough.

"Sand?" I said.

"It doesn't h-h-hold heat well. When the sun goes d-down . . . *poof.*" She raised a hand with a magician's flourish. "Gone."

"I don't think . . . we're on Earth anymore. No Big Dipper."

"Mmmm."

"You don't find that w-w-weird?"

"No Big Dipper?"

"That we're on a different planet?"

"Maybe we're i-i-in . . . the southern hemisphere."

I hadn't thought about that. "What constellations are"—I clenched my teeth to stop them from rattling—"in the southern hemisphere?"

"S-s-southern Cross."

I raised my eyes to the night sky but had no idea what I was looking for.

"You're pr-pr-prob-ly right," I said. "The Sahara is in the suh-suh-suh. In the s-southern hemisphere, and this f-feels like the Sahara."

"I'm sorry, Joe. You never wanted to g-go to The No-End House. It was my idea."

"You wouldn't have known about it if I did-did-didn't tell you 'bout it."

"I lied. When I told you we just ended up in the gugh . . . Gothic Quarter. I l-led us there. Are you mad at me?"

"No."

"You are."

"I'm not."

"You didn't want to sign the contract." She coughed sharply, cleared her throat. "You would have left. I made you sign it."

A bottomless hole opened in my gut. Frowning, I said, "She gets our souls, you know."

Limned in the silver moonlight, Helen's face was grim. "Only if we don't finish this."

"What do you thuh-thuh-thuh . . . think she's going to do with them?"

Helen shook her head. "I don't want to talk about that, Joe."

I didn't either. We walked in morose silence.

"Hey," I said, struck by a novel thought. "You kn-kn-kn-kn-know where else we might be? In the *future*."

"Mmmm."

"The last room was m-millions of years in the past," I said, despite her apathetic reaction. "So m-m-maybe this one is m-millions of years in the future . . . where the c-continents . . . have all turned into deserts. That's what always ha-ha-happens in post-apaw-apaw-apaw . . . in those sci-fi movies. Everything turns to deserts."

"Would explain the stars."

"Huh?"

"Stars mu-mu-move. Not in our lifetime. But over hundreds of thousands of years, the Big Dipper would probably . . . look more like . . . a kitchen knife."

"Wonder what happened to humanity."

"We probably bu-blew ourselves up."

"Or colonized uh-uh-other planets—"

"*Joe?*"

Something in that whispered word raised the hackles on the back of my neck. I looked behind us, expecting Jason to be within striking distance.

He was behind us, all right, but still fifty or maybe a hundred yards away. It was difficult to judge in the dark.

"No, *there*, ahead," Helen said in that same hushed tone, and I realized what I was hearing in her voice wasn't fear; it was cautious optimism. "Do you see-see-see-see that?"

"See what?"

"Please tell me you see-see-see—"

"See *what*—"

The question died in my throat.

Chapter 19

"When reality can no longer be trusted, imagination becomes a necessity."
—The Book of Nine

Several white spires of varying sizes soared into the night sky. They protruded from what I thought was a shadowed jumble of rocks until I realized the lines were too straight, too geometric.

It was some kind of building.

"We made it!" I exclaimed.

"You see it!" Helen said.

"It's gotta be the exit!"

"Has to be!"

We ran toward the building, falling in the sand in our eagerness to reach it, bouncing back to our feet, groaning with effort. The shadows peeled away from the structure, revealing expansive sheets of glass separated by steel beams. The design reminded me of a modern, minimalist house.

We stopped before what turned out to be a revolving door with four glass partitions. We placed our hands on the outside panel and pushed.

It didn't budge.

"Shit," I said, glancing behind us.

Jason was still there, still coming, slowly yet inexorably.

Grunting, Helen threw all her weight into the panel. I did, too. After several long seconds, there was a loud *pop!* like a gasket seal unmating, and then the panel rotated easily around the vertical axis.

We swept through the cylindrical enclosure and entered the building. The air was warmer than it had been outside and smelled stuffy and stale. Dozens of tables and chairs were arranged in neat rows before us. Beyond them was a peanut-shaped bar with a tall feature wall stacked with a variety of bottles. The ceiling was composed of acoustic tiles yellowed with age. The white-and-black floor tiles were arranged in a checkered pattern. Unlike the building's exterior, there was nothing modern about the interior. Everything looked like it was from the 1970s or '80s.

I beelined to the bar. Grabbed a bottle of gin from one of the shelves.

Empty.

All of the bottles were empty.

"What the fuck?" I said, running my tongue over my dry gums.

"Hurry," Helen said, dashing past me down the wide corridor.

We rounded a corner and discovered that the block at the center of the building was an elevator bank. There were three sets of anodized steel doors. We went to the closest one. Helen jabbed the up and down buttons on the call box. Amazingly, they both lit up.

"Power in the middle of a desert?" I said.

"Come on, come on, come on," she said impatiently, glancing back the way we had come.

"He might be too stupid to use a revolving door."

"Come *on*," she said.

A ping sounded. Helen cheered in delight. The metal doors parted, revealing a gleaming, brightly lit cab. We stepped inside it.

Helen's finger froze before punching a floor button.

There were 110 floors.

"That's impossible," I said. "How could there be that many floors beneath us?"

"We're in a skyscraper . . ." she said with amazement. "Joe, we're in a *skyscraper*. We must be . . . has to be . . . a *buried* skyscraper."

Instinctively I knew she was right. The spires—or, more likely, antennae—all the glass panels, the numerous elevators—we were on the observation deck at the top of a skyscraper.

A skyscraper buried by over one hundred stories of sand.

I could barely get my head around that and didn't try.

Helen jabbed the *G* button for the ground floor. It lit up, but nothing else happened.

"Why that one?" I asked.

"It's where the entrance is—and the exit." She jabbed the button again.

Still nothing.

"It's not working," I said.

Helen hit other buttons at random. They all lit up, but the cab didn't move. She hit more and more buttons, faster and faster, and then she pounded the panel with her fists while sobbing.

"Hey," I said, gripping her by the shoulders. "Stop it."

The fisting became open-hand slapping. The sobbing rose several octaves, turning into awful shrieks.

"Helen!" I shouted, spinning her around to face me. "Stop it! You're going to break the fucking thing!"

"This isn't fair!" she sobbed, backing into the wall. She

slid down it until she was on her butt, her knees bent, her head in her hands. "This isn't fair. We came so far, and there's nowhere left to go. He's coming, and there's nowhere left to go. There was never anywhere to go."

Leaving Helen in the cab, I returned the way we had come. She didn't ask me where I was going, didn't try to stop me. After being the strong one for so long, she'd finally reached her limit. She'd given up.

I rounded the corner of the elevator bank.

The revolving door that we had entered through was rotating, and then Jason stepped into the observation deck. He stared directly at me through the single eyehole in the burlap sack.

Then he started my way.

I kept the peanut-shaped bar between us. I had no plan other than not to let him get too close to me. I needed a weapon, of course. Yet none were available. Certainly none to rival his hatchets.

We played ring-around-the-rosie until we stood on the opposite sides of the bar from where we'd started. High on adrenaline, I was as physically exhilarated as I was terrified. I was also confident enough to taunt Jason with creative obscenities as I backed away into the rows of tables and chairs. He followed, indifferent, silent, implacable.

I grabbed a chair by the backrest. It featured a metal frame and had some heft to it. Still no match for hatchets, but it was something. I raised it as though I were a lion tamer keeping a lion at bay.

Jason swung the right hatchet. The blade twanged off one of the chair legs.

I drove the chair forward. The legs poked his chest. He swung the same hatchet in an overhead cleave. I danced backward, avoiding the attack.

And saw Helen approaching out of the corner of my eye.

I kept my focus on Jason so he didn't realize the odds were about to change.

I kicked a table toward him. He kicked it aside. I slid chairs between us. He stepped around them. I called him a walking bag of monkey shit that died in every one of his movies.

Suddenly he lunged, swinging the hatchet. His quickness caught me off guard, and I barely raised the chair in time to deflect the blow.

I drove the chair at him again. He batted it aside.

Helen was behind him. I didn't realize she had empty liquor bottles in her hands until one of them shattered across the back of Jason's skull. Barely fazed, he swung the left hatchet in a 180-degree arc. Helen ducked, and what could have been a decapitating blow sailed over the top of her head.

Still gripping the chair by the backrest, I cocked it like a baseball bat and swung it at Jason's knees. They buckled. He dropped the right hatchet as he sank to that side, bracing himself with his now free hand. Helen shattered the second bottle over the top of his skull. I shoved the chair into his chest, then scooped up the hatchet.

Jason was getting back to his feet.

With an unrecognizable, barbaric cry, I lodged the blade in his face. It made a sickening, thick *wud!* on impact. He stiffened as if he'd just touched a ten-thousand-volt live wire. The burlap sack darkened as blood saturated it from within. Then, with no more grace than a cardboard cutout, he fell flat on his back.

"He's dead," I said.

Helen kept kicking his head.

"Helen, he's dead!"

She wouldn't listen to me, and I let her exhaust her rage. Finally she turned away from the pummeled head, stumbled a few steps, and collapsed to the floor.

I knelt next to her and said a few things I thought might comfort her. She said nothing back. Her eyes were closed, her face at rest. I lay down and wrapped an arm around her torso.

I listened to her breathing. I inhaled the citrus scent of her hair and the sweetness of her sweat. I enjoyed the warmth of her body.

Seconds later I, too, was asleep.

Helen was shaking my shoulder. I opened my eyes to stark white light streaming through the large glass windows.

It was daytime again.

I pushed myself into a sitting position. Although I must have been asleep for hours, I hardly felt rested. At least I no longer felt like a walking corpse.

Despite the sun damage etched into Helen's prematurely aged face, she seemed to be feeling better. The vivacious brown was back in her eyes, and she was grinning at me.

"We killed him," she said happily.

Blinking rapidly, I looked past her to Jason's still form. A pool of blood circled his head-turned-butcher block.

"We're lucky he's not like the Jason from the movies."

"What d'you mean?"

"That Jason always came back from the dead."

"He picked the wrong motherfuckers to mess with."

That sounded like a line from a movie. Coming from Helen, it almost made me laugh.

"Picked the wrong foot to mess with," I said. "You must have kicked him in the head a hundred times."

She shrugged. "A girl's gotta do what a girl's gotta do. Motherfucker deserved it."

"Would you stop speaking like that?"

"I'm just glad to be alive. I actually feel *good*. How do you feel?"

I took a moment to assess my battered body. Everything seemed to be working. "Thirsty."

"I looked everywhere for the vending machine but couldn't find it."

I frowned. "What vending machine?"

"The one that was here when I was a kid."

"When you were a kid?" I said dubiously. Maybe she wasn't okay, after all.

"This is the Sears Tower, Joe."

I blinked. "In Chicago?"

"It's called the Willis Tower now. But it was called the Sears Tower when I was there."

"What are you—?" And then, all at once, I understood. "You conjured this . . ."

She nodded, still grinning. "My dad was a marketing executive with Sears," she explained. "He worked in this building until Sears moved out in the nineties. One day Sears had this bring-your-kid-to-work thing for its employees. My dad showed me around the building, everywhere from the mailroom to the cafeteria to random floors filled with those partitioned cubicles. Afterward, we went to his office, where I just sat around while he did his job. Anyway, at lunchtime, he took me up here, to the observation deck. All these tables had been set up for a special employee-kid lunch. When we finished, I asked him if I could stay up here instead of going back to his office. He gave me five dollars and told me not to get into trouble. I remember playing make-believe, going from one window to the next, pretending I was a queen at the top of my castle, lording over all the tiny people way down on the streets below. The best part was, there was a vending machine in a nook on one wall. I wasn't usually allowed junk food, so it was a real treat when I could get my hands on some. And five bucks went a long way in the eighties. I stuffed myself with chocolate bars, potato chips, sodas . . ."

"It took you a while to recognize this place."

"The observation deck?" She looked around. "I still don't recognize it, not really. I was only six or seven when I was here, Joe. And kid memories are just general feelings, blurry pictures, nothing specific. That's what I experienced when I woke up—a vague feeling that I had been here before. I can't explain it any better. But the more I thought about it, the more convinced I became that I *had* been here, with my dad, on the bring-your-kid-to-work day. I'm positive of that now."

"Huh," I said, shaking my head but hardly surprised by the revelation; I doubted anything could surprise me anymore. "Well, that explains the building, but not why it's buried in the middle of a desert—"

"I used to have a sandbox in my backyard," Helen said promptly. "My dad built it for me one summer. I was the only kid on our block to have one. My neighbor—this little brat my age that I never liked—used to climb the fence and play in it with his plastic army men. I always told him to get out, but he'd say these stupid things like I couldn't tell him to get out because it wasn't my house; it was my parents' house. He was a dork. Anyway, our family had a poodle. It was harmless, but it liked to bark and nip at heels, so whenever I saw this kid in my sandbox, I'd sic the poodle on him. You'd never seen anyone scale a fence so fast."

"And this sandbox has something to do with this desert?"

"During the bring-your-kid-to-work day lunch, a woman gave all the kids a toy replica of the Sears Tower. Just like the T-Rex was one of your favorite toys, this was one of *my* favorite ones. It probably doesn't sound like anything special. But the Sears Tower was the tallest building in the world back then, and I was proud that my dad worked in it. That was before . . . well, that was then. Anyway, yeah, I thought the toy was neat. I used to play with it every day—until one day I couldn't find it. I looked everywhere. I had no idea where it went. Not until the following spring. The snow was melting in the backyard. I lifted the big piece of plywood off the top of the sandbox and began cleaning out all the dead leaves that had somehow gotten into it—when I saw a white antenna sticking out of the sand." She shrugged. "Sound familiar?"

"Christ, Helen," I said, both annoyed and amused. "Don't you remember us agreeing to empty our minds when we entered this room? It sounds like—"

"I *did*, Joe," she said. "I wasn't thinking about any of this. We probably conjured the desert together because deserts are a good representation of nothing. And we'd been walking in it for ages before the tower appeared. So if you want my psychoanalysis, the desert reminded me of the sandbox, which reminded me of the buried Sears Tower. Which my subconscious, in its crazy own way, decided could serve as an exit, something we were desperately searching for. We were lost, exhausted, desperate. My mind latched onto something that meant a lot to me, a beacon, a lifeline, just as yours did with the T-Rex."

"It's crazy shit, Helen. But I suppose it all fits." I sighed, which turned into a groan as I shifted my stiff and aggrieved body. "Too bad you went to all the trouble of conjuring the entire Sears Tower but left out the vending machine . . ."

"Don't complain. We're alive thanks to my imagination, aren't we? After all, it added that revolving door. Otherwise we would have been stuck outside."

"I'm guessing you added the bar, too," I said. "Unless booze was flowing freely at the employee-kid luncheon."

"I wonder if I did that so we'd have the bottles to attack Jason with?"

"They did come in handy. . . . Anyway, have you figured out what we're going to do now? With the elevators out of order, we still don't have any way down to the ground floor."

"*Au contraire*, Joe," she said with a pretentious, self-congratulatory air. "The clues to the next room have always been right in front of our noses. And who's been in lockstep with us for almost the entirety of *this* room?"

I looked at Jason's lifeless body, then back at Helen.

"He's the clue?" I said, confused.

"Check out what I found in one of his pockets."

She opened her fist, revealing a toothy key on a silver chain.

Back in the elevator, Helen stuck the key in the keyhole at the bottom of the control panel. It was a perfect fit. She turned it to the right.

"I knew it!" she said. "Do you want the honors, Joe?"

"You figured it out. You do it."

She pressed the button marked *G* triumphantly. Nothing happened.

"No!" She jabbed the button again. "It has to work! It *has* to."

"Wait a sec," I said. "The rooms have always been numbered. Maybe the exit's not on the ground floor. Maybe . . ." I pressed the button for the eighth floor.

The elevator began to descend.

Chapter 20

"Memories are toxic. The good ones turn nostalgic while the bad ones remain bad."
—The Book of Nine

The elevator doors of the Sears Tower opened on the eighth
floor to a lighted cubicle farm festooned with balloons,
streamers, and other celebratory accoutrements.

"This is supposed to be Room Eight, not Room Nine, right?"
I said.

Helen counted on her fingers. "Fatty, the mirrors, Vampmilla, Smurf Land, the blackout room, Jurassic Park, the Sahara—that's seven. So this is definitely Eight. Besides, you
pushed the button for Eight."

"It looks like our subconsciouses are celebrating one room
early then."

"The house is just messing with us," she said. "But screw
it. Two rooms left. We can do this."

I nodded. "We will," I said, and I meant it. I felt it. This
challenge was cruel. It played by its own rules. It defied what
anybody knew about time and science and reality. But The
No-End House was beatable, and we were going to beat it.
Seven rooms behind us, two to go. "Which way?"

Helen shrugged. "Don't you think that question's redundant by now?"

"I just mean . . . pick one."

"I'm left-handed, so left."

We started that way. I guessed there were about fifty partitioned workspaces on this side of the floor. The cheerfully colored helium balloons were gathered in bunches and tied to chairs, lamps, plastic plants. The tinsel streamers strewn over everything were mostly silver and gold. Despite being eight stories in the air, there was no view beyond the floor-to-ceiling windows. There was only hard-packed yellow sand. It made me think of a glass ant farm I had as a kid—and I quickly pushed that thought from my mind, fearful of inadvertently conjuring a colony of enormous, man-eating ants.

I said, "I didn't know you were left-handed."

Helen said, "Why would you?"

"I wouldn't—it's just funny how little I know about you. After everything we've been through, I feel like . . ." I didn't finish the sentence.

"Feel like what?" she asked, looking at me wryly. "Do you *love* me, Joe?"

"What?" I frowned. "Where did that come from?"

"That's what people typically say after an opener like, 'After everything we've been through . . .'" She impersonated a fawning Southern belle: "After everything we've been through, Joe, I do believe I've fallen head over heels in love with you."

"So you love *me*?"

"Hardly. But I can't do a man's voice."

"Hardly?" I said. "That's a bit rough."

"All right, Joe. I love you. There, I said it."

I had no idea whether she was being sincere or not.

"What?" she said innocently.

"I was actually going to say something along the lines of—"

Helen stopped. She was staring straight ahead at the glass-walled offices at the far end of the floor.

And then I saw why.

The office directly before us was occupied. A man sat in an executive chair with his feet up on the desk. He was speaking into a telephone with a rotary dial and a coiled cord. He hadn't noticed us.

"Dad . . . ?" Helen breathed softly.

As if hearing her, the man looked our way. He raised his hand to beckon us over.

Beige and chrome-accented filing cabinets occupied much of the office. An L-shaped desk filled one corner. On it sat a dated computer and printer, a gold goose-neck lamp, numerous gray binders, a yellow coffee mug stuffed with pens and pencils, an empty in/outbox, and a black ashtray overflowing with crushed cigarette butts.

The man in the executive chair wore a V-neck cardigan over a shirt and tie, brown slacks, and brown loafers. Wavy black hair and an unkempt beard not unlike mine channeled a young Steve Jobs. He held up a finger while he finished speaking on the phone. Then he dropped the handset onto the cradle and swung his feet off the desk.

"Kiddo," he said, his eyes taking in Helen. "Look at you, all grown up now. An old woman, and that's too bad; I heard what happened, but still pretty as a peach, just like your mother."

"*He's* your dad, Helen?" I said.

She was nodding, her face ashen.

"He's white . . ."

"My mom was from Senegal. The other half of me, *him*, is Irish."

"What's wrong then?" If I'd conjured one of my parents, still in their prime, I would have been admittedly rattled. But Helen wasn't simply rattled; she appeared terrified.

"You're dead," she told her dad, ignoring my question. "You can't be here."

"He's not real," I reminded her. "He's just—"

"You're *dead*!" she said. "Go away! Go *away!*"

"Go where, kiddo?" he said, unfazed by her outburst. "This is my office. This is where I wasted the best years of my life to earn a living for us, to provide for you and your mother—"

"I hate you!" she shouted. "I hate you! *I hate you!*"

She lunged at him. He sprang to his feet, raising his arms to deflect her pounding fists. I pulled Helen back and held her until she stopped kicking and screaming.

I said, "What the hell's going on, Helen? He's your *dad*."

Panting heavily, glaring at the man who was her father yet paradoxically several decades younger than her, she said in a flat, emotionless voice, "He should be dead. He *is* dead. I bashed a mirror over his fucking head and killed him."

It took me a dumbfounded moment to process what she said, and when I did, I felt sick to my stomach. Helen had never mentioned her kidnapper's name. Was that because it had been her father? Had he kept her imprisoned in the basement of the house she'd told me about? But why would a parent do such a thing to their child?

I said, "He's the one who kidnapped you?"

Still glaring implacably at her father, she said, "He's a child molester."

"And a pretty damn good one at that, if I do say so myself," he said.

"My mom found photographs hidden in his office, photographs of the little girls he kidnapped, sexually assaulted, and murdered."

"Bitch had no right snooping around my office," he said. "I should have known better. When she started accusing me of having an affair, I should have known she might go snooping. Should have gotten rid of the photos."

"He came home when she was in his office," Helen said.

"The photographs were on his desk. She was on the phone with the police. He strangled her to death and left before they arrived. He picked me up in his car while I was walking home from school. He took me to the big house I told you about."

"Fuck's sake," said her father, tugging a pack of Winstons from a pocket and lighting one up. "If you want to tell it all, tell it all then, but don't go making me look bad."

"Helen . . ." I didn't want her to go through this again, to relive her childhood trauma (especially in the ghostly presence of her tormentor), and I would have told her to stop. Yet her father was here for a reason. Nothing in The No-End House was random or superfluous. Helen and I were not only creating the challenges we faced, but we were also creating the solutions. We were both contestants and game masters, blind and omniscient. Her subconscious had conjured her father for a reason, and distressing memories or not, we had to go with the flow.

"Whose house was it?" I asked her.

"A widow in her nineties. He told the neighbors he was her son, she was in poor health, he was helping her out, which explained all his comings and goings. She never went outside much when she was alive, so they never suspected she might be dead. But she was. He strangled her to death, too. When he took me there . . . it was like I told you. He locked me in the basement. There were bars on the windows. What I didn't tell you: there was another little girl in the basement, as well. She was a couple of years older than me. She had bruises all over her body and wouldn't speak to me. After about a week, my dad took her upstairs, and I never saw her again. He killed her. I learned that later. I learned a lot about him later."

"I should've killed you, too," said her father, blowing two streams of smoke from his nose. "But with you being my little girl and all, I guess I had a soft spot for you. Never thought you'd have murder in you. Didn't see that coming, I admit. Actually, I'm kind of proud of you, kiddo. You're just like your old man. Anyway! That's all in the past." He took a step forward. "Now that you're here, all grown up, why don't you and me pick up where we left off? I don't mind older women much—"

"Don't!" Helen shrieked, backing away from him. "You lay a single hand on me, you sick son of a bitch, I'll kill you, I swear to God I will. I'll kill you *again*."

She was trembling violently. I pulled her into an embrace, stroked her back. Over her shoulder, I said to her father, "Where's the exit?"

He extinguished his cigarette in the ashtray on the desk. "The exit?"

"To the next room."

"You think it's going to be that easy, do you? I'm just going to usher you on your way? Get real, man. I haven't seen my little Petunia—"

Helen whirled toward her father. "Don't call me that!"

He grinned. "But that was your nickname, kiddo. Don't you remember your mom and me taking you to that farm with all the animals? That field of petunias, and you saying they were the most beautiful flowers in the world—"

"We need to go," she said to me. "I can't stand him. I can't listen to him. He disgusts me."

"We can't go, Helen," I said. Then, "The clues are always right in front of us . . ."

"Listen to the schmuck, kiddo," said her father. "I'm the clue. You need me. So drop the *I'm-more-righteous-than-thee* act. You love me, deep down, I know you do. Back when you were just a tot, visiting me right here in this very office, you told me I was the best dad ever. Told me that was the best day of your life—"

"That was before I knew who you really were," she snapped. "*What* you really were. I don't love you, Dad. I hate you. I hope you're rotting in hell."

"Rotting in hell!" He spread his arms. "Does this look like hell, kiddo? Does this look like I'm dead? I sure as heck don't feel dead. I feel great. I'm young, healthy. Got my little girl here, just like old times. Why don't we celebrate? That's right. We should be celebrating. This reunion's been over thirty years in the making, hasn't it? Celeste!" he yelled suddenly. "Bring in that cake!"

Helen and I spun toward the office door as a little girl with two black eyes and swollen lips entered. She was carrying a large silver platter. On it was a round chocolate cake prickling with slow-burning sparklers.

"You!" Helen gasped.

The girl set the platter on the desk. Keeping her eyes glued to the floor, she said in a timid voice, "Would you like me to cut the cake, Chip?"

"It's not going to fucking cut itself, is it? Three pieces, and don't skimp on mine."

"Don't," Helen told her. "You don't have to do anything he says."

The girl ignored her, removed the sparklers, and began cutting the cake.

"You remember your old roommate, don't you, baby?" her father—Chip, as she called him—said.

"You killed her," Helen hissed.

"Of course I did. What good are they when they break? When they lose their spirit and will to live? *Their fear of me?* Where's the fun in that? I do them a favor when I end their miserable young lives. Now eat up, Petunia. I know how far you've come to see me. You must be famished."

Helen looked at me. Given the crazy shit she was dealing with right then, you'd figure cake would be the last thing on her mind. But food was a basic physiological need, and we hadn't eaten in days.

She was as hungry as I was; I could see that in her eyes.

I grabbed a slice of cake with my hands, careful not to let it fall apart, and gave it to her. I took a second piece for myself . . . and when I saw Chip reaching for the third piece, I slapped the silver tray off the desk. It clattered against the floor. The chocolate cake splattered across the tiles.

Helen chirped with glee around her full mouth.

"Aren't you a hoot," said Chip, scowling at me as I wolfed down my messy piece. "I'm going to enjoy watching you die slowly." He nodded. "That's right, that's how it's going to happen, you schmuck, you better believe it. Slowly and painfully. Jen! Get your ugly face in here!"

Chapter 21

"A game is not unlike torture. Each provides entertainment at another's misfortune."
—The Book of Nine

I went weak all over when Jen appeared in the doorway. Balloons, not clothing, covered her body. Beneath the balloons, bare flesh was visible, as well as the white bandages that wrapped around half of her torso. Bandages also wreathed much of her face, and it was clear that she had no lower jaw. Her eyes, however, were visible. Large, hazel, heavily lashed, just as they were in every tormented memory. I could see that she recognized me, and if she had been able to, she might have been smiling.

I rushed over to hug her . . . but didn't. The balloons would make that difficult. Also, she was missing her left arm and shoulder. So I stopped in front of her and tried to smile. It was forced and probably ghastly. Seeing her in the condition she was in, I was on the verge of tears. I wondered if Jen knew what had happened to her. She'd been in a coma following the accident right up to her death. Yet since I'd conjured her, did that mean she knew everything I knew? Was that how this madness worked? I had no idea, and I hated The No-End House more right then than I had ever hated anything in my life.

I took her right hand in mine. It was warm, soft, delicate.

"Jen," I said so quietly that I wasn't sure she heard me. "I'm so sorry . . ."

Tears shimmered in her eyes.

I turned to Chip. *"What the hell is this?"* I demanded.

He was leaning against his desk, ankles crossed, grinning smugly at me. He took his time lighting another cigarette. "You tell me, chump," he said, exhaling a veil of blue smoke that wafted up his face. "You're the one who brought her here."

"The balloons?"

"Well, that I *do* know something about. They're necessary for the game that you and my Petunia are about to play."

"What fucking game?" I asked, thinking about the two previous games Helen and I had played and lost.

"I'm not playing another game," Helen said defiantly.

"You most definitely are, kiddo," said Chip, "if you want to reach the final room."

"What's the game?" I demanded.

He slid open a drawer in his desk and produced a handful of darts. He held them toward me. "Go on, take them."

I looked from the darts to Jen, to the balloons, and went cold with dread.

"What's the game?" I asked again.

"I've got nine of these right here, nine darts," he said. "All you got to do is pop nine of the balloons covering the cripple. You do that, and I'll show you to the exit. Easy as pie."

"What's the catch?" Helen said.

"Catch?" said Chip innocently.

"There's always a catch," I said.

"Did I mention the darts are filled with the venom of a Brazilian wandering spider? No, huh? Surprise, they are! And there's enough venom in each one of them to guarantee the death of your pathetic, disfigured wife."

"That's it?" Helen said, sounding surprised. "*She* dies? She's not even real!"

"She's as real as I am, Petunia. As real as you and your schmuck boyfriend are. You're mistaking time as linear. It's not. Death isn't permanent. In fact, it never really happens at all. The merry-go-round of life never stops to let anyone off. It just keeps turning."

I made eye contact with Jen. I wanted to ask her if it was true, but of course she wouldn't be able to respond. I wanted to whisk her away from this sick game. I wanted to tell her that I wasn't Helen's boyfriend. I wanted to apologize for buying her the flight lessons . . . and for privately blaming her for dying in such a profoundly stupid way. I wanted to tell her so many things.

"You're full of shit," Helen told her father. "You're not alive. I *conjured* you. You're from my mind. She's from Joe's mind. When we leave this room, neither of you will exist anymore. We know how this works, how this house works. So cut the bullshit, Dad. What's the catch? The *real* catch?"

Chip rolled his eyes. "Oh, *all right*. There *is* something else, Petunia. It was so obvious, I didn't think it needed mentioning. But I guess it does, so here it goes: if the cripple dies, the game is over. You lose. You and the chump both lose. You don't make it to Room Nine. You don't pass Go, you don't collect two hundred dollars—you don't ever leave this building. *Ever.* Can you dig that, kiddo? You get to spend the rest of your life with *me*."

"Are you sure you want me to throw them?" I asked Helen.

"I've never played darts in my life," she said.

"Jesus." I looked apprehensively at the nine darts in my left hand. They were light, plasticky, toylike. No brass barrel or aluminum shaft, no metal at all except the tiny point. Presumably, this was so the dart's forward momentum would be stopped by a balloon. But if it missed a balloon and struck flesh . . .

Jen dies, and Helen and I never leave The No-End House.

"Jesus," I repeated. My heart was racing. My nerves were all over the place. I didn't think I could do this.

"You can do this," Helen said, as if reading my mind.

Exhaling steadily, I faced Jen. She had moved to stand next to the desk, framed by one of the large, sand-cataracted windows. Chip was back in the executive chair, his feet up on the desk. The little girl who'd brought the chocolate cake knelt stiffly between his legs, facing us, eyes haunted, while he massaged her shoulders.

I transferred the first dart to my right hand and assumed a throwing stance. The distance from me to Jen, decided by Chip, was about ten feet.

"Aht, aht, aht," said Chip, shaking his head. "Get that toe behind the line, chump."

For the first time, I noticed there was a piece of tape on the floor that might or might not have always been there. I adjusted my stance so my toe was safely behind it. The last thing I wanted was to lose this game because of a technicality.

I raised the dart to eye level and focused on a green balloon attached to Jen's midsection. But my nerves were too much. I lowered the dart and shook out my arm. I'd had a dartboard as a kid, and I remembered my dad telling me once: *Darts is a game of touch, Joey, not force.*

"Take your time," Helen said. "There's no rush."

Nodding, I exhaled again as I raised the dart, this time

gripping the torpedo-shaped barrel less tightly. I threw it with a snap of my hand and wrist. The green balloon exploded with a loud *pop!* Helen squealed with joy.

One down, eight to go.

Pop! Pop! Pop!

My confidence should have been surging with each successful throw, but the exact opposite was happening. On the last throw, I had been aiming for the yellow balloon to the right of Jen's belly button, but I struck the red balloon below it. So not only was my aim not as true as it needed to be, but each deflated balloon revealed more flesh—which meant less room for error.

Nine balloons had originally covered Jen's front side. The first three I struck were over her breasts and abdomen. The yellow balloon I had missed was the only one remaining above her waistline. Two more covered her pelvis, adjacent to the red one I'd accidentally popped. A blue one was stuck to her left thigh, an orange one to her right thigh.

And I had to hit all of them. No more mistakes.

If I'm even an inch or two off . . .

I lowered my arm. "I can't do this . . ."

"Yes, you can, Joe," Helen said. "You're doing great. You're almost halfway done."

"Each throw has to be perfect, Helen. These darts are crappy. I can't control them." I clenched my jaw. This kind of thinking wasn't helping the situation.

"You can do it, Joe," she insisted. Her voice changed, hardened. "You *have* to do it, Joe. We're so close to the end of all this. *One more room.*"

"What's the holdup, chump?" said Chip. He was still massaging the little girl's shoulders with one hand while now smoking a cigarette with the other. "Hurry up and miss so the kiddo and I can start spending the rest of our lives to-gether."

I concentrated on Jen—and noticed her twitch her head to the left. Had that been involuntary? It almost seemed as though she were trying to tell me something . . .

She twitched her head again. I frowned. There was noth-ing to her left.

Unless, I thought, she meant *behind* her . . .

"Jen?" I said, tempering my sudden optimism in case what I suspected was wrong. "Can you turn around for me?"

She turned around, revealing nine unpopped balloons stuck to her back, buttocks, and legs.

"For fuck's sake," grumbled Chip, stabbing his cigarette out in the ashtray.

"Good thinking, Joe!" Helen exclaimed.

I nearly thanked Jen, but I wasn't sure whether her helping us was against the rules, and so I held my tongue.

Working my way down, I popped the two balloons cover-ing her upper back first, then the two below them, always aiming a little lower in the belief that if my throw was off, I could still get lucky and strike the lower balloon.

Nevertheless, I didn't miss. I popped all four I had been aiming for.

Eight balloons down, one to go.

Three purple balloons were taped to Jen's buttocks, while two more were taped to the back of her legs. It was almost identical to what I'd faced on her front side. Of course, that was a very different situation. Then, I thought I needed to pop all five. Now, I only needed to pop one.

I really could do this.

"Go for the middle purple balloon," Helen instructed me, as she had been doing for each of my throws. "If you miss it, you might still hit the ones on either side of it."

"But if I go for the left or right one and miss," I said, "I might still hit the middle one or the one below it."

"Yeah, yeah . . . but the middle one just seems like the safer bet." Her advice had been spot on so far, and I went with it again.

"Okay, middle purple," I said, as if calling a shot during a game of snooker.

"You got this, Joe. Take your time."

"No pressure, chump!" said Chip. "No pressure at all! Just think what I'll be doing to my little Petunia every night when you miss—"

"Shut up!" Helen yelled at him.

On the count of three, I thought, as I assumed a throwing stance for the final time. Raising the ninth dart to eye level, I rocked slightly forward. *One . . . two . . . three . . .*

I missed.

The dart was wildly off its mark, striking Jen in the middle of her back.

At first I thought the shriek of horror I heard came from Jen as the poisoned tip pierced her skin, but it had come from Helen beside me.

"No!" she cried. "No!"

The room spun and blurred as I stumbled backward. Chip was laughing from impossibly far away.

Helen was sobbing.

I bumped into a wall and slid down it to my butt. I could barely think as my mind grappled with the enormity of my fuckup.

We lost. The challenge is over. We're stuck here forever.

I watched in a dreamy kind of stupor as Helen went to Jen, who had collapsed to her side, already incapacitated by the neurotoxins invading her bloodstream. Yet Helen didn't attempt to help her; she simply snagged a dart from the floor and swerved toward her father. The little girl with the haunted black eyes darted out of the way as Helen lunged at him, driving the dart toward his face.

I snapped back to myself, leaped to my feet, and ran to the struggle. Chip and Helen were both yelling. Chip had both his hands around Helen's wrist. The tip of the dart hovered inches from one wide eye.

"Helen, be careful!" I said, fearful she might prick herself.

"Stop her!" said Chip. "I'll give you a second chance!"

"Helen!" I said, seizing her wrist. Her father might have been lying, but the possibility he was telling the truth was something we couldn't ignore. "Hear him out!"

She didn't relent.

"Helen!" I said again, as her fist—and the dart protruding from it—inched closer to her father's eyeball. "*Stop*—"

With a resigned scream, she backed down, tearing free from me. Chip tried to get out of his chair.

I shoved him back into it.

"What's the second chance?" I demanded.

"Give me some space, pal, will you? What are we, goddamn animals?"

I looked at Helen. Her eyes were shiny, manic; I didn't recognize her in them. But when she spoke, she sounded preternaturally calm.

"Let him up, Joe," she said. "There are two of us. He's not leaving this office alive. You hear me, Dad? You have two options. You show us the exit, or you die. I don't care if that means we spend the rest of our lives trapped here. At least it won't be with you."

I stepped back from Chip. He got to his feet and adjusted the knot of his tie indignantly. "Look, Petunia . . ." Clearing his throat, he reconsidered his choice of words. "Look, kiddo. I can't just show you the way out of here. That's not how it works." He held up his hand. "But what I *can* do is

222 Jeremy Bates

offer you a second chance—as long as the risk is in the ball-park of the reward."

I said, "What the fuck are you talking about?"

He said, "One last dart, one last throw."

I glanced at Jen on the floor. It took all my willpower not to go to her. She wasn't real, or if she was, she wasn't part of my reality. My Jen was dead. This one would either vanish into nothingness when Helen and I left Room 8, or she would go back to whatever afterlife she came from.

In either case, she wasn't moving. If she wasn't dead, she was going to be very soon.

I said, "She can't stand, and I'm not throwing—"

"She's not the target anymore, you schmuck," said Chip. "You are."

I frowned. "Me?"

He went to Jen, tore a purple balloon from her behind, walked back to me, and stuck it to the top of my head. "There you go. All set."

I could guess what he had in mind, and I didn't like it one bit.

Chip said to Helen, "Three's a crowd. Spending the rest of our lives together with this chump hanging around was never in the cards. I was always going to offer you a second chance—although, to be honest, I was on the edge of my seat there for a bit. Didn't think you would get as far as you did. Eight out of nine balloons—holy shit, talk about close. Anyway, the fact is, you *did* lose. So here's your second chance. One dart, one throw. And you gotta be the thrower, kiddo. You pop that balloon there on top of this schmuck's head, I show you both the way to the next room. But if you miss . . ."

I die, I thought bleakly.

"What if I miss?" Helen said, looking as queasy as I felt.

"Like, miss everything? I've never thrown a dart before. What if I don't hit either the balloon or Joe?"

"You keep on throwing. Until you hit the balloon or your schmuck boyfriend. And if that happens, it's just you and me, baby, together 'til the end. So what do you say? Do we have a deal or what?"

Chapter 22

"Second chances are quite often last chances."
—The Book of Nine

Helen kissed me on the lips, then whispered in my ear, "I can do this."

I nodded. What was there to say?

Helen went to the strip of masking tape on the floor. I remained standing next to Jen's body—she was no longer breathing; I'd checked—in front of a window. I would have been quite the sight. A haggard-looking, scared man dressed in filthy, sweat-stained clothes . . . with a purple balloon taped to the top of his head.

Helen lined up behind the tape. I thought about offering advice but didn't. If she'd never thrown a dart before like she'd said, whether she hit me or the balloon would come down to pure luck.

I watched her until she raised the dart. Then I closed my eyes and held my breath. A moment later, I heard the dart strike the window behind me and clatter to the floor.

I opened my eyes.

Helen said, "I missed."

"You weren't even close!" Chip trilled.

"Better high than low," she told me.

I nodded.

Closed my eyes.

Waited.

Another *clack!* as the dart hit the window, but much lower than the last one, somewhere to my left.

"Closer?" I asked, opening one eye.

Helen was very pale. She nodded.

"Closer to me or the balloon?" I knew the answer.

"You," Helen said.

I swallowed the corrosive tightness in my throat.

Chip was cackling as he watched from his chair. The little girl was now seated on his lap, and he was absently stroking her long black hair.

I closed my eye and waited for the next dart to prick my skin. It wouldn't hurt much, I knew. Not the prick. The venom would. I was bitten once by a rattlesnake while hiking in Arizona. It hadn't been a very big rattler, but the area around the bite burned until I received treatment at a hospital. I was under no illusion that the venom of a Brazilian wandering spider would be any less toxic than that of a rattlesnake. And the dosage in the dart would be much greater than what one would receive from a bite from anything in the wild. So the pain was going to be bad. Jen would have been screaming right up to her death if she had been able to.

Yet this concern was ancillary, a flashing warning in the back of my mind, that was all. The truth was, I couldn't have cared less about the pain. I could deal with pain.

What mattered—what terrified me to my core—was that I would die.

Two or three minutes after the dart pricked me, I would be dead.

And this was going to happen because Helen couldn't throw

a dart for shit, couldn't hit the broad side of a barn . . . let alone a balloon taped foolishly to the top of my head—

Pop!

My eyes snapped open. Given the dazed look on Helen's face, I was certain she'd hit me. But then her face transformed; it radiated joy.

I touched the top of my head—and felt the withered latex remains of the balloon.

"I did it!" Helen cried. A moment later, she crashed into me, throwing her arms around my neck, laughing.

I was alive. I *felt* alive. My thoughts, my senses, the world—alive, alive, alive. The citrus scent of Helen's hair, the feel of her muscles beneath her sweater, the softness of her flesh, the stale taste of the office air, the drumming of my pulse inside my head, the pounding of my heart, and the knowledge of being alive when I should have been dead—it was all as beautiful as a white picket fence on a bright blue day.

I'm alive!

I planted my lips on Helen's and felt the kiss tingle through every inch of my body.

When it finished, Helen said to Chip, "We won, motherfucker! Show us the way out, motherfucker!"

Because I felt so good, I added with goofy exaggeration, "That's right, *motherfucker*. That's how it works, *motherfucker*."

Sneering at us, Chip shoved the little girl off his lap. She squawked but landed on her feet. In the next moment, she vanished into thin air. I looked to where Jen had been on the floor. She was gone. Chip yanked open a desk drawer and took out a red emergency hammer of the sort found on buses and trains to shatter tempered glass.

He went to the window behind us and said, "Outta my goddamn way."

Helen and I moved toward the office door. Chip smashed the window with the hammer's metal tip. Cracks in the glass spiderwebbed away from the point of impact. More and more cracks appeared, crisscrossing the entire pane.

Suddenly large shards of glass fell free from the frame, and sand began to pour into the small office.

If the Sears Tower was indeed buried beneath more than a thousand feet of sand, the office—and the entire eighth floor—should have filled with sand due to pressure and equalization and other factors. But The No-End House didn't follow the rules of physics, and only enough sand spilled through the broken window into the office to reveal the mouth of a stone tunnel.

I boosted Helen up into the tunnel, then climbed into it after her.

She was looking back into the office, frowning. I looked, too.

Chip was gone.

"I'm sorry, Helen," I said. "What you went through as a kid . . ."

"Forget it," she said promptly. "He's gone, and there's only one room left. After what we've just been through, it's going to be a piece of cake."

I wished I could believe that.

Chapter 23

"Like any good story, a journey has a beginning, a
middle, and an end."

—The Book of Nine

Fiery torches in ornate wrought-iron wall sconces illuminated the tunnel, which was identical to the very first few
we'd encountered beneath The No-End House.

"I think we're back where we started," I said hopefully.

"We're so close, Joe . . ." Helen said. Her voice was thick
with longing and desperation.

"I wonder how many contestants make it to the last room."

"Maybe we're the first," she said.

"You think highly of us."

"This hasn't been a walk in the park. How many people
do you think could have done what we've done?"

"Depends on how many people have taken the challenge
before us. There might have only been a handful."

Helen shook her head. "The No-End house has to be at
least seven hundred years old. That's when Barcelona's Old
Quarter was first developed. So even if as few as one or two
people took the challenge every month . . . well, that would
number in the thousands."

"Then I definitely don't think we're the first to reach the last room."

Out of the blue, she asked, "Where are you going to take me when we finish this?"

I looked at her. "Where?"

"We're going to have to celebrate," she said. "So where will you take me to celebrate?"

"Oh." I thought for a moment. "Where do you want to go?"

"I'm asking *you*, Joe. If I wanted to take myself out, I'd do that. But I want you to take me out, and that means you have to choose."

"I guess it would be somewhere nice. But I don't know Barcelona's restaurant scene. I usually stick to street meat and fast food in big cities."

"We don't have to go out to a fancy restaurant. You could come over to my place. We could order in Chinese and watch *The Twilight Zone*."

"You like *The Twilight Zone*?" I asked.

"I never watched it as a kid, but I discovered it on Netflix. The episodes are trippy. Sort of like watered-down versions of The No-End House."

"Maybe we should pitch our story to Hollywood . . ."

We continued with the nervous banter until, a short time later, the stone tunnel passed beneath an iron portcullis, and we emerged in a huge oval room. Multiple bonfires lit the open space before us, revealing a sandy floor littered with what appeared to be thousands of human corpses.

Terror rose swiftly and monstrously inside me, and it took several long moments before I found my voice again.

"Room Nine," I said.

Although the oval space was about the size of a baseball field, the curved stone walls didn't lead up to spectator seating; instead, they soared uninterrupted beyond the light of the bonfires into the impenetrable bowl of darkness above us.

Helen said, "I hope those aren't the bodies of previous contestants . . ."

I said, "They can't be. We make the rooms. They come from us. We made this one, too."

"Unless this room is different. It's the final one. It must lead back to the palace. So maybe it's the same for every-one—"

A tiny yellow light appeared high up in the wall. A figure stood silhouetted in a rectangular window. The familiar, accented voice of Doña Isabella carried down to where we stood.

"Congratulations, Joe from Arizona and Helen from Chicago on reaching Room Nine! I have been following your journey with much interest. You have proven to be tremendous contestants. And alas, you now stand in the presence of some of the greatest contestants to have ever walked the rooms of The No-End House. Yes, señorita, those are the remains of previous contestants, men and women just as accomplished as you, as they had all defied the odds to come this far, as well."

Helen's hand found mine and gripped it tightly.

"So do not rejoice, even though the end is in sight, señor and señorita. Your most difficult challenge yet awaits. Beginning in one hour, an opponent will arrive to do battle with you to the death. If you defeat he, she, or it, a new opponent will arrive precisely one hour from then, and these battles will continue ad infinitum until either you are dead or you discover the exit. Good luck, young travelers. I look forward to the entertainment."

The light went out.

Silence reclaimed the crypt.

Chapter 24

"It is not impossible to escape the mind of a god,
but it is not terribly easy either."
—The Book of Nine

After about a minute of freaking out over what Doña Isabella had revealed to be in store for us, I said, "We're wasting time. We need to figure out how to get out of here."

"Fight to the death!" Helen said, apparently not hearing me. "She wants us to fight to the death!"

"Helen!" I said. "Get over it! We're wasting time we don't have!"

Her eyes cleared, then sharpened. "What are we supposed to do, Joe?" she snapped. "Do you see any way out of here?"

I looked around the arena—and that was definitely what it was, an arena, but one designed not for basketball or ice hockey but blood sports—and spotted metal glinting in the light of a nearby bonfire on the far side of the oval. It was some sort of weapons rack.

"Weapons!" I said, pointing to it. "We can arm ourselves."

Helen squinted. "I have no idea how to use a sword, Joe. I've never even *held* a sword in my life."

"We're not going to fight whoever appears with our bare hands."

"Or *what*ever. That's what Izzy said. It could be a he, a she, or an *it*." Although the wild panic had left her eyes, it remained in her voice.

I didn't blame her for being afraid. Standing among what had to be more than a thousand corpses was frightening enough, but knowing that the chances were good you soon might be joining them was terror on an entirely different level.

Nevertheless, I'd tucked my fear away for the moment, and Helen needed to do the same. Death was coming for us, and we had to prepare.

I said, "Whoever or whatever appears, Helen, we need those weapons to win. Follow me."

Without waiting for a reply, I pioneered a path through the corpses and heard her follow. At first I tried not to look at any of the skeletal remains we were stepping around or over, but soon there was nowhere else to look; they were everywhere. Their clothing (in most cases dirty and torn and bloodstained) offered a sad insight into the people they might have been. The skeleton dressed in a simple brown robe with a rope belt had likely been a monk or poor farmer. The skeleton in a high-necked dress adorned with pearls was undoubtedly some sort of noblewoman. Ditto for the one in a silk dress embroidered with an intricate flower motif . . . yet perhaps she had been from the East, visiting Spain with her husband on a diplomatic mission.

I began to invent backstories for all the poor souls we passed. The man in a wool military uniform accented with gold braids and buttons: an officer in the Anglo-Spanish War. The man in tea-green breeches and a matching knee-length waistcoat: an upper-class French or Italian youth on his grand tour of Europe. The woman in an Edwardian gown with puffy sleeves and lots of chiffon and lace: an aristocrat who liked nothing better than meddling in royal scandals and courtly intrigue.

It seemed The No-End House didn't discriminate with its contestants. People of all castes, occupations, religions, and races had been welcomed to participate in its challenge. Here, a man in a Japanese kimono, and another in a Turkish robe woven from luxurious fabric. There, a priest in a clerical collar, and nearby, a nun in a wimple. An Arab in a loose chemise, baggy trousers, and turban. A peasant in a dull gray tunic. A knight wearing a tabard over a suit of chain-link armor.

The deceased contestants weren't only from the distant past. A flamboyant 1940s zoot suit with wide lapels and voluminous pants. A double-breasted business suit and paisley necktie. A coral-colored flapper dress with a decadently beaded fringe. A houndstooth blouse and pleated skirt that could have come straight from a *Leave It to Beaver* episode.

At one point, I started at the sight of what I thought had been a large animal, but it was the remains of a woman in a fur coat.

I turned around to tell Helen it was strange we had yet to come across any of the opponents these people had faced . . . and found her some distance behind me, staring at a corpse at her feet.

I backtracked and looked at the corpse, too. Judging by the personalized leather jacket, the guy had been a punk or skinhead. The steel caps of BIC lighters lined the jacket's collar and cuffs, while tiny silver skulls and pistols dangled from the many zippered pockets. A Ramones logo, which parodied the presidential seal, had been cut from a T-shirt and safety-pinned to one sleeve. Below this were buttons reading WHITE PUNKS ON DOPE and LEMMON AID, as well as a felt patch depicting the Union Jack. A chain and bicycle lock wreathed his skeletonized neck.

"He was just like us . . ." Helen said quietly.

"I'm not much into Quaaludes," I said, referencing the LEMMON AID button, which itself referenced a company that had produced the sedatives.

I glanced at Helen to see if she'd gotten the attempt at levity. She was crying silently. The tears angered me. They showed weakness, and we needed to be strong. We needed to be damn near indestructible if we were going to accomplish what all the dead had failed to do: escape this room.

"He had a family, friends," she went on. "He liked music. Nobody would have known what happened to him. He just disappeared one day. Just like us. Nobody's going to know—"

"We're not dying here," I said tersely. Then, to change the topic: "Have you noticed we haven't come across the remains of any of the opponents?"

Helen wiped the tears from her cheeks. "How do you know we haven't? They could be mixed in with the contestants."

"I haven't seen anybody dressed like a fierce gladiator. And I definitely haven't seen anything not human."

We resumed walking toward the weapons rack.

Eventually Helen said, "How are we supposed to defeat a minotaur, Joe? Even with all the weapons in the world, I can't see us slaying a minotaur."

I frowned. "Why do you think we're going to face a minotaur?"

"I think The No-End House . . . it's not just in Barcelona. Maybe now it is. But I think it appears wherever in the world it wants. Look at the contestants. They're from every country. When I started wondering about that, I started wondering about other places the house could have been, other *palaces* it could have inhabited throughout history, and the first that came to mind was the one on the island of Crete in Greece. You know the legend."

"I know there was a labyrinth and a minotaur that ate people."

"The queen of Crete had sex with a bull," she said, "and their baby had the head of a beast and the body of a man. When the minotaur grew up, the king built a labyrinth in his palace to hold it, and he would send young Greek men and maidens into it to feed the minotaur."

"I have no idea where you're going with this, Helen . . ."

"People entering a palace and never exiting—that sort of sums up this place, doesn't it?"

"You think at one point The No-End House was that palace in Greece?"

"Why not?"

"For starters, that palace was excavated. A labyrinth was never discovered in it."

"Because there wasn't a *literal* labyrinth, Joe. That was simply a metaphor. The people who survived all nine rooms and lived to tell their stories . . . that was how they described the palace and its impossible rooms: a labyrinth. And maybe they all fought minotaurs in the final room. Everything else—King Milos, the origin of the Minotaur, Theseus—was all legend, but legend built up over time from the bits and pieces of what really happened."

"Why would everyone have to fight minotaurs in the last room?"

"To even the playing field. Think of The No-End House as an open-world video game. Players can usually get to the end of the game any way they want, but to finish it, they all have to defeat the same final boss."

I contemplated this until we came to a deposit of corpses so dense that we had no choice but to walk over them. I avoided stepping on any skulls, but I couldn't say the same thing about other bones, many of which splintered beneath my weight.

On the other side, I waited for Helen to catch up. I offered her my hand as she tiptoed over the final few bodies.

"This is so not right," she said.

"There was no other way around," I said.

"So what do you think?"

"About what?"

"My theory. What if all these contestants had to fight minotaurs to the death? He/she/it? Minotaurs are all those things, depending on whether a male or female one shows up. So maybe each opponent is a minotaur. Maybe we have to fight minotaurs ad infinitum until . . . well, until we find a way to escape . . ."

"I don't know, Helen," I said carefully, wanting to be diplomatic. "It's all a bit . . . out there . . ."

"Out there?" she fumed. "The No-End House is the very definition of *out there*, Joe! How do *you* explain it?"

I shrugged. "We can't explain it, and we don't have to. We only have to escape this final room. And on that note, you should stop thinking about minotaurs, in case you end up conjuring one."

"But that's the thing, Joe. If minotaurs *are* the final challenge for everyone, then we don't have a choice but to fight them—"

"Helen, stop it!" I told her, realizing with a slippery and unpleasant sensation that she was losing her shit. "There are no minotaurs! Your theory doesn't make any fucking sense! So stop thinking about minotaurs, because the only way we'll face one is if you conjure it, and if you do that, we're as good as dead!"

Fighting a new flood of tears, she brushed past me and took the lead through the corpses.

I followed her until we reached the weapons rack. It was a sprawling wood structure finished in black lacquer, and it held a well-used arsenal: straight swords, curved swords, rapiers, clubs, maces, twin blades, spears, polearms, axes, flails, katanas, war hammers, and even a deadly-looking bow made from the horns of an animal.

Helen selected a curved sword, seemed surprised by its weight, and exchanged it for a katana. I chose a mace with half a dozen flanges protruding from the metal ball at the top of the shaft. I swung it experimentally.

Helen was looking at the katana in what appeared to be disgust.

"Go on," I told her. "Swing it."

With both hands choked high on the hilt, she performed an awkward chop that made me think of a fisherman casting a line into the sea.

"Hold it lower and—"

"This is crazy, Joe! I don't know how to use this stupid thing!"

"You can learn," I told her. "You just need a bit of practice—"

"I don't want to do this," she said petulantly. "I *can't* do this."

I clenched my jaw in frustration. "You can, and you have to, Helen. There's no other option. Believe it or not, I'm no expert with a mace. I'm going to need your help defeating whoever or whatever arrives."

Her face had gone slack in the flickering torchlight. "We're going to die," she said flatly.

"We're not going to die, Helen! Stop saying that!"

"We might."

"We're not!"

"Look around us, Joe! Look at all of the bodies! There are thousands of them! Why are we any different? Why are we so special? Why are we going to survive when none of them did?"

"You're only seeing the dead. You're not seeing the survivors. Who knows how many contestants *didn't* die? There could be just as many! More! And if that's the case, then we have a better than fifty-fifty chance of surviving, too."

Helen pressed her lips together tightly. I could tell that she didn't believe what I was saying, and I wasn't sure I did, either.

"Anyway, we have each other," I told her more gently. "Izzy admitted it was an exception for two people to participate together. That increases our odds exponentially."

Helen practiced swinging the katana again; it was just as awkward as her first attempt. She blurted, "I won't even tickle a minotaur!"

"Stop thinking about minotaurs!"

Tossing the katana aside, she stalked away into the darkness.

I retrieved the discarded katana and carried it to where Helen had slumped against the stone wall. She was staring stoically at the sandy ground in front of her.

"You need to practice," I told her, offering her the sword. She didn't look up. "You really need to practice, Helen. We likely only have half an hour until the first opponent arrives."

"It's to soak up the blood . . ."

"What?" I said, trying to keep the impatience from my voice.

"The sand," she said. "The Romans covered the floor of the Colosseum with sand, because it soaked up all the blood and vomit and urine."

"Maybe it's the key," I said.

Now she did look up. "The sand?"

"The clues are always right in front of us. So maybe the sand's a clue."

"How's the sand a clue?"

"I have no fucking idea," I said, and laughed at the absurdity of the discussion.

Helen surprised me by laughing, as well.

"Oh, Joe," she said. "I'm sorry. I'm flaking out, I know . . ."

"Hey," I said, kneeling in front of her. "You're doing amazing. You figured out the clues to the other rooms. You can figure out this one, too."

"I did not figure them out," she said. "You did. You discovered that arrows were behind the mirrors. You realized the oven door had five sides . . ." She shook her head. "How you noticed that with the stick thing trying to get us . . ."

"Wild Child was pointing right at it."

"The blonde girl?"

I nodded. "That's how I thought of her."

"She *was* rather feral . . ."

"It was your idea, Helen, to make our way to the smoke signal. You suggested the T-Rex might be there to help us. And you're the one who found the key to the elevator on Jason."

"Okay," she said, smiling—albeit halfheartedly—for the first time since we'd entered the crypt, "so we figured out the clues together . . ."

"We make a good team."

"Fuck Izzy."

"Fuck Izzy."

Helen's eyes shifted to the katana in my hand. "Think you can still teach me how to use that thing?"

By gripping the sword's hilt with one hand near the pommel and the other a few inches above it, and using her hips and shoulders to execute strikes instead of her elbows, Helen's form improved quickly. I retrieved a longsword from the weapons rack, and we practiced thrusts, slashes, and parries, as well as proper distance and timing.

After only ten minutes or so, I became much more confident in her ability to attack and defend. She was certainly no samurai, but she was no longer a fisherman, and that would have to be good enough.

While we continued to clash swords, we brainstormed ways out of the room. These included searching each corpse for a clue, attempting to scale a wall, and even returning to the Sears Tower in case we had missed something there that could help us here.

None of those ideas were very good, of course, but the discussion was a welcomed distraction as the final minutes of the hour-long wait counted down.

Chapter 25

"Old scores tend to get settled, one way or
another."
—The Book of Nine

We'd figured our opponent would arrive via the passage-way beneath the portcullis, as there was no other visible entrance to the arena, so we'd returned that way and flanked the gate to hopefully get a jump on whoever/whatever came through it.

Instead, a thunderous rumbling rose from somewhere below us, and then a large circular section of the ground in the center of the arena began to turn slowly in a clockwise direction as it lowered out of sight.

"Holy shit!" I said, as vibrations shot up my legs. I had to shout to be heard above what could have been the grinding of colossal stone gears.

"*What's happening?*" Helen said, looking more surprised than frightened.

"Come on!" I said, and started cautiously forward.

We stopped when we were still a good twenty feet away from the hole. The sand spilled over the rim like a golden waterfall, taking some of the nearest corpses with it. We didn't want to join them.

"It's like a sinkhole," Helen said.

"Only a man-made one," I said.

"You mean *god*-made."

We ventured closer when the sand stopped falling and peered into the hole. The cross-section revealed that we stood on top of three or four feet of sand. Below that was solid gray-black rock that stretched down into darkness. The light from the bonfires didn't extend far, and we could barely see the sand-covered disc as it corkscrewed deeper into the ground.

"What could be powering it?" Helen asked.

"No idea," I said, even as I pictured in my mind something akin to a cattle wheel—only giant stone golems, not oxen, labored to turn the wheel around the axle.

Suddenly the grinding noise ceased, leaving a tinny ringing in my ears.

"It's stopped," Helen said redundantly.

"Guess it's at the bottom," I said.

She retrieved an arm bone from the sleeve of a nearby corpse and lobbed it down the hole. We never heard it land.

She looked at me.

"What were you expecting to hear?" I said. "The ground's covered in sand."

"What's it doing?"

"Picking up our opponent, I imagine."

"Maybe we were supposed to go down with it?"

I sure as hell hoped not. The only place worse than where we were right then would be at the bottom of the hole in the pitch black.

The rumbling started again so abruptly that I jumped at the sound of it.

"Get ready," I told Helen, as a fresh wave of adrenaline surged through me. "It's coming back up."

We moved away from the hole and raised our weapons. I held the longsword in my right hand and the mace in my left. Helen gripped the katana with both hands.

Neither of us spoke as the ancient contraption rose inexorably toward the surface. And to my dismay, I found myself thinking that on it would tower an eight-foot-tall minotaur with smoldering red eyes, flaring nostrils, and devilish horns curling outward from its forehead. My imagination wouldn't quit there, cycling dangerously through every little detail of the bovine-like creature from its dark mane down to its hooved feet, from its broad shoulders and powerful chest covered in coarse fur to its muscular arms and short, tufted tail.

Clawed hands gripping an immense bronze axe that could effortlessly cleave me in two . . .

Stop it! I told myself, and thought about anything else.

"You!" Helen said when our opponent appeared.

It was as though he'd choreographed his entrance, because the first glimpse we had of him as he rose from the ground was the back of his head and shoulders, but when the rotating lift came to a stop, he faced directly toward us.

"Hello, my darlinks!" the midget Nazi said, grinning from beneath his slug-like Hitler mustache. "Did you miss me?"

He wore the same black pants and jackboots as before. Now, however, his upper body was bare, revealing a large black swastika painted on his chest. He held a red chainsaw—just like one I had once owned—in his small, sinewy arms. He yanked the starter cord. The engine roared to life.

"Who shall die first?" he shouted over the high-pitched whirring. "I will try not to be too messy. Merchant Belmont pays much more handsomely for neatly severed limbs."

I looked at Helen. She nodded almost imperceptibly.

We began moving toward the Nazi—Moritz, I recalled Lard-Ass calling him—while spreading away from each other as we had practiced.

"Oh, I see, my darlinks," he said. "You want to flank me. No, I do not believe zat is going to work."

He strode confidently toward us, revving the chainsaw while swinging it back and forth between Helen and me, saying in a singsong way, "Eeny, meeny, miny, moe, cut a contestant head to toe. If zey holler—oh, and zey will holler, zey most definitely will—I will *not* let zem go ... eeny ... meeny ... miny ... *moe!*" He ended the children's rhyme with the chainsaw pointed at me. "It looks like you are first, *mie Schlappe*. Ready or not, *here I come!*"

He rushed me, chainsaw screaming.

It took all my willpower to stand my ground.

When he came to within striking range, I lunged forward with a swift and sure thrust. He swung the chainsaw in a wide arc that caught the sword midair. Sparks flew as metal met metal.

We broke apart. I saw Helen approaching from the side. Moritz did, as well.

To keep his attention focused on me, I attacked again, this time with a diagonal slash that would have split the swastika on his chest in two had it connected with his flesh.

But he was too quick, dodging and swinging the chainsaw in a low sweep. I smashed the cutting bar away at the last moment with the blunt head of the mace.

Yet the blow knocked me off balance. I tripped on a corpse and fell onto my back. Moritz raised the screeching chainsaw high above his head and seemed about to leap on top of me ... but turned at the last second toward Helen, who had tried sneaking up on him. She swung the katana in an overhead chop. He bashed the blade aside with a shrill, gleeful "*Yieeeeeeee!*" He also knocked the sword from her grip, leaving her unarmed and defenseless.

Nevertheless, her intervention provided me with the window of opportunity I needed. I swung the mace horizontally.

The flanged head struck the Nazi's knee with bone-crushing force. Shrieking, Moritz collapsed to his side.

I swung the mace again, this time at his head. Hs skull and jaw cratered inward with a loud and snappy *whup!* The chainsaw dropped to the sand, where it continued to buzz angrily as it chewed through his left boot and the flesh beneath. Moritz's surviving eye glowered balefully at me, even as he rocked forward and fell face-first onto my lap.

Disgusted, I scrambled out from beneath his bleeding, broken head.

Helen was staring at the convulsing body and appeared to be in shock.

I reached forward and flicked the kill switch next to the chainsaw's trigger. The engine shut off. Blissful silence reigned for several long seconds.

Finally I said, "It was either him or us, Helen. We didn't have a choice . . ."

"I don't give a shit about that bastard, Joe . . ." As the vacant look left her eyes, a smile spread across her lips. "I just can't believe we *won*."

Chapter 26

"If in each moment an infinite number of possibilities exist, then anything is fair game."
—The Book of Nine

It's gotta be the way out," Helen said. "It's the only way out." We were standing at the edge of the mechanical lift.

"You want to ride it down?" I said skeptically.

"We're in some sort of colosseum. And beneath the Roman Colosseum were a bunch of rooms to hold the gladiators and animals and props before they rose through trapdoors into the arena. There were also passages and tunnels leading to places *outside* the Colosseum, like stables and barracks and stuff. So maybe there are tunnels down there that lead out of *here*, too?"

"And what if it's just a deep pit?"

She shrugged. "Then we come back up."

"What if we can't make the lift come back up? What if we get stuck down there—?"

"*What if? What if? What if?*" She threw up her hands. "I don't know, Joe! What if we *don't* try it? What are we going to do up here? Sit around and wait until the next opponent arrives?"

She was right, of course. I exhaled heavily. "Do you have any idea how to make it move?"

"I imagine we just have to step on it."

"It has a built-in motion detector?"

"Let's try and see what happens, smart aleck."

"Better grab the katana."

Helen picked up the weapon and said, "Should we take the chainsaw, as well?"

I raised the longsword and bloodied mace. "My hands are full." She appeared to weigh the pros and cons of chainsaw-versus-katana and decided to keep the sword.

We walked side by side onto the lift, picking our way through the countless bodies in our way.

When we reached the center, Helen said loudly, "Abracadabra!"

Nothing happened.

She hopped up and down.

Nothing.

I was quietly relieved. "Looks like—"

"Come on, Izzy!" Helen shouted tauntingly into the empti-ness above us. "We figured it out! We know we have to go down! So send this stupid contraption—"

The gears beneath us rumbled to life.

The deeper we went, the darker it became, until we were cocooned in inky blackness. The already cool air seemed sev-eral degrees cooler.

"Do you think Izzy did that?" I asked Helen.

"Lowered this? Why not? She admitted she's been watch-ing us."

"Maybe you should have asked her where the way out is."

"This *is* the way out, Joe. It has to be."

"I hope you're right."

"Are you afraid of the dark?" she teased.

"This darkness, yes."

"There's gotta be a light at the bottom."

"What if . . ." I hadn't planned to bring up what had crossed my mind, but I said it anyway. "I know you hate my what-ifs, but what if . . . we're descending into our subconsciouses?"

"Cut it out, Joe."

"I mean it."

Although I couldn't see her, I could feel her staring at me. "Literally? You literally think we're descending into our subconsciouses?"

"Every room in The No-End House has been built by our subconsciouses. Maybe this is where everything comes from. This hole. Maybe every single contestant we could ever imagine is already imagined and down here, waiting for us."

"Holy moly, Joe," Helen said, with an uncertain laugh. "And you thought *my* theory about this house was out there."

The darkness lessened, and then I realized we were no longer surrounded by stone. We'd passed through some kind of borehole and were once again descending through open space.

"I told you!" Helen said excitedly. "We're in another room!"

Soon we could see bonfires dotting the darkness below us, each one growing larger and brighter as we wound slowly downward.

The lift stopped when it reached the ground, and we found ourselves in the center of another arena filled with just as many corpses as the previous one.

"It's no different than the last room," Helen said dismally.

"Bit anticlimactic," I said, although this was much prefer-able to what had been brewing inside my head.

"More like a *waste of time*. We've just wasted ten minutes. And that means ten fewer minutes to figure out the way out of here before the next opponent arrives." She made a frus-trated sound. "I feel like we're in a goddamn Borg ship."

I frowned. "Borg?"

"You don't watch *Star Trek*?"

"Never."

"I have every *Next Generation* episode on DVD. We can watch them together when we get out of here . . ." Her voice faltered, and she turned away from me. She raised a hand to her face, presumably to wipe away tears.

"Maybe we should try going down again," I said. "This lift is here for a reason. The opponents could have come through the gate. But they came up through here. Why? What are we missing?"

Helen turned back to me, once more composed. "Can I use one of those what-ifs you like so much?"

"Go for it," I said.

"The doors to each room have always been numbered. The fancy *One* on the first door. The *Two* on the fat guy's wagon. The *Six* on Izzy's other fancy door."

"That's only a few doors—"

"The others were still numbered, just indirectly. Three fleurs-de-lis on the big mirror you broke. Four people in front of the hole under Vampmilla's table. Five sides on the oven door. Seven horns on the triceratops. The number eight on the elevator panel. The nine balloons taped to the front of your wife. So what if we have to go down *ten* floors?"

I was surprised. "Ten?"

"We're in the ninth room. But to pass through nine rooms, you need ten doors. So what will be on the last door, the one that leads back to the real world? Probably *Ten*, right? Which means that if there's a clue to finding that door, it would involve the number ten. And if this lift is the clue, then . . . well . . . lifts only do one thing, right? They lead to different levels or floors. So if this lift *is* the clue, like you say, then we should ride it for ten floors, because that's where the tenth door would be . . ." She had been nodding more and more assuredly as she spoke, and now she smiled hopefully at me. "I think I'm right, Joe. I really think that's it, that's the way out of here. . . . We need to take this contraption down eight more floors."

I considered all that, and I wasn't as enthusiastic about it as Helen was. For starters, the solution seemed too similar to the one in the Sears Tower elevator, and I didn't think The No-End House would rehash old material. But more, the numbers signaling the next door, directly or indirectly, were always in plain sight. Even the *8* in the Sears Tower elevator was right there, right in front of us, on a button on the control panel. What Helen was suggesting now was an intangible, invisible *10*—and that veered too much from the established script.

Unfortunately, I had no other ideas to offer, so I told her with a shrug, "I guess it's worth a shot."

Before we attempted Helen's plan, I cleared a few corpses to reveal a small patch on the arena floor. Using the heel of my shoe, I drew a single word into the sand.

This time, Helen didn't have to invoke Izzy's help to get the lift to descend again. As soon as we reached the center of it, the unseen gears churned, and the platform began to rotate.

"You're wrong," Helen told me nervously.

"I hope I am," I said, as the darkness around us became complete. We traveled the rest of the way down in silence.

*   *   *

When the lift emerged into the next room, Helen and I went carefully to the edge of it so we had a view of the ground below spinning slowly into view.

We were still fifty or sixty feet above it when Helen said, "No!"

I made out the word I'd drawn in the sand a moment later: *JOE*.

Chapter 27

"Family is bonded by blood . . . until that blood is
spilled."
—The Book of Nine

It can't be the same room," she stated stubbornly.
I didn't say anything.

"It can't be, Joe!"

"It is, Helen."

I went past the clearing with my name in the sand and
looked for Moritz's body among all the others. I didn't see it
anywhere.

"He's gone," I said. "The Nazi."

"See!" she said, with a fierce kind of desperation. "That
means—"

"No, it doesn't, Helen. My wife disappeared. Your dad
did, too. When someone's no longer needed here, they disappear."

"I hate this house!" she said, kicking her foot through my
name.

Then much louder, almost a wail: "*I hate this fucking
house!*"

Grim-faced, I started toward the weapons rack.

Helen called after me, "Where are you going, Joe? Don't leave me here!"

"We need to prepare," I told her.

Although I was comfortable wielding the longsword and mace, I would have fared even better against the chainsaw with a polearm or spear. Consequently, for the upcoming fight, I wanted to have the best weapon to counter our opponent's, and that meant camping out by the weapons rack instead of in the middle of the arena.

I spent the next twenty minutes mucking around with a variety of weapon classes, getting a feel for each, before laying seven weapons on the sand so they would be easily accessible, depending on who or what arrived next.

Eventually I sat down next to Helen, who was still in a funk about her exit strategy not panning out.

To try to cheer her up (not that either of us could ever be genuinely "cheery" while trapped in this diorama of death), I said, "So you're a *Star Trek* fan, huh? I didn't know you were such a nerd."

"I'm not a nerd," she said flatly.

"I'm just kidding around—"

"I'm a geek."

"Much better."

"It is. Nerds have nothing going for them except their intelligence. Geeks are just as smart as nerds, but they're trendy, too."

Even as I chuckled at that, I found myself thinking morbidly, *I don't want to die here. I want to spend time with Helen, real time. I want to order in Chinese food with her. Watch* Star Trek *with her. It doesn't matter that she's older now. We could be happy. We could have a lot of good years together.*

I said, much too seriously, "You're not a geek, Helen."

"Uh, have you noticed my hair lately? I dye it bright orange."

"Okay, maybe you are one . . ."

She took my hand and squeezed it.

"You're a good guy, Joe."

"Thanks," I said, but that was all. I no longer wanted to talk. Her tone had changed just as mine had, becoming far too serious.

She said, "Resistance is futile."

Here we go, I thought, and said, "Don't say that, Helen."

"It's what the Borg say."

"From *Star Trek?*"

"They're an alien race of cyborgs. They have a hive mind and assimilate other cultures and technologies into their collective consciousness. And that's what they always say before they assimilate you: 'Resistance is futile.' "

"You mentioned this room reminds you of their ship?"

"They fly around in ginormous cubes. In one episode, Picard and the away team beam into one of the cubes. The interior is the same everywhere. You could be on any level, and the miles of corridors are all identical." After a long pause, she added, "When we took the lift and emerged in the same room we came from, I pictured a million identical rooms all stacked on top of each other, all stacked side by side, all connected like in an unending, inescapable cube."

I tried picturing that, and the unfathomable enormity of it scared the shit out of me.

"Resistance isn't futile," I told her. "We wouldn't be here if it was. We're on the doorstep out of here, and we're getting out—"

The lift was moving again.

"Hiya, Petunia!" Helen's father called, waving to us from the middle of the arena as the lift made its final, grinding rotation before stopping. He was dressed in the same drab, dated business suit he'd worn in his office. "I see you're still with the schmuck! He would never have gotten my blessing, you know. My little girl could do much, much better."

"All right!" Helen grinned at me. "It's just my *dad*!" She started toward Chip with the katana raised in the way we'd practiced.

"Helen, wait," I said.

She stopped, turned. "What are you worried about, Joe? He doesn't even have a weapon!"

"He's holding something behind his back."

She looked again at her father, who was coming our way, apathetically trampling on the corpses in front of him.

"What do you have behind your back, Dad?" Helen called.

"Nothing, kiddo! Nothing at all."

And then I knew.

"Darts," I hissed. "Shit, Helen, he has the *poisoned darts*! We won't be able to get close to him."

Her confident and vengeful—and I would even say blood-lusting—grin faltered.

"Dammit!" she said.

I tossed aside the mace and longsword and picked up a bow and quiver, one of the weapons I'd laid out on the sand. The bow was made from the rather lightweight antlers of a deer or elk. I looped the quiver's strap over one shoulder, withdrew a feathered arrow, and nocked it on the gut bow-string.

Helen appeared uncertain. "Can you use that thing?"

The only time I'd ever used a bow and arrow was during an archery lesson when I was a kid at summer camp. Nevertheless, I said, "It's not hard. Point and shoot."

I aimed the arrow at Chip, who was still at least thirty yards away. I drew the bowstring toward the tip of my nose until the limbs of the bow refused to bend farther.

He said, "Who do you think you are, chump? Robin Hood? Don't be such a little pussy! Fight me like a man!"

I released the arrow. It whooshed through the air and struck a corpse near his feet.

"Jumping Jesus!" said Chip, leaping backward. "Careful, you son-of-a-whore! You almost hit me!"

I nocked a second arrow.

"Okay, wait, wait, wait . . ." He raised the hand that had been behind his back. As I'd suspected, he was gripping a fistful of darts. "Look here. I'll get rid of these. You get rid of that. Then we can fight on even terms, mano a mano. The winner gets Petunia all to himself. How does that sound to you—?"

I fired the arrow. It whizzed past his left side, narrowly missing him.

"Fuck you, asshole!" he shouted. "Fuck you, you cowardly bitch!" He turned and fled.

Helen and I chased him. We didn't know if Chip would simply vanish when his successor arrived on the lift in a little less than an hour, but if he didn't, then it would be two versus two, and there was a very good chance either Helen or I (or both of us) would end up with a poisoned dart in our backs.

The obstacle course of corpses made the pursuit difficult. Chip showed no respect for the dead, charging over the bodies as if they were driftwood, demolishing bones beneath his feet, kicking others free of their clothing. We did our best to minimize the carnage by following in his wake, yet we also crushed an uncomfortable number of brittle remains beneath our feet.

"He's too fast!" Helen said from behind me after several minutes of this rigmarole. She was panting.

"He'll get tired soon," I told her.

"I'm already tired . . ."

I was, too, and I knew the dynamics of the chase needed to change. Not only was her father younger than us, but he also seemed to be in great shape.

I said, "Should we try . . . splitting up? Cutting him off?"

Helen said between breaths, "I think . . . think he's going back to . . . the Sears Tower . . ."

Chip had been leading us in big loops up until then. But indeed it appeared he'd changed tactics and was making a bee-line toward the portcullis.

Which would not be good.

In the wide-open arena, the bow was ideal for picking him off before he could get close enough to throw a dart. But in a confined space like an office, with everything he could hide behind, it would be much more difficult to land a clean shot from a distance—

Chip tripped on one of the corpses and went down face-first. He seemed momentarily stunned and didn't move for a couple of seconds. Then he got to his knees . . . and looked back at his right foot. He shook it aggressively. It appeared to be stuck inside a rib cage he had stomped on.

"Get him now, Joe!" Helen cried.

Her father gave up trying to free his foot and transferred one of the darts to his throwing hand.

I slowed, slipped an arrow from the quiver, and nocked it.

"Come on then!" Chip shouted at me. "Come and get me, you pansy-ass chump!" He launched the dart in a desperate Hail Mary. It landed far short of us.

I loosed the arrow. It flew straight and true, and the flashed steel tip impaled him in the center of his chest.

"Yes!" Helen cried.

Chip dropped the darts. His hands went to the shaft protruding from his sternum.

I nocked another arrow.

"No," Helen said. "I want to do this."

She hurried toward her father and stopped a few feet before him. I stood beside her, the arrow trained on him in case he tried going for one of the discarded darts. His face was fish-belly white and covered in a sheen of perspiration.

Helen raised the katana. "You have no idea how good it feels to be able to kill you again, Dad. Oh, man, you have no idea. I should probably have something witty or mean to say. But you know what? There's nothing to say. You're just not worth the effort."

She swung the blade.

Chip's body slumped forward. His decapitated head dropped next to it, rolled past his shoulder, and stopped against the corpse he'd tripped over, his lifeless eyes staring up into the black void above us.

Chapter 28

"Lying is the quickest way to make a stranger of a friend."
—The Book of Nine

While picking our way through the corpses to the weapons rack, Helen said, "That was a pleasant surprise. I mean, it was my dad, of all people. We got to take down an easy opponent, and I got some sweet revenge to boot. Two birds with one stone."

Her voice might have sounded upbeat, but her eyes were flat, stony, defeated.

She knew as well as I did that we couldn't keep this up. In another forty minutes, the next opponent was going to be here.

And then another one, I thought despondently, *and another one, and another one . . .*

I said, "I'm tired, Helen. My body's tired, but my eyes are even more tired." When the adrenaline spiked before and during each fight, I'd never felt more alive. But like with any drug, when the high faded, it took that energy with it—plus a lot more. "I need to rest."

"We can't rest, Joe. We need to figure out how to get out of here."

"I understand that, Helen. But I don't know how I'm going to do that when all I can think about is putting one foot in front of the other."

"We're *going* to get out of here."

"I really want to . . ."

"We are, Joe! No *want to* bullshit! We *are*! Because if we don't, we lose our souls. I don't even know what that means. I can't comprehend it. But it's not going to be good. It's going to be right down there at the bottom of the list of Worst Things That Can Happen to You. So I don't care how tired we are; we're getting out of here. Okay?"

"Okay."

"Say it like you mean it."

I opened my mouth, closed it.

"Say it, Joe!"

"I can't, Helen! *Okay?* I can't! We're fucked!"

We walked in silence. I hated yelling at Helen. I hated giving up even more. But that one additional straw that broke the camel's back had landed on my back some time ago. Yet I persevered because I had to. There was no other choice. That sad fact hadn't changed any. However, it wasn't just my back that was broken now. My spirit was broken, as well. Despite all our bluster, all our talk of getting out of here, I knew—deep down, far enough from my thoughts that I couldn't fool myself—I knew we weren't getting out of here. Our fates had been sealed the moment we'd signed Izzy's godforsaken contract.

When we reached the weapons rack, I slumped down against the stone wall behind it with a bone-weary sigh.

Helen eyed me disapprovingly. But what she said was, "You should rest."

"I can't," I told her. "As soon as I close my eyes, I'll be out like a stone. I'll never hear the lift pick up the next guy."

"I didn't say *we* should rest. I said *you* should. I'll stay awake. I'll wake you when the lift starts to move. And when we beat the 'next guy,' I'll rest, and you'll keep watch."

I was so exhausted that I didn't think Helen could wake me even if she had a bucket of ice-cold water to splash over my head. Yet the temptation to close my eyes, even for a few minutes, was so great that I nodded in agreement.

"Good," she said. "We probably have another half an hour, so make the most of it and recharge. I'm going to go find a new shirt."

Blood soaked the bottom half of her cream sweater. It wasn't from her; when she'd decapitated her father, a jet of blood had spurted from his neck.

"You're going to take a shirt off a corpse's back?" I said.

"It will be better than this one. The smell's making me sick."

I watched Helen as she waded into the sea of corpses, stopping to study one or another, sometimes squatting, perhaps to feel the material of the shirt she was about to appropriate. I found myself strangely intrigued by what she would eventually choose . . .

When my eyes flashed open, I was momentarily confused. Not by where I was—that had never left the forefront of my mind, not even while I was asleep—but by what had woken me.

Helen stood ten feet away. Her back was to me, bare except for the silver straps of her bra. She held a shirt in front of her and seemed to be looking down at it.

I was pretty sure I'd heard her gasp, and that had been the sound that had roused me. It had been exclamatory and frightened.

"Helen . . . ?" I said.

"You're awake?" she said, without turning around. There was something in her voice . . .

"What's wrong?"

"Nothing. Go back to sleep."

"I heard you." I pushed myself to my feet. A wave of dizziness roared over me. I braced a hand against the wall until it passed.

Helen had put on the shirt she'd been holding. It was a rose-colored, button-up silk blouse with a pointed collar and short sleeves. It had survived the owner's death largely unscathed.

"Are you okay?" she asked me.

"Just dizzy. What happened?"

"Happened? Nothing. I'm fine." She attempted a smile. "Some of the blood from my old shirt"—she pointed to her sweater on the ground—"got on my stomach. Grossed me out. But I rubbed it all off."

I might not have known Helen for long, but I had come to know her well enough, and in all our time together, I didn't believe she had ever lied to me. But she was lying to me now. I was sure about that.

"How long was I asleep?" I asked her.

"Twenty minutes. Maybe thirty. Probably closer to thirty."

I looked toward the mechanical lift.

"It hasn't moved," Helen said. "I guess it should be descending soon, right?"

"I guess," I said, thinking, *What the hell are you lying to me about?* I almost came out and asked her this. But if she was lying to me, she would most likely lie about why she was lying.

"Don't you like it?"

I realized I had been frowning at her blouse. It had been in her hands when she'd cried out. She'd been looking at it.

What's going on?

I said, "It suits you."

"I almost chose a polka-dotted one, but it didn't really go with my jeans."

I tugged at the hem of my shirt. "Maybe I should look for something cleaner, too."

"No! What? Why? That shirt's still in good condition—"

Something huge swooped down out of the darkness.

Chapter 29

"Everybody fears monsters."
—The Book of Nine

I saw it at the last moment and threw Helen to the ground. I landed on top of her and felt a gust of air as the thing's wings propelled it past us.

"*What is it?*" Helen shrieked.

All I'd seen had been a flash of brown fur, compound eyes, and a mouth that resembled a bear trap.

I rolled off Helen and scanned the darkness above us. It was gone.

"Did you see it?" she asked breathlessly.

"Briefly," I said, with a calmness that belied the fear pumping through me. "Get your sword."

Helen scrambled to where she'd left the katana protruding blade-first from the ground. The bow and quiver were next to me. I ignored them. Hitting a stationary target with an arrow was hard enough; hitting an airborne one, regardless of how large this creature was, would be a considerable challenge.

Instead I went to my stash of weapons on the sand and selected a six-foot-long halberd. Helen was hurrying toward me in a crouch, as though she expected another dive attack at any moment.

"Why the fuck didn't you tell me?" I said when she reached me.

"*Tell you what?*" she said shrilly.

"That the next opponent had come!"

"I didn't know!"

"Don't lie to me, Helen! You had to know!"

"I didn't!"

"You never saw—or heard—the lift go down and come back up?"

She shook her head. "It didn't move! I swear!"

I jabbed a finger in the air. "Then how did that fucking thing get here?"

"I don't know, Joe! It has wings! It could have come from *above* us."

That possibility jolted me. As we'd discovered, the hole below us was the same hole that was above us. And if our opponents could rise through the one below us on the lift, there was no reason they couldn't also descend through the one above us on wings. They would, contradictorily, be coming from the same place.

"There!" Helen said, pointing. "It's there!"

I saw it, too, far above us, a black shape soaring erratically before disappearing into the higher shadows.

"Holy, holy shit," I said. "It's a giant moth."

Helen crouched defensively.

"Here it comes!" I yelled, and gripped the halberd tightly in both hands.

The moth swooped toward us in an unpredictable, jerky flight pattern. It had a wingspan of at least ten feet and a cylindrical body the size of a small car. Sharp barbs edged the tattered, leathery wings. White markings that resembled omniscient eyes covered the chitinous membranes. Slender, segmented antennae protruded from the mottled forehead above its two real eyes, which were bulbous and multifaceted, reflecting the torchlight in a thousand directions.

But it was the mouth that turned my blood to sludge.

A circular hole staggered with rings of needle-sharp, inward-facing teeth.

Although I had observed these details in the few seconds it took the moth to bomb toward us, all I was thinking right then was where to strike the blasphemous insect.

I decided on the exposed belly and thrust the halberd.

The moth dodged upward with gravity-defying ease. Its powerful wings created a downdraft that knocked Helen off her feet. I staggered backward against the flurry of wind but held my ground and thrust the halberd again.

The six-inch hammered spearpoint atop the axe-like blade glanced harmlessly off its thick exoskeleton.

The moth dropped on me. I ducked its hellish mouth and took the impact with its body with my left shoulder. The bristly fur smelled awful, a noxious chemical scent that seared my nostrils. Grimacing, I swung the halberd in an upward thrust. The blade sliced through its right wing with a satisfying crunch.

I had been under the impression that moths couldn't vocalize, and if they could, it would be somewhere in the ultrasonic range.

Not this one. It released a thin and utterly otherworldly screech.

And dropped on me again.

It was so quick that I barely had time to raise the halberd. The beartrap mouth sprang closed over the wooden shaft between my hands.

Its wings beat loudly. My feet left the ground.

"Helen!" I shouted, kicking in vain while I glanced peripherally at her. "Cut its other wing!"

She was standing off to the side, katana raised in front of her, watching the monstrous moth lift me into the air—and doing nothing about it.

I considered releasing the halberd, but then I would be defenseless. And the moth and I were hovering only a few feet off the ground; despite how furiously it flapped its wings, it couldn't seem to gain any more lift.

A stalemate.

"Helen!" I said again. "Cut its wing! If it gets me, it'll get you next!"

A moment later, she bounded forward and swung the katana. The blade ripped through the scaly membrane of the moth's good wing.

It screeched again. Hot, fetid air blasted me in the face as I fell—still gripping the halberd—to the ground.

I landed on my feet, stumbled, regained my balance.

The moth was skating back and forth above me as it struggled to remain aloft.

I jabbed the tip of the halberd up and through the same wing I'd attacked earlier. This time I used the hooklike beak on the back of the blade to rake a three-foot gash through the membrane before it tore the weapon from my hands.

Nevertheless, the damage was done.

The moth crashed to the ground. Its disgustingly plump body nearly crushed me. Its wings fluttered helplessly. Its antennae flailed back and forth like heat-seeking whips.

Helen sliced off the latter with the sword so she could get close to the bug's head. Standing in front of it, wailing like a banshee, she drove the katana down between its eyes.

The moth went still.

Chapter 30

"What becomes of morality when there is no right choice?"
—The Book of Nine

Limbs rubbery with fear and exhaustion, I lowered myself to the sand and scanned the airy darkness for any more moths.

"I hope that was the only one," I said.

"I don't see any others," Helen said, also looking up.

My revulsion for her right then sickened me, but I kept it hidden the best I could. I wasn't going to tip my hand until I knew what she knew.

And why she wanted me dead.

"Took you a while to get into the fight," I said.

She averted her eyes. "I know . . . I . . . I just froze up. I *hate* moths."

"Hate them enough to conjure one?"

"I told you earlier that I hate bugs."

"Moths are pretty harmless, as far as bugs go."

"Not that one."

She glanced at the giant moth—and retched. Her hand went

to her mouth as she swallowed the gastric acid that had come up her throat. Then she doubled over and vomited. "Ugh," she said when her diaphragm relaxed. She wiped her lips with the back of her wrist. "That thing is so disgusting— and it stinks. Did you see its mouth? If it bit you, it wasn't letting go."

"I did see its mouth, Helen. My face was an arm's length away from it."

"I'm sorry, Joe. I really am. I froze. But we got it in the end. That's all that matters. We got it; we won."

"We haven't *won*, Helen," I snarked. "That was only our third opponent. There are a thousand more waiting in line, a million more. We're living on borrowed time until we find a way out of here." I couldn't help myself and blurted, "*Do you know the way out?*"

"What?" She appeared thrown off guard by the question and huffed. "Right, Joe. I know the way out, but I'm keeping it a secret because I'm having such a good time here."

I stared at her impassively. She was either telling the truth or a damned good liar.

"Come on, Joe!" she said. "How many times do I have to apologize? I can tell you're angry with me, and I'm sorry I froze. And I guess while I'm at it, I should also apologize for conjuring the moth in the first place."

"What's your thing with moths?" I didn't care. But the more she talked, and the less I talked, then the less likely she would figure out that I was onto her.

"I just hate them," she said. "They give me the creeps. Some people hate spiders. Some hate snakes. I hate insects. Every one. I always have. Even ants, and ants are just *ants*."

"So why not conjure an ant? Why a moth?"

"If I knew how this worked, Joe, I wouldn't have conjured either. It's just . . . subconscious shit." She shrugged. "Maybe because I used to pluck the wings off moths, and this is my guilt getting back at me."

I blinked. "You used to torture moths?"

"I tortured all sorts of insects when I was a kid. But moths a lot, yeah, because they didn't bite, and they were easy to catch. You just turn on an outdoor light at night, and when one of them gets attracted to it, you whack it with a dishtowel. That usually dazes it long enough to bottle it in a jar."

"I thought you hate bugs?"

"I do. That's why I tortured them."

"But weren't you afraid of them?"

"If they were crawling all over me and stuff, I'd go schizo. But I never let them get too close. I used pliers and other tools from my dad's shed—"

"Jesus Christ, Helen. What are you? A fucking serial killer? That's how they start, with bugs, then pets, then people . . ."

"That's so insulting, Joe! I hope you're joking . . ."

I coughed up a bitter laugh—and it really was a cough as much as a laugh. Soon it was a full-on coughing fit.

When it ended, Helen said, "You need to rest."

I shook my head. "It's my turn to take watch. You rest."

"I'm not tired. I'm not. So go on, rest. I'll keep watch again."

She seemed way too eager to keep watch again, and I had a feeling she'd been waiting for a turn in the conversation to make the altruistic offer. I also had a feeling—in fact, I was certain—that whatever she had up her sleeve would play out when I was asleep.

"Seriously, Joe," she said, "get some rest while you can. I'll keep an eye on the lift *and* the sky this time."

"All right, Helen," I said, pretending indifference with a

half-assed but mostly real yawn. "Wake me as soon as you hear anything."

I leaned back against the stone wall and closed my eyes. But I didn't go to sleep.

There was no chance in hell I was going to sleep.

About ten minutes later, I heard Helen approach. She was moving stealthily, but in the crypt-like quiet of the arena, I could make out the soft scuttling of her footsteps on the sand.

She stopped when she was a dozen feet away. The wait, the not knowing, was unbearable . . .

Had she gotten the bow and quiver? Was an arrow nocked and aimed at me? Was she drawing back the fifty-pound bowstring?

I was about to open my eyes when she said, "Joe?"

I didn't answer. My heart hammered inside my chest. I focused on breathing evenly and deeply, mimicking sleep.

She started toward me again.

"Joe?" she said softly, and now she couldn't have been more than six feet away.

I said nothing.

She took two more steps—

I opened my eyes and snagged the halberd, which I'd kept at my side.

Helen froze. She held the katana before her, arms outstretched, the tip of the blade pointed at me.

I rose swiftly to my feet and said, "Get. The fuck. Back."

"I . . . I was just checking on you," she stammered. "You were . . . speaking in your sleep."

"Lift your shirt!" I told her.

She stiffened. "What?"

"Lift it!"

"Joe, you're . . ."

"I know! All right, Helen? I *know*." I yanked up my shirt. I didn't need to look to see what was there. Shortly into my feigned sleep, I'd had an epiphany and checked my chest, discovering a large, jelly-red *1* carved into my flesh. Unlike the raw, stitched incision in my side, the *1* appeared well-healed, like it had always been there, which explained why I'd never felt it before. "Now lift yours."

With a sullen, sheepish expression, she removed one hand from the katana's hilt and lifted her shirt, revealing a *1* nearly identical to mine. Tears shimmered in her eyes. "It was the only way, Joe . . ."

"You were going to kill me," I said stoically. "You were actually going to kill me." This was the reason I'd waited as long as I had before opening my eyes; I'd wanted to catch her in the act, wanted indisputable confirmation of her intent.

I needed that if I were going to bring myself to kill her first.

"Joe . . ." she said, shaking her head, tears flowing freely. "What else was I supposed to do? I've thought about it. God, I've been thinking about it nonstop. And it's the only way. One of us has to die."

I glowered at her. "You should have told me when you first knew, Helen. We could have talked it through. Found another way."

"There *is* no other way, Joe! There's no *Ten* anywhere! There's no tenth floor, no tenth door. We were wrong. But there's a *One*. There's one right here! And there's one right there!" She emphasized these last two points by pointing to her midsection and then mine.

"And you think if you kill me, you'll be offered the way back to the first room?"

"Don't you?" she said. "The clues are always right in front of us. *Right in front of us.*"

"Fuck, Helen!"

"I'm sorry, Joe. I'm so, so, so sorry. You think I *wanted* to kill you? It breaks my heart. It breaks my goddamn heart. But if I didn't do it, you'd kill me. When you figured it out, you'd kill me. You're bigger and stronger, and you'd kill me. *I had no choice.*"

"I wouldn't have killed you, Helen . . ."

"I think you probably believe that. I really do. And if you're noble—or stupid—enough not to, then we'd both die to the next opponent or the one after that. We'd both die, and that would be so pointless. *I had no choice.*"

I tilted the tip of the halberd toward her. "So what happens now? I should let you kill me?"

"What was I supposed to do, Joe? What was I supposed to *do*? I don't want to die. I don't want to . . . lose my soul." The last few words were almost incomprehensible, buried beneath wretched sobs.

Tears warmed my eyes. Could I kill her? Murder her in cold blood? Could I do that to save my life? To save my *soul*? It should have been a no-brainer. I barely knew Helen. If I didn't kill her, we both would die at the hands of a future opponent. It was a no-brainer.

But I didn't think I could do it. I couldn't.

Despite the stakes, I couldn't kill her.

"This is bullshit, Helen," I said finally. "This can't be the only way out. That means one of us was never meant to leave The No-End House. That's bullshit! That's not fair—"

"You think *this* is fair?" she wept, waving one arm dramatically. "You think fighting opponents ad infinitum is *fair*? You think a giant motherfucking moth with a thousand teeth is *FAIR*?" She backed away from me, both hands on the hilt of the katana. "I'm so scared, Joe. I can barely think straight. I don't want to be here anymore . . . I don't want to be here . . ."

I grimaced. Regardless of the fact that Helen had tried to murder me in my sleep, I felt sorry for her. Because I knew the fear she was experiencing, the fear of eternal damnation; it was an ice-cold, bowel-numbing terror that was nearly impossible to describe.

Lowering the halberd, I watched as she continued to back away from me before turning and running for her life.

Chapter 31

"The most cunning fighters are those who have
everything to lose."
—The Book of Nine

I didn't pursue Helen. What would be the point if I wasn't
going to kill her? Instead, I decided to use however much
time we had until our next opponent arrived to figure a way
for the both of us to leave this room alive.

And that began with the 1s carved into our abdomens.

I agreed with Helen that they meant the way out of The
No-End House was via the first room, from where we could
walk back to—and exit through—the door to Izzy's study. I
also agreed with her interpretation that one of us had to die
for the other to survive. It made sense in the twisted and morbid workings of the challenge.

Nevertheless, I didn't think it was the *only* interpretation.
Helen had said The No-End House wasn't fair; she'd yelled
that at the top of her lungs. I disagreed. The house was difficult. The house was brutal. The house was sometimes mind-
bendingly frustrating. But it didn't cheat. It played by the same

rules—regardless of how twisted and morbid they might be—as we did.

That suggested there had to be another way out for the both of us.

What that was, I had no idea. And the clock was ticking.

Something to do with 11? *Each of us alone is a* 1, *but together we're* 11 . . . *an eleventh room? But that's just as unenlightening as a tenth room . . . and now that I think about it,* 10 *could also be interpreted as* 1 + 0 . . . *and that goes back to what Helen believes: one of us escapes, one dies . . .*

I rubbed my aching eyeballs. They felt like they were wrapped in sandpaper.

None of my furious ruminations were making sense. *I* wasn't making sense. I was too tired, too stressed. The last twenty minutes had been nothing but a white-knuckle race of one hairbrained idea after another—

I frowned.

Helen had previously been pacing along the edge of the arena opposite me.

Now I couldn't see her anywhere. She was, I realized angrily, staying out of the light of the bonfires, hiding in the shadows, no doubt in the hope that whoever or whatever emerged from the hole ignored her and came for me first.

This was self-defeating, because even if that scenario played out, and the opponent bested me, it would come for her next. And if she/he/it could kill me, then Helen was as good as dead, as well.

We needed to stick together. Fight together.

It was the only way to survive . . . for a little bit longer, at least.

All at once, the bonfires went out.

The overwhelming blackness lasted for an excruciatingly

long period, during which the only sound was the ancient lift grinding slowly down through the borehole—and then back up.

Then nothing.

Silence . . .

A bright light clanked on far above me. Then another, and another, half a dozen in total. They were like concert LEDs that directed the light toward the performers on stage—and in this case, the performer standing in the center of the lift was Helen.

I stared at her in confusion, wondering what the hell she was doing, and more importantly, where our opponent was—

From the darkness on the opposite side of the arena, someone yipped with joy.

I stiffened as Helen—the real Helen—emerged from the shadows and cautiously approached her doppelgänger on the lift.

"Are you . . . on my side?" she called.

"Of course I am, silly!" said her twin. "Girls gotta stick together, don't we?"

"How do I know you're not going to hurt me?"

"Why would I hurt *you*? You're *me*. And you conjured me to get us out of this mess, so here I am. Now, are we going to finish this or what?"

Helen looked in my direction. "What are we . . . supposed to do?"

"You know what we're supposed to do."

As the two Helens approached me, lit up like haggard rock stars in the harsh overhead illumination, I expected them to spread apart and try to flank me, yet they remained side by side, perhaps realizing—correctly, I believe—that because of the reach of the halberd, I could have rushed and incapacitated one of them before the other had a chance to attack.

"Helen," I said, talking to the one on the left, the real one, "don't do this. I'm not the enemy. She is. She's tricking you." I was gripping the halberd so tightly, I had to willfully relax my hands.

"Shut up, Joe," said the doppelgänger. Her expression mirrored Helen's: frightened, a little unsure, yet resolved.

"This isn't going to end well for anybody," I told the real Helen.

"Stop talking to me, Joe," she said. "Please . . . just stop."

I raised the halberd. Began circling to the right, eyeing the doppelgänger, waiting for an opening. If I could take her out, Helen would back down; I could talk some sense into her.

With an Amazonian cry, Helen feinted toward me, sword raised.

I pointed the halberd at her to keep her at bay. The doppelgänger leaped forward, her katana slashing through the air. I parried. Metal clanged. The impact sent shockwaves through my arms but also knocked the twin off-balance. I used the halberd's hook to disarm her, then swung the weapon back toward Helen, who had been about to attack.

The other Helen went down—I figured she'd tripped on a body—and I swung the halberd back in her direction to strike before she recovered her sword.

She was faster, springing to her feet and tossing a fistful of sand in my eyes.

Grunting, I turned my head to the side. I couldn't see anything.

However, I sensed them coming and brandished the halberd in reckless, wide arcs as I stumbled backward. A skull shattered like an eggshell beneath one of my feet; my ankle twisted; I collapsed.

They charged.

Still unable to see clearly, I no longer knew who was whom, and thrust the halberd at the nearest attacker. The spearpoint ran through her chest. I released the shaft and rolled just as the blade of a katana struck the ground where I had been a second before.

I scrambled to my feet and ran.

Considering I was no longer armed, I was surprised when the remaining Helen didn't give chase. She simply shouted, "Joe, wait!"

I looked over my shoulder, felt comfortable with the distance between us, and stopped. I was breathing hard.

The Helen who had called my name was facing me with her katana lowered. The other Helen lay on her side, motionless, on a bed of corpses.

"Helen?" I said, uncertain which one I was talking to.

"It's me, Joe . . ."

"How do I know that?"

"Because it's *me*, that's how! I'm sorry. I'm so sorry I attacked you. But I think . . . I think it's over now."

"What do you mean?" Hope and skepticism warred inside me.

"Because *she's* dead . . . the one I conjured. . . . She might not be real, but she's still me. She still has . . ."

She knelt next to her doppelgänger and lifted her shirt until it caught on the halberd's blade.

Even from where I stood, I could make out the *1* carved into her bloodied abdomen.

"See!" Helen said triumphantly. "Look! She's got a *One*, too! We beat the challenge, Joe! We killed one of us *without killing one of us*! We can leave now!"

"How?" I said, my pulse racing at the possibility. *Could this be true?* "How do we leave?"

"I don't know, but I imagine . . ." Standing, she surveyed the arena. "I imagine we take the lift again. But this time, it won't take us back here. It will take us *out of here*."

A tsunami of relief washed over me. She was right. I knew she was right. I felt it with every fiber of my being.

She came toward me, smiling.

"Wait," I said, retreating a step.

She stopped, frowned.

"How do I know it's you, Helen? *Really* you?"

"Joe, it's me. I swear, it's *me*. You just have to believe that. *Please* believe that."

My mind raced. I said, "When we met on the patio of the hostel . . ."

She was nodding. "Hola Hostel. I was working on my laptop. You were drinking a beer."

"When we were getting ready to leave, you wanted me to come over to your place . . ."

"Uh, duh . . . I *liked* you, Joe. I *like* you, Joe. I've *always* liked you, Joe, from the very beginning."

"But I couldn't go with you. I told you about my wife, what happened to her, how she died . . ."

"And I'm so sorry about that . . ."

"How did she die? Tell me what I told you to prove you're really Helen, *my* Helen."

"She walked into a spinning airplane propeller. I'm sorry, Joe. I am . . ."

I swooned, almost fainted.

"Joe!" Helen hurried toward me, laughing, crying.

I opened my arms. Embraced her in a powerful hug. Inhaled the lemony scent of her hair.

She was saying something, kissing my neck. I cupped her head in my hands, planted my lips on her forehead—and twisted her head sharply to the left, breaking her neck.

She slid down my chest and collapsed in a heap on the ground. I saw in her wide, shocked eyes that she wasn't dead, only paralyzed.

"I never told you how Jen died," I said.

Then I picked up the katana to finish the job.

Chapter 32

"There is little value to life without death."
—The Book of Nine

I went to the real Helen's body, trying and failing to avoid her vacant, accusing stare. I pressed my fingers on her eyelids and held them closed for a few seconds until I was sure they wouldn't open again, and then I removed the halberd's spearpoint from her chest. I lifted her limp body in my arms and made my way through the corpses to the lift.

I stopped in the center of it.

And waited.

And prayed.

And thought, *I'm right. This is the real Helen. Has to be. She never conjured the other one; I did. My subconscious, believing Helen was a threat to me, conjured a doppelgänger as an opponent. That's the only explanation for the twin knowing something only I knew, something Helen had never known. She came from me . . .*

After the longest ten seconds of my life, the mechanism began to turn—in a counterclockwise direction.

It rose slowly into the air.

Around and around, up and up.

Head tilted skyward, I looked up as we passed into darkness, passed through the borehole. I continued looking up the entire ride, and eventually, a distant light appeared. That turned out to be the two-tier medieval chandelier hanging from the center of Merchant Belmont's vaulted chamber.

When the lift came to a stop, I was facing the fat man himself. He was seated on the back steps of his stagecoach, a book in one hand, a cigar in the other. Everything was as it had been when Helen and I had first reached this room—everything except the table and the mystery boxes, which were gone.

"Ah, my friend!" Merchant Belmont said, smiling at me as if just noticing my dramatic entrance. "You have returned! Care for some cheese? A sausage or two? Bratwurst, black pudding, green chorizo, cotechino—I have only the finest. Only the finest! Come and sit and tell me all about your adventures!"

If I'd had the presence of mind to bring the halberd, I more than likely would have butchered the bastard. Instead, I left the room through the arched doorway, ignoring his jolly entreaties to dine together on a future date.

I went from one torchlit hallway to another, my legs leaden, my feet dragging on the stone pavers. Helen's body was impossibly heavy in my arms, but I didn't set her down or stop to rest, fearful that if I did, I wouldn't be able to muster the strength to move again.

Soon the dry ice appeared, swirling around my thighs. I passed the hatchet lodged into a crack in the wall, and then the alcove with the copulating skeletons (still rocking back and forth, albeit without the glowing red eyes or orgasmic squeals). I climbed the steep staircase that led to the final hallway. As I approached the door at the end of it, I heard the electronic whirring of the locking mechanism, the dead bolt releasing.

The door swung wide open, welcoming me inside.

I stepped into Doña Isabella's opulent study. Although Helen and I had only spent half an hour or so in it previously, I felt as if I knew it intimately: the priceless art and statues and antique furnishings, every detail engraved on my brain, never to be forgotten.

Wearing a white dress with a high demure neckline, a tight bodice, and a skirt that flowed out from her hips, Izzy stood behind the rolltop desk where we'd signed the contract. Her black hair was piled high on her head, fastened with a tiara of shining diamonds.

Rosy blush on her sharp cheekbones and pink lipstick accompanied her gobs of mascara. Her green eyes studied me with haughty indifference.

"Welcome back, Señor Joe," she said. "You have proven yourself to be an enormously worthy contestant—"

"Fuck you," I told her. "Fuck you, and fuck this house." I continued through the room to the entrance hall.

"Señor!" Her high heels clicked rapidly on the marble floor behind me. "Where are you going with the señorita? You cannot expect to walk down the streets of Barcelona carrying a lifeless body."

"Watch me," I said over my shoulder, as I went to the large front door.

"She lost the challenge. She belongs to The No-End House now."

"Fuck you!"

"Señor Joe!"

I gripped the brass door handle—awkwardly given my burden—and yanked the heavy oak door open. I crossed the gallery lined with Gothic sculptures. I went down the external staircase into the lush courtyard.

The sky was bright and blue, just as it had been when Helen and I had first arrived at the palace. It might have been mid-afternoon, yet I saw nobody on the street on the other side of the stone archway.

I hesitated. Doña Isabella was right. I couldn't simply walk through Barcelona carrying a lifeless body. I'd make it all of two blocks before I was arrested—and how would I explain the ragged hole in Helen's chest? I needed some time to think. I needed to rest so I *could* think. Right then my head felt stuffed with nothing but air. The only thing I knew for certain was that I wasn't leaving Helen behind.

I glanced at the gnarled, timeless olive tree in the center of the courtyard. The twisted branches stretched in all directions. The small silvery leaves offered shade from the sun.

I went to it, sat down with my back against the trunk's rough bark, and held Helen tightly and protectively in my arms.

Moments later, I was asleep.

Chapter 33

"Some goodbyes are forever."
—The Book of Nine

Someone was in the house with me. I'd heard them, and they weren't trying to be very quiet. I passed through the living room without banging my shins on anything—the lights were off, yet the furniture was all familiar—and then entered the kitchen. The intruder stood in front of the refrigerator. The door was open, the inside light silhouetting her body.

I slapped on the wall light switch.

Helen spun around, a hand going to her chest in surprise. "Joe! It's just you. You scared me."

"What are you doing here, Helen?"

"Don't sound so happy to see me."

"It's the middle of the night . . ."

"I came to see you. But first I wanted something to eat. I'm starving."

I realized I was hungry, too—both hungry and impossibly thirsty. I went to the sink and filled a large glass with water and drank it in a single, uninterrupted swallow.

"I like your house, Joe," Helen said. "It could use some feminine touches, though."

"You have to go," I told her. "If you wake Jen, she won't be happy."

"What's *she* doing here?"

"She lives here. She's my wife."

"But she's dead."

You are, too, I thought, and for the first time, I realized the halberd wound in her chest was gone. Her silk blouse was untorn and unbloodied.

"Why are you here?" I asked again.

"To say goodbye to you. Oh, and I brought you something to remember me by."

She handed me a peach-colored bundle of fur. It began cooing and squeaking, even though I couldn't see a mouth or other features.

"It's a Tribble," she said.

"From *Star Trek*?"

"You *have* watched the show before. I knew it! Anyway, they're born pregnant, and they reproduce, like, *a lot*. Just so you know."

"Thanks, Helen," I said, setting the fuzzball on the counter.

"Can I get a hug now?" she said. "I'd like to say goodbye with a hug rather than . . . you know . . . how things ended . . ."

We held each other in the middle of the kitchen for a very long time.

"I need to go, Joe," Helen whispered into my shoulder at some point.

"Don't go," I told her.

"I have to."

"Don't," I said, knowing the word meant nothing, hating the emptiness in it.

"Please, Joe . . . you need to let me go."

"You can't leave me, Helen. I need you. I can't keep going without you . . ."

"I have to, Joe. I'm sorry. It's not my decision to make . . ."

I held her as tightly as I could until—

I shot awake with the dream fresh in my head. It was powerfully vivid, more like a memory than a dream, an encounter that might have happened only yesterday—

I'm in a bed, I realized.

I sat straight up.

I'm in the hostel.

The other beds were unmade, piled with backpacks and clothes. Sunlight streamed through two street-facing windows. I heard traffic below.

I swung my feet to the floor, went to one window. People, cars. A dark-haired woman riding a red bicycle with a basket on the handlebars filled with vegetables.

A dream? I wondered feverishly. *Could it have all been a dream?*

I yanked up my shirt. No number *1*. No stitches. And my clothes . . . they were clean. I sniffed an armpit. I didn't smell like I'd just spent a week in hell.

"Could it . . ." I said, but what came out was a lumpy croak. I was parched. I'd never been so thirsty in my life.

I saw a Font Vella water bottle on the top mattress of one of the bunks. I twisted off the cap and gulped the water, much of it spilling down my chin. I went to the communal bathroom at the end of the floor's hallway and filled the water bottle at the sink repeatedly, drinking until my stomach felt swollen.

Back in the room, I searched my backpack for my phone but couldn't find it—because I'd dropped it during the mad dash through the oven in the mushroom house, or because I'd lost it sometime last night while on acid or whatever

Helen had slipped me?—and then took the stairs to the lobby.
I recognized the surfy German staff member behind the reception counter. He was the same guy who manned the bar at night.

He grinned at me. "Good time Friday?"

I frowned. "Friday?"

"The girl. She was sexy sexy, yes?"

"Orange hair?"

"You were with more sexy sexies?"

"What day is it?" I demanded.

His grin wavered. "It's Sunday, man. Hey, everything okay?"

Everything really had been a dream! I thought ecstatically. It had to be. I'd slept for twenty-four hours after whatever drug-fueled bender I'd been on, and I'd had the mother of all dreams.

The street outside the hostel bustled with people. I was walking at about twice the speed of everyone else, weaving in and out of the crowds as I went looking for Helen's hotel.

"She's not answering, señor," the Spanish woman at the reception desk told me, hanging up the telephone.

"Have you been here all morning?" I asked her.

"Only for the last two hours."

"Did you see a woman with orange hair coming or going?"

"No, señor. But I know Señorita Sembène. She has been staying with us for several weeks. Do you want to leave a message for her?"

"Yes—no," I said. "I lost my phone. I'll come back again later."

I left the hotel.

Almost as soon as I'd turned south on Passeig de Sant Joan, the large boulevard that Helen and I had walked along to find a coffee shop in my "dream," I realized that it hadn't been a dream, after all; everything that I remembered had happened.

The epiphany began with a vague sense of déjà vu. A building I thought I recognized, an intersection. The trickle of recollections quickly became a deluge, and by the time I reached the Starbucks that Helen and I had patronized, I was in a cold sweat.

I went inside and sat at the same corner table where we had sat. My memories of that morning were crystal clear. The cappuccino she'd ordered. The latte I'd ordered. The barista mistakenly calling her Hilda. Talking about UNICEF, about my sojourn around the world. Telling Helen about the Kiwis, the "haunted house," and her insistence that we check it out.

I remembered everything. It had all happened.

And that meant everything else that had followed had happened, too.

The Starbucks seemed to melt around me. I was having trouble breathing. I stumbled to the bathroom, locked the door, sat down on the toilet. The stack of pennies in my throat was so corrosive that breathing became even more difficult. A prickling sensation spread across my skin. I tried to ignore it, but the sensation grew more intense with each passing second. My vision blurred to nothing. I was convinced I was dying. I was going to have a heart attack right then and there.

I fell off the toilet and curled into a ball on the floor. I squeezed my eyes shut and tried desperately to ride out the storm of overwhelming panic—and eventually the worst of the anxiety attack passed.

Drained and drenched in sweat, I felt as though I had just run a marathon, and it took me several long minutes before I could pick myself off the floor.

I left the café, ashamed and embarrassed by what had just happened.

But those emotions paled in comparison to my fear and despair.

It exists, I thought.

The No-End House exists. Helen had died there.

And now it had her soul.

It took me another twenty minutes to reach the Gothic Quarter.

Halfway along the alley-like street named Carrer de Montcada, I found The No-End House. The courtyard was in shambles. The lush vegetation was years dead, replaced with overgrown weeds. Only the olive tree remained, although it had seen much better days. The monogrammed front door to the palace stood ajar. A chain had at one point secured it closed. Now severed, it lay coiled on the stone pavers. The many rooms were dusty and abandoned. Trash littered the floors, and graffiti covered the walls.

Doña Isabella and her circus-like challenge had packed up and left town.

Chapter 34

"The mind . . . oh, the powers of the mind."
—The Book of Nine

I returned to the hostel, got my stuff, and walked south through the Gràcia district. Walked southwest from there through the Sants-Montjuïc district. Kept walking through the Baix Llobregat region of Catalonia, and then along the coastline until nightfall.

I camped out on a stretch of deserted beach, tore through a loaf of rye and some hard cheese I'd bought earlier, and slept like a zombie until just before dawn. I finished the bread and cheese for breakfast and hit the road again at the first light.

Instead of heading south, I very nearly backtracked to the international airport I'd passed the day before to buy a ticket home to Arizona. It seemed like the sensible thing to do after the experience at The No-End House. Return to my old life, putter around the garden, and find one hell of a good psychiatrist.

Continuing to walk around the world, spending all that time alone with only my thoughts for company—and no longer any meds—that wasn't going to be good for me. I might very well go crazy.

And if I were being honest with myself, I wasn't sure I wasn't already crazy. Like completely fucking insane.

I mean, a goddess who could control time and space? A house that manifested your innermost thoughts?

An obese merchant who ate your body parts, and a vampiric woman who stole your age?

How could any sane person believe any of that shit? Not to mention that one of the defining characteristics of being insane was that you didn't know you were insane. If a schizophrenic who believed government agents were stalking him understood that it was all in his head, then he wouldn't be a schizophrenic, would he?

So how did I know I wasn't crazy?

How did I know the trauma of Jen's death didn't push me toward the edge of the abyss?

How did I know all the solitude and loneliness of the last three years didn't push me *over* the edge?

I didn't. I couldn't. I was caught in a catch-22 situation where I didn't trust my perceptions of reality, but to determine what I trusted, I required those very perceptions.

So flying home, ending this fool's journey, seeing a shrink— that was what I needed to do.

I told myself this repeatedly, hour after hour, day after day, even in the cold hours after midnight when I lay awake in my sleeping bag, unable to sleep because of my most recent nightmare.

Nevertheless, I kept walking south through Spain.

And walking.

And walking.

And walking.

*   *   *

I reached the Spanish port town of Tarifa eight days after setting out from Barcelona. Inside the ferry terminal building, I purchased a one-way ticket across the Strait of Gibraltar to Morocco. I went through the security screening and queued for the immigration checkpoint.

The Spanish official who waved me to her booth was female and young, her platinum-blondehair tied back in a ponytail. I gave her my passport as well as my visa, which I had applied for at the Moroccan consulate when I'd first arrived in Barcelona.

"Why are you going to Morocco?" she asked me in English, as she flipped through my passport with a practiced eye. She seemed surprised by all the entry/exit stamps and inspected the pages a second time more slowly.

"Travel," I said.

"You've been to many countries . . ."

I was used to this reaction and gave my typical response: "I'm walking around the world. I left the United States three years ago. So far, I've been to eighteen other countries. Spain is the nineteenth."

Sometimes the immigration officers would crack a joke or two. Sometimes they would seem genuinely interested and ask me questions that weren't the usual fare intended to trip up drug traffickers, human smugglers, fraudsters, and the like. Sometimes they wouldn't bat an eye.

This woman fell into the last group. She simply swiped my passport through a scanner and read the information on her monitor.

Then she picked up the telephone and spoke in Spanish for thirty seconds or so. I didn't know what she was saying, but I was suddenly uneasy.

I looked at the impatient queue waiting behind me, looked back at the immigration officer.

"Is there a problem?" I asked when she hung up the phone.

"A moment, señor."

She returned her attention to her monitor. Shortly two burly men dressed in the dark navy-blue uniforms of the Spanish National Police arrived and conversed with the woman.

One of them said to me, "You need to come with us, sir."

They led me to a small interrogation room with a single table and two chairs. A video camera watched me from the corner. I could think of only one reason why I was here. The police knew that Helen was missing, and they'd figured out that I was the last person who'd been with her.

I didn't sit in one of the chairs; I was too upset, too wired. Instead I paced from one wall to the other, my mind racing to get my story straight.

It had been eight days since Helen disappeared inside The No-End House. That meant she would have gone an entire work week without showing up at her office. Her coworkers would have been concerned. Someone might have gone to her hotel. They might have been allowed inside her room. They would have learned she wasn't there, and when she failed to return that day, or perhaps the next, they would have reported her missing. The police would have talked to the receptionist that I'd talked to on Sunday. But how did they find out who I was? They would have had no reason to suspect Helen had gone to Hola Hostel on Friday night; it was two blocks away from the hotel. However . . . if her disappearance had made the news, and a photograph of her were broadcast, someone at the hostel could have recognized her. Told the police that Helen and an American guy had spent the night drinking together. The hostel had a photocopy of my passport. The police would have flagged it so they would be alerted when I attempted to leave the country.

Which seemed to be exactly what had happened.

So the police knew I had spent Friday night with Helen. All right.

That didn't prove anything. Did they know I'd met her again the following morning? I should probably assume they did to avoid being caught in a lie.

In fact, I thought, they would almost certainly know we'd met again. They would have gotten a court order to obtain our data from the phone companies. They would have been able to follow our movements all morning.

Nevertheless, I was quite certain our phones wouldn't have pinged from inside The No-End House. For one, almost from the start, we'd been deep underground, where reception was no longer possible. Moreover, as we'd progressed, we might no longer have been in this fucking reality.

So the police would know I was with Helen on Friday night. They would know we were together on Saturday morning.

But that would be all. I could work with that.

Eventually I sat down. I had been in the interrogation room for over an hour now, and nobody had shown up to question me. Were they playing mind games? Trying to psych me out? I didn't know, but it was their time they were wasting.

At some point, they would have to charge me with a crime or let me go.

It was another three or four hours before the door to the interrogation room unlocked and opened. I wasn't sure, as I'd been dozing with my arms folded on the table. I raised my head and looked at the man who entered.

He was tall and imposing, with a rugged air of toughness. A thick beard framed a square jaw. His dark eyes appeared deceptively aloof, as though this interrogation was just one more task to check off for the day. Which was bullshit. He wore a tailored brown leather jacket, white dress shirt, and olive-green slacks. The civilian clothes suggested he was a detective, likely the one in charge of Helen's case, and if that were so, his jurisdiction was in Barcelona.

He had flown down here to see me.

Which, coincidentally, explained all the waiting around.

He slapped a manila folder on the table and sat in the second chair, close enough to me to crowd my personal space. He reeked of tobacco.

When he spoke, I saw that his teeth were stained brown. "Joe Hadfield," he said, opening the folder and checking an official-looking form. He studied me. "Do you know why you're here?"

"No," I lied.

"No idea?"

"No," I said. "And I hope there's a good reason. I missed my ferry."

"You want to take a guess?"

"I'd prefer for you to tell me what's going on."

His eyes went to the form, back to me. "You are walking around the world, huh?"

"Yes."

"Not many people do that."

"I haven't met any others."

"Must be difficult?"

"It's rewarding."

"You probably need to be pretty tough up here, huh?" He tapped his head with a finger. "You running from something, Joe?"

"Look—I never got your name . . . ?"

"It's Big Carlos. You can call me Carlos."

"Look, I'm happy to voluntarily answer whatever questions you have, Carlos. That being said, you know as well as I do that I don't have to cooperate. And if you don't get to the point soon, I'm going to invoke my right to legal counsel."

"Hey, Joe, don't get so upset," said Big Carlos, raising his hands. "We're just talking, *sí*? So you want to talk about something else, huh? Okay. How about we talk about Helen Sembène?"

"What about Helen?" I asked, almost adding the cliché, *Has something happened to her?*

"She's missing."

"Missing?" I frowned. I wasn't a very good actor, and I figured the less I said, the better.

"Since last Saturday." He glanced at the form again. "The fourteenth."

I appeared aghast. "She's been missing for a *week*?"

"Any idea where she might have gone?"

"Why would I know where she went?"

He lifted the thin stack of papers from the folder, shuffled to a new page, studied it for a few seconds. "You spent an evening with her at the hostel where you were staying in Barcelona. Hola Hostel. Friday night. Did you know Helen Sembène before then?"

"No," I said.

"How long were you with her?"

"We hung out . . ." I shrugged. "I guess until midnight."

"And then what?"

"Nothing."

"Nothing?"

"We said goodnight. She went to her hotel. I went up to my room."

"How do you know she went to her hotel?"

"I don't. I imagine that's where she went. It was late."

"Did you get along well with her?"

"Yeah, I did. She's been missing for a *week*?"

"She was an attractive woman, *si*?"

Was, I thought. I doubted that was accidental. More likely he wanted me to talk about her in the past tense. "Yeah, she is. Do you have any idea where she might be?"

"Are you married, Joe?"

"No."

Big Carlos held up his left hand, wiggled his ring finger. The light winked off a gold wedding band. "You know, before I became a happily married man, if I spent a night with an attractive woman, I usually went home with her."

"Lucky woman."

He grinned humorlessly. "You didn't go back to the hotel with Helen Sembène?"

"I've told you what happened." Then, to take some semblance of control of the interrogation, I said, "I didn't see her again until the next morning."

Something like surprise crossed Carlos's eyes, and I enjoyed a small measure of satisfaction in that. If he had our phone records—as I was sure he did—and if he knew I'd spent Saturday morning with Helen, and knew the pings had stopped around midday . . . and suspected that was when I might have murdered her and destroyed our phones . . . then he'd probably been betting that I'd deny seeing her on Saturday.

I returned his scrutinizing gaze with my best poker face.

He said, "You saw her Saturday?"

"I woke up early and was leaving the hostel to get a coffee. She was sitting on the patio."

"Just sitting on the patio, huh?"

"She was having a coffee."

"She came to the hostel to have a coffee?"

"She told me nothing was open near her hotel. She knew from the night before that the hostel's breakfast opened at six. Also, I think she wanted to see me again."

"She came to the hostel to see you, huh?"

"As I mentioned, we got along. She might have wanted Friday night to have ended differently than it had."

"Are you gay, Joe?" Carlos asked me pointedly.

"No," I said.

"Yet a beautiful woman wants to spend the night with you, and you say no?"

"I'm not married because I'm a Lothario, as you seemed to have been in your prime, Carlos. I'm not married because my wife died. But that's none of your fucking business, is it? Are we almost done here?"

"No, Joe," he said. "We're not almost done. We're just getting started. Where'd you go with Helen Sembène on Saturday?"

"To the Gothic Quarter."

"Any particular reason?"

"I've always wanted to go there."

"Why so much hostility, Joe?"

"Next question."

"Where did you go after the Gothic Quarter?"

"I walked Helen back to her hotel."

"You walked her back to her hotel?" he repeated. A spark had ignited his eyes; he thought he had me.

"Our phones were stolen," I told him, as a way to explain why our phones had stopped pinging; it was reasonable to conclude the thieves would have removed the SIM cards, thus preventing the phones from being actively tracked. "Helen was pissed off. She wanted to go home."

Carlos studied me closely. He didn't appear to be happy about falling one step behind. "Who stole them?" he asked tightly.

"A couple of kids. One snatched mine from my back pocket. The other grabbed Helen's handbag."

"You didn't try to get them back?"

"They disappeared into the crowd before we could do anything."

"Did you see Helen Sembène later that day?"

"No," I said.

"You didn't meet up with her again?"

"I just answered that."

"What did you do after you walked her to her hotel?"

I didn't know how I had ended up in my bed in the hostel. Did I walk back in some kind of trancelike state? Did Izzy teleport me there? Regardless, I didn't think it mattered, and said, "I don't remember. I might have walked around the city a little more. But eventually, I went back to the hostel."

"And you never saw Helen Sembène again?"

"We seem to be going in circles, Carlos."

"Did you attempt to get in touch with her?"

You know I did, I thought. "I stopped by her hotel on Sunday."

"Why?"

"I wanted to see her."

"Any particular reason?"

"I wanted to say goodbye."

"Goodbye?"

"Tell her I was leaving Barcelona."

Carlos was nodding. "And?"

"And?"

"What happened when you went to her hotel?"

"The receptionist called her room. There was no answer. I left."

Carlos kept nodding. He seemed to be mulling over something.

Finally he said, "You think you're pretty smart, don't you, Joe?"

I blinked. "I'm sorry?"

"You think you've got this all worked out. Covered all the bases."

"Jesus Christ, Carlos. I don't know how much more help I can give you here. Am I worried about Helen? Of course I am. Do I think something's happened to her? I hope to God not. But it's more likely she's gone off somewhere without telling anybody. She has a fiery, unpredictable streak. Whatever you think about me, whatever you think I might have done, you're wrong—"

"You know, Joe," he interrupted, "I'd like to believe that Miss Sembène decided to pull a week-long sickie without calling in. I'd like to believe she's on a beach somewhere, snorkeling and drinking margaritas. But I've been at my job for a long time now. I'm good at what I do. I trust my instincts." He leaned forward. "And they tell me you're full of shit."

I waited patiently, as he clearly had more to say.

"So how about you answer one more question for me, Joe? Put my mind—and my instincts—at ease, because there's something that's been bothering me." He paused a beat for emphasis. "Why'd you decide to leave Barcelona so abruptly?"

I frowned. "Abruptly?"

"You'd booked four nights at the hostel. You checked in on Friday afternoon." He counted patronizingly on his fingers. "Friday night, Saturday night—that's only two nights, it seems to me. Yet you'd paid for Sunday and Monday nights, too . . . and you decided to leave Barcelona sometime on Sunday. Didn't even try to get a refund from the hostel for the unused nights. So, yes, Joe, *abruptly*. You left Barcelona very abruptly. Can you tell me why? I'm listening."

I shrugged. "I wanted to move on."

"You wanted to move on?"

My response came naturally, because it was the truth: "That's what I said, Carlos. I wanted to move on. It's been three years since I left Arizona to walk around the world. Days, weeks, even months blur together. I have a general idea of what I'm doing, where I'm going, but I also go where I want to when I want to. Sometimes I'll book a hostel for one night, and if I like the place, the city, I might decide to stay for three. Sometimes I'll book a hostel for three nights, hate the place, and stay for one. It depends on how I'm feeling on any particular day."

Big Carlos scowled. "You're a lucky man, Joe. Money doesn't seem to be of concern to you."

"No, Carlos, it's not," I told him bluntly. "I haven't worked a day in the last three years, and I'm not going to work again in the next two years or however many years it takes me to finish my journey. So, no, money is not a concern at all. I don't give a second thought to how much a hostel costs each night—regardless of whether I end up staying there or not."

After Big Carlos left the cramped interrogation room, I played over everything I had said, and I didn't believe I'd incriminated myself in any way. Carlos had all sorts of speculations but no hard proof. And without hard proof, without Helen's body, all his speculations amounted to nothing.

When the brawny detective finally returned sometime later, he had my journal in his hand. He sat on the edge of the table, showed me the inside of the battered book, and said, "Missing a lot of pages, Joe. Wonder what happened to them? Didn't like what you wrote—or just getting rid of incriminating evidence?"

I frowned; I wasn't sure why pages were missing.

Big Carlos read from one of the existing ones: " 'She's been sitting on the bench there for a while now, next to a potted palm, working on her computer but also watching the activity on the street, like she wished she had something better to be doing. Reminds me of a Norman Rockwell. Sweet, nostalgic, lonely. A stranger in a strange place, an outsider . . . sort of like me, I guess you might say.' " The detective looked up. "Sounds to me like you were creeping on Miss Sembène."

"Creeping? I was writing in my journal. That illegal?"

Big Carlos flipped to the next page: " 'We went to an old palace in the Gothic Quarter. It was probably built in the twelfth century by an aristocrat or wealthy merchant. That was the neighborhood to live in back then, the Upper East Side of the Middle Ages. It's abandoned now. I had a look around a couple of days ago. It was massive. There were even tunnels beneath it. Seemed like they went on forever. A palace that grand needs a name, and I figure The No-End House is fitting.' " The detective looked at me again. "Want to tell me where exactly this palace is, Joe? We're going to find it anyway."

I said nothing.

Carlos flipped through more pages. "You got one fucked-up mind. I don't even know what to make of half this shit. A Nazi and evil witch and dinosaurs? Sounds like the ramblings of a crazy person. Are you crazy, Joe? Because you said something somewhere . . ." He flipped back and forth through the pages. "Here it is: 'Probably shouldn't have thrown away my meds.' Then a lot of mumbo jumbo. More mumbo jumbo. Blah, blah, blah . . . this isn't even stream of consciousness. It's verbal diarrhea. Ah: 'Doc calls it a mood disorder. Mood disorder, my ass. It's no mild mood disorder when you got two people living upstairs rent-free inside your head.' " He closed the journal. "Which one of those two people am I talking to right now, Joe?"

I frowned once more, confused. Yes, I'd had a mild mood

disorder since Jen's death. Yes, I was on meds, and yes again, I threw away my meds when I arrived in Spain. But that was because I was doing better. Walking around the world had given me the headspace I needed. I certainly wasn't a fucking schizophrenic . . .

But then why would I have written that I was? And why couldn't I remember writing it?

Something that had crossed my mind a few days ago came back to me, vague and imprecise but in my voice, something about a catch-22 and not trusting my perceptions of reality even though I needed those very perceptions to determine what I trusted.

I said, "I want an attorney."

Big Carlos said, "I'm sure you do, Joe. You got a lot of explaining to do. But why don't you tell me one last thing first. Why'd you change the name?"

"What?"

He showed me the cover of the journal. Scribbled in black marker on the red leather was *The Book of Nine*. However, "Nine" was scratched out, and there was a haphazardly drawn *10* beneath it.

I was unsure when I'd done that or why.

"Let me tell you what I think, Joe," said Carlos when I didn't reply. "You started this journal while walking around the world. Maybe you were bored, or maybe you just wanted to remember all the sick shit you did back home. How you took a chainsaw to your wife and daughter—"

I shot to my feet, appalled. "What the fuck are you talking about?" Was he trying to goad me? Get me so worked up I confessed to Helen's murder? "My wife walked into a spinning airplane propeller, you asshole. And I don't even have a daughter—"

"That's two," said Carlos, slipping off the table so we

stood eye to eye. "Two murders. But then there are the seven little girls that disappeared not too far from where you lived. All of them under ten years old, and all of them found in the desert, chopped up with a hatchet. Cops put you in the vicinity where some of them were last seen—"

I clenched my jaw. "They were grasping at straws. They had a different suspect every other week. They interviewed me and let me go—"

"Because they couldn't prove anything for certain. But they were sure you were their guy, and they kept eyes on you. You knew that. You knew the heat was on. And you grew paranoid. So paranoid, one day you packed a bag and just walked right out of your little town and kept on walking. And when you got to Barcelona, and met Helen Sembène, you thought you were in the clear, and you couldn't help yourself. Sick fucks like you can never help yourselves. And so you killed her, too. And that's ten. Ten people you murdered, you son of a bitch. Ten murders you decided to write about in your sick fucking journal before feeling the heat again and ripping the incriminating pages out—"

"You have no idea—"

Big Carlos snagged my shirt with his fists. "The FBI might not have been able to nail your ass, Joe Hadfield," he hissed. "But I will. Trust me, *capullo*, you're going down."

Furious at what he was accusing me of, knowing it couldn't possibly be true, I gripped his wrists firmly to force them off my shirt—and saw his cuff links.

Each one was a fleur-de-lis.

I stared at them in horror, paralyzed by revelations I could barely digest or comprehend.

Until they all clicked in appalling synchronicity.

I never left The No-End House! I never left Room 9! I was tricked. Izzy tricked me. I simply went back to Room 1. I'M

STILL IN ROOM 1. I'm back at the beginning of the challenge, going through it all over again . . .

My knees went weak. The world canted. I shoved myself away from the detective.

And that was when I saw the number 2—everywhere.

It wasn't just Carlos's two cuff links with the two fleurs-de-lis. There were two gold wreaths on the badge clipped to his belt. Two prongs on his buckle. Two chairs at the table. The wall clock read two o'clock . . .

"This isn't real," I said out loud, speaking to myself. I pointed a finger at Carlos. "You're not real. I'm still in the house. *I'm still in the house.*"

"The No-End House, Joe?" said Carlos evenly, looking up and past me.

I spun around. The camera. The camera was watching us. "This isn't fair, Izzy!" I shouted at it, knowing somewhere beneath my reckless terror that Izzy would never need a video camera to spy on me. "I did it! I beat the challenge, you bitch! *Let me out of this fucking house!*"

"Where's the house, Joe?" said Carlos, more urgently. "Where's the fucking house?"

I spun back toward him. He flinched, and I knew I must have looked like the craziest motherfucker he'd ever seen right then.

"Is *that* the door?" I demanded.

"What door?"

"The exit! To the next room!" I jabbed a finger at the door. "*Is that the exit to the next room?*"

I lunged for the handle. Carlos crashed into me, driving me against the wall. He had my shoulders pinned, so I couldn't use my arms. I headbutted him.

"*Mierda!*" he cried, releasing me. He cupped his nose, which was gushing blood.

I clocked him with a right hook. He dropped to the floor, struggled to get up. I kicked him in the face over and over until he went still. I threw back the hem of his leather jacket and tore his firearm from the holster on his belt.

Flipping the safety from *on* to *off*, I went to the door, yanked it open.

Two police officers were running toward me. Seeing I was armed, they scrambled for their guns. I fired four rounds, hitting them both.

A woman screamed. People scattered.

"*Which door is it?*" I yelled madly, swinging the gun from one fleeing person to the next. Yet I was finding it difficult to concentrate on anything in the large room. My vision had tunneled; I was seeing everything as if through the wrong end of a pair of binoculars. "*WHICH ONE'S THE EXIT?*"

Firecrackers went off so rapidly, I couldn't count how many.

And then I was on my back, staring at the ceiling, excruciating pain locking up my chest.

The room was suddenly very dark.

Helen was kneeling next to me.

"It's better this happened now, Joe," she said in a soothing tone, despite the chaos I heard just out of sight. "There was never a way out of The No-End House. It's named that for a reason. You would have just kept going from one room to another, again and again and again. It's better this way."

"Which way?" I asked, although I didn't think I'd moved my lips. The darkness surrounding us began encroaching on Helen, erasing her from the edges.

"Dying," she said. "It's the only way to end the challenge for good."

"We're trapped in The No-End House forever?" I might have been crying.

"It's not so bad, Joe," she said, taking my cold and clammy

hands in hers. She was almost completely erased. "At least we won't be alone. We'll have each other."

There was so much more I wanted to say, wanted to know, but the darkness was relentless, eating up the last of her until she was no more.

Then there was only a stygian expanse, and then there wasn't even that.

Acknowledgments

Thank you to my agent, John Talbot, and my editors, Kimberly Orr and James Abbate. A big thanks as well to the team at Kensington.

Visit our website at
KensingtonBooks.com
to sign up for our newsletters, read
more from your favorite authors, see
books by series, view reading group
guides, and more!

BOOK CLUB
BETWEEN THE CHAPTERS

Become a Part of Our
Between the Chapters Book Club
Community and Join the Conversation

Betweenthechapters.net